RHODES

THE MOJAVE-STONE

Also by M.M. Gornell

Uncle Si's Secret
Death of a Perfect Man
Lies of Convenience
Reticence of Ravens
Counsel of Ravens

Rhodes
The Mojave-Stone

M. M. Gornell

Champlain Avenue Books, Inc.
Henderson, Nevada, USA

Published by
Champlain Avenue Books, Inc., Henderson, Nevada

International Standard Book Number ISBN-13: 978-0-9908256-7-8
Library of Congress LCN: 2014922931

Cover by *LAWRENCE*

FIRST EDITION
2015

Printed in the United States of America

To:

Dolores Bucholz

PREFACE

Between Needles and Victorville, California, many Mojave Desert locations have called out—*"Stop awhile, listen to what I have to say."* Special places where one can envision future dramas unfolding and evolving, while simultaneously eavesdropping on tales from long gone times. Then add into such flights-of-fancy, kaleidoscope-like memories of Chicago mansions and childhood neighborhoods; followed by the improbable thought of a homestead—*indeed a whole town*—rising out of the rugged and desolate ridges along a familiar stretch of Route 66.

All these images commingled to tickle my imagination.

There are many events and stories hidden underneath shifting desert sands, and quite possibly many of these tales are doomed to ride *ad infinitum* on relentless desert winds—ghosts trapped on a plane-of-existence they can never escape. The town of Shiné *(Shy-knee)* is a fictional concatenation of several of these magical places, fanciful thoughts, and hidden dramas. A place where provocative and unanswered questions actually escape the entrapment of Mojave winds and take center stage.

Hopefully, the small fact Shiné does not exist will not dissuade you from visiting...

De Mortuis Nil Nisis Bonum
Of the dead, (say) nothing unless good

What Leigh Cooper Rhodes Started

December 25th, 1990, Shiné, California

Leigh Cooper "LC" Rhodes knew this was a singular day—and he, a singular man. It was a Tuesday.

Swaddled as he was in the comfort of his massive and plush four-poster bed, in Rhodes Castle's warmly appointed master-suite, and surrounded by two generations of offspring, LC remained mentally strong enough to ponder for the last time a concept he'd recognized and embraced from his earliest of days. A concept he considered the guiding principle of his life. Somehow, someway, he knew even in childhood: the perceived traumas of his youth, egregious or slight, *could* end up controlling his life. Further, if he let himself become so consumed, hurt, or even victimized, it would destroy his chances for achievement far beyond his days of youth.

LC's eyes were closed, the air on his face cool, while his body was cocooned in warmth. Just the way he liked it.

Admittedly, there must have been a few others like himself, who instinctively *knew* to brush away early negative experiences as trifles. *Knew* they were nothing more than unavoidable annoyances based upon ignorant words and ill-conceived acts of the uninformed. Or most probably, just plain stupid children doing hurtful things. For a moment, he thought of the Coopers, and quickly dismissed their part in his early life. Now was the time to let past slights and disagreements slide into the universe.

Also quite early on, he further concluded such cruel acts and taunts of youth were actually a primeval "outsider" reflex—disguised as "boys will be boys." *And girls too*—he'd learned later in life.

Thinking about his perceived wisdoms, LC thought he smiled, but wasn't sure. He also thought he heard Everett click out the corner of his mouth—just like he was also prone to do. But again, he wasn't sure. His mind felt sharp as ever, but LC realized his hearing was failing, he wasn't fully in control of his muscles, and his visual focus was turning fuzzy. But even though all his familiar senses might be fading, there was a new sensation, a kind of electricity LC wasn't familiar with— seemingly charging and intensifying every molecule of reality he was still able to experience.

For example, he could still make out the vision of Viola sitting beside his bed, *almost glowing*, and most importantly, feel the pressure of her hand in his—the touch of her skin, the pressure of her fingers feeling slightly electrical. Magical, almost. Near sixty years of marriage, two sons—*one waiting for me in the hereafter*—and four grandchildren, *of course I know about the other one.*

It was faint, but he could still smell the warm fragrance of one of Viola's spice blends "lightly dancing on the air," as she might say; becoming part of his final breaths. Part of him.

Viola—just thinking her name touched his heart and made him feel like he might have shivered. Funny to feel a shiver that probably didn't actually happen.

A small family by some standards. *But my family.*

Continuing to look back over his life, his guiding principle, and the subsequent building of his family, LC remembered again how his early years were peppered with youthful persecutions—and how such experiences had not destroyed. *No,* those episodes had in fact fostered in him the determination, strength, and cunning needed for his eventual successes. Even pushing him not to remain just a Cooper, but to change completely, and become a Rhodes.

Luck also played a role, he knew. Even now, LC still marveled how just at the right time, Doc Rhodes gave him the money to head out into the world to make his fortune—and most remarkably, lent LC his surname along with the funds. An amount meager by today's standard, but a phenomenal amount to him at the time. Twenty-one years old, heading west out of Chicago, a new name and a "no return required" grub-stake of sorts.

My life ahead of me.

LC sighed with pleasurable pride, but doubted any of his family members gathered around him heard. His breathing felt too shallow. An odd feeling, that—but not particularly unpleasant. For a moment LC's eyes found and rested on his grandson, Leigh-Everett Rhodes, and for a flickering moment, he felt *something*, but didn't know what, or why.

LC next thought he might have sighed once more—but again, doubted anyone noticed.

On many fronts, his life had been event-filled, sometimes tumultuous—but immensely fulfilling. And in these, his waning moments, he was a happy man. *It is a blessed man indeed*, he thought, *who can pass into the hands of the Lord having accomplished everything he'd set his mind to.*

Oddly, his bedroom seemed to take on a glow, *no*, more like a brightness of its own making. LC sighed for the third time since he'd started counting, knowing this time, his breathing was slight—barely noticeable. His son Everett had placed his leather-bound bible under his left hand—now resting on his stomach. And though his grasp was slight, LC could feel the leather, experience its weathered smoothness more deeply than ever; indeed, the touch of his favored book was more comforting than any time in the past. He considered the bible a story-book of sorts, "But the best damn story ever written," he'd proclaimed to family and friends on numerous occasions.

Then quite dramatically, as if orchestrated by what he called a "Director of the Universe," *a biblical God I hope*—though even at this special moment LC wasn't unequivocally sure—he could somehow *see* outside his room, his home. *See* the sun setting; its glow dramatically exuding red, orange, and turquoise brilliance across his piece of the Mojave. And with some sense he didn't know what to name—he not only *saw*, but also *felt* the world surrounding him.

It is indeed a singular day.

And Shiné—*my addition to the Mojave is aglow and shining*. No matter what his critics wanted to say. Oh yes, LC knew quite well, many only considered him a hard businessman. But he hoped, even those with that view of him, also saw his toughness was modified by fairness to all—and most importantly, appreciated his Shiné legacy.

Few though—*maybe one besides his dear Viola*, knew the sensitivity of his true soul. *Knew* like him, sometimes you just needed to stop, take pause. Smell the roses, or flowers—similar to what that golfer Walter Hagen said. And LC hoped his touches of appreciation for the softer parts of life would survive the generations through his offspring. He could no longer tell where Leigh-Everett was standing, but he sent him a thought, a message of sorts.

And now? Well, today everything was as it should be—his family, his land and house, his substantial wealth, his town, his journal, and his jewels. He wanted to smile at the thought of the jutting and lovely hills behind his house, Lookout Loop across what was now called Shiné Valley, and his row of Pindo palms out front—which he could amazingly now see, spread panoramic and vivid across his mind's eye.

All possessions paled, however, when compared to his legendary Mojave-Stone. Thinking about his "treasures-of-treasures," LC took a few seconds to thank back across the years the unknown Humboldt County miner who had bartered away his chunks of rocks.

LC sighed a last time—more like catching a deep breath. Leigh Cooper Rhodes felt at peace with all his memories and accomplishments. He closed his eyes and imagined he was floating peacefully on the surface of a small lake in a black-pearl darkness. It was a *moment* like no other in his entire life. A *moment* when nothing mattered, where nothing could harm. He thought it the first, last, most sensuous, and only true *moment* of unadulterated contentment in his whole life.

But before leaving this world, LC *once again* reflected upon his singularity among men, and *once again* fleetingly wondered, *who among my offspring's offspring, or maybe even further down the road—will read my journal and understand?* About Viola, about lingering intents, about destinies? And who, like himself so many years ago, would gaze at a seemingly worthless handful of rocks—all potential fiery opal Mojave-Stones—and become mesmerized and transformed for life.

PART ONE
Around Shiné

Chapter One

From LC's journal: *Got to have all the old things from Europe. Not a fancy place without the "things." Learned that way back in Chicago doing yard work for rich folks in Winnetka. Fancy folks, fancy house, fancy stuff. Thank God I have my Viola to help me.*

Saturday night—years later

"You want another?" Leigh-Everett "Leiv" Rhodes asked while making a pouring-gesture with a bottle of Harvey's Bristol Crème. He'd just topped-off his own cordial glass. "It's a brand new bottle." *Nice stuff,* he reminded himself as the sherry's aroma reached his nostrils. A throat warming and sweet smelling counteractive to the dank odor and pervasive feeling of coldness Rhodes Castle often exuded. *Especially in winter. Especially tonight.* Tonight he was worried, but couldn't quite put a name to what was nagging at him.

"You know I never have more than one. Besides, I still have to write my sermon for tomorrow." Pastor Lloyd Apply shook his head and absently brushed the front of his sweater as if there were crumbs needing immediate dispatch.

Leiv saw real anguish in his friend's expression, and guessed it wasn't because he couldn't have another sherry, but concern over what to put in his sermon tomorrow morning.

It was Saturday night, a special time for Leiv. A time to enjoy his Shiné friends, good food, and his favorite sherry. He was forming a new life here, and these gatherings were crucial to making it work. *And yes,* it was also a time to play dress-up and don his vintage-styled and admittedly pretentious smoking jacket. A present from his wife before she died. Didn't matter he didn't smoke, Melissa had thought he would like the era it represented—and for him now, wearing it was his way of reaching out and touching her memory. Remembering all her kindnesses. *Dear, dear, Melissa,* he mentally whispered across the years.

Outside and unseen, but visually imagined from the reality of many such evening shows he'd seen, Leiv knew a richly-colored sun was setting across his grandfather's Shiné desert. Another hot winter day turning into the cold of a desert night.

Mojave winter days often flipped from scorching hot to bone-chilling cold in less than twenty-four hours. Consequently, Leiv didn't mind they were cloistered inside, warm and comfortable. Shut off from the rest of the world on many levels. He was happy "imagining" the sunset from the comfort of an armchair.

Yes, his special Saturday nights were made for sharing with company inside, in the comfort of his great-room. As with much in Shiné, Leiv learned about them from LC's journal. This larger-than-life room's purpose was suggested by Viola. A room his grandfather started calling the "withdrawing room." *Pompous and folksy at the same time.* "That was Leigh Cooper Rhodes," Leiv said aloud.

"Were you actually talking to me?" Lloyd shook his head again and smiled. "Or completing one of your internal thoughts in the external world?"

"You know me too well." Leiv chuckled. "Guess that's why you're a priest."

"Pastor," Lloyd said, with an exaggerated sigh. "And you know the difference."

"You could be a priest."

Lloyd laughed. "Does that mean you want me to hear your confession?"

Leiv liked the sound of them laughing together. "Heck, *NO.*"

They were ensconced in identical well-worn leather armchairs, and with his friend's refill refusal, Leiv sat the bottle of Harvey's on the small Edwardian nested side table between them. He'd done his part to be a good host—now he could sit back and further enjoy Lloyd's company. Leiv wiggled his rear-end around in his armchair's deep cushions. *Yes,* he was quite comfortable—and as he often was—reminded of LC. The chair frames were original, purchased by his grandfather in the nineteen-forties, then his father Everett had the leather and cushion-stuffing replaced in the sixties. *And still comfy.*

After exhaling a long slow breath, Leiv let his neck relax against the plush comfort of his chair's headrest. *Healing and reflective moments.* The kind of moments he'd come to expect from his Saturday nights with Lloyd and his father's old friend Margaret Deers.

"Too bad Margaret couldn't come tonight." He missed her. Indeed, her pleasant and often smiling oval face, silver hair, and fifties styled attire were comforting on several levels.

Since his return to Shiné, Margaret, like Lloyd had become a cherished inner-circle friend. *And probably more,* he reflected. *I need them both.*

"Not quite the same without her, is it?" As if toasting their absent friend, Lloyd raised his almost empty cordial glass several inches into the air.

Leiv followed with an identical gesture.

They sat facing a monster-sized wrought iron grate-protected fire—burning modestly in the quite immodest fireplace Leiv called "grandfather's stone monument." More often than not, Margaret would have been sitting on the settee to their side. Her view: the two men and that floor-to-ceiling rock fireplace with its centered, circular, but rather disappointing plain rock pattern above the firebox. Almost a star with a center stone, and almost a circle, but not quite either.

"Well, at least we have Dobie," Leiv said, pulling his attention from the fireplace to his rescued female Doberman. She was stretched out across the fireplace hearth on a handmade Anatolia Terrain hearth-rug—snoring. He thought, *she's finally comfortable enough to relax and enjoy her new home.* Margaret had suggested it might take awhile, but Dobie surprised them both, quickly making Rhodes Castle her home without missing a doggie-beat. The simple fact of Dobie's perceived doggie-happiness caused Leiv to inwardly smile. Nonetheless, despite all the pleasantness surrounding him, he couldn't shake the feeling tonight was the beginning of something very unpleasant. *And I don't have a clue what it is.*

Lloyd interrupted his reverie with, "I'm worried about Tucker." His friend paused and also placed his aperitif glass on the highly polished surface of the antique table between their chairs. "I want to say something tomorrow that might help him." Then lightly running his hand over the table's corner, the pastor mumbled absently and with characteristic wonderment, "You're lucky to have HM."

That's it, Leiv thought. *Tucker's problem is also what's worrying me.* Leiv knew Lloyd was referring firstly to the pastor's proposed Sunday sermon at Shiné Community Church and the circumstances surrounding Shiné's mayor, Tucker Oakes; then secondly, to the Rhodes housekeeper, Hester Miller Junior, dubbed affectionately and un-affectionately, depending upon the speaker—as HM, aka, Her Majesty. He couldn't remember a time when a "Hester Miller," mother or daughter, hadn't been around.

The pastor having led him to a likely source for his apprehension, Leiv relaxed more and allowed his thoughts to continue meandering. Rhodes Castle was one of the few things he, Lloyd, and Margaret shared past memories about. Lloyd explained more than once, how as a child, he was told by LC personally the significance of this room, along with the importance of the care required to maintain everything. Leiv, himself, was told by his own father, Everett, years later— furniture, tables, fireplace, *everything*—remained just the way LC wanted it. And that was due to Miller women dedication. A thought Leiv tried keeping in mind when HM was at her most annoying.

Silence between the men was easy, and in the quiet of the next few moments, Leiv's thoughts turned to the comfortableness of their friendship. It seemed as if they'd become instant friends after Leiv's return to Shiné. Often intuiting each other's thoughts or intentions. Indeed, they seemed to share a kindred philosophical and emotional view of the world. *Except when it comes to religion.* Leiv's past history as a lawyer, then as a judge, didn't seem to matter to Lloyd. He was LC's grandson—and consequently okay.

For his part—even with Lloyd's prior relationship with his mother and father—he liked Lloyd for himself, not because of past connections. Though it was nice they could share pieces of the past.

Like tonight regarding HM.

Breaking their silence, Leiv asked, "Is your sermon going to be about Naomi's death in particular?" He certainly hoped not. Leiv was uncertain Tucker could handle a direct assault on his guilty feelings. *Feelings,* he feared that could lead to terrible consequences.

"No, I can't be that direct." Lloyd made a kiddingly-derisive sound. "Have you never heard of parables?"

Ignoring Lloyd's provocative tease, Leiv said, in a reflective tone, "You want to say something general that Tucker will take personally." *Circumspection,* Leiv mentally mused while remembering several defense attorneys in particular.

"That's the idea." Seemingly reading Leiv's mind, the pastor added, "I need to be circumspect, you know. Infer, not tell."

Leiv knew Tucker felt responsible for Naomi Hall's death. Regardless of their mayor's "feelings," he and Lloyd agreed early on the young man's guilt was self induced. Leiv also knew, some in town were of a different mindset. And guilt, manufactured or real, was a heavy burden. Indeed, his days in the courtroom had taught him a lot—and seeing "guilt" up close and personal, and in many of its manifestations had convinced him of its corrosive effect. *My own guilt and regret included.*

"Can't you just talk to him in private?" A smidgen of tease edged Leiv's question. "Isn't that what a pastor's for?" Not a believer or follower of anything religious, levity sometimes crept into his comments. It was not a serious impediment to their relationship; indeed, Leiv knew full well the positive effects of churchly counseling from back during his days on the bench. He would also *never forget* watching his father give LC his bible on his grandfather's death bed. *Never forget,* the look of peace on LC's face.

"I did," Lloyd said, then turned his head to look at Leiv directly. "He says everyone thinks he killed her, you know, because of the land feud thing. Even though there isn't any evidence he did. And he can't remember doing it." He sighed.

Tucker being flat-out drunk—without one single memory during the time she died. But there really wasn't a shred of evidence implicating Tucker. Of course, Lloyd had a personal interest in the situation, being Naomi Hall's distant cousin and the executor of her estate.

"Bad situation." Leiv took a deep breath, and for a second, he felt the oddest sensation. Like he'd gone back in time and was in an Edward Hopper painting of two men and a dog—centered on a massive fireplace in an European styled and appointed great-hall. A picture emotionally capturing a moment of time marking the beginning of something—if that was possible. A flight of fancy of course, but Leiv felt throughout his being *something* was starting—*and this was the moment.* He felt an urge to shiver, but controlled it. Leiv did reach for his Harvey's bottle.

Well, whatever he was sensing couldn't be anything bad, *could it?* He felt too good sharing sermon-talk and sherry with his friend.

After Leiv replenished his cordial glass—he reckoned a full shot this time—he patted his smoking jacket pocket. *Yes,* the letter he received this morning was still there. The return label had been clear, hand written in neatly aligned capital letters—NADYA RHODES COLLINS. His deceased Uncle

André's daughter. *My first-cousin.* He'd considered discussing the implications of her letter with Lloyd. The pastor had met her when they were children, and maybe he could help him decide how worried he should be.

But for some reason, Leiv pulled his hand away from his pocket like it held a hot potato. *Not tonight.* Leiv's instincts told him whatever Nadya was bringing into his life wasn't good—but he certainly couldn't *know* that. *No,* he would not spoil tonight with conspiratorial silliness. Nonetheless, another sliver of a shiver surfaced, and this time washed over him quite thoroughly. He was surprised, but quickly recovered.

I am definitely not the same man who sat on the bench for so many years. Good or bad—he wasn't sure.

To further mock Leiv's perceived sturdiness of his former self, somewhere in what he knew to be his emotional being, fear took hold—in particular, he suddenly realized, Sunday, tomorrow, scared him. Tucker was not the entire explanation. *Nadya? Something unknown?* It took Leiv several moments to cajole his emotions back into enjoying Saturday evening with Lloyd and Dobie.

La nuit. The night, *a beautiful time in Shiné,* she thought.

Sitting on her expansive wooden-railed porch, Margaret Deers was also in a ruminative mood—with several paths of thought winding in different directions through her mind and occasionally converging. Her cats Samara and Silky her only companions.

One such thought-trail was her view of Shiné. Similar to Leiv's place, her vista was panoramic, but from a different angle. Both their properties were aeries, but Margaret's was west-facing, and Rhodes Castle looked toward the east. He saw the morning light as it first touched Shiné, while she enjoyed the brilliance of fading-light sunsets across a seemingly infinite desert horizon. On a closer to home perspective, looking down into the valley separating Shiné and Lookout Loop, she could experience the darkness of night encompassing their town as indoor lights popped on in various spots around town.

On one important psychological and emotional level, however, Margaret thought their perspectives quite similar. She and Leiv were both in the right place—Shiné—at the right times in their lives.

But things change. And with those changes, she'd found her perspective on life changing. A good thing, she thought— except when the change was based on loss. As with her dear friend Naomi.

Swiftly, Margaret tried whisking the unwanted thoughts surrounding Naomi away. But remembrances of her friend weren't so easily dispatched. *Things have already changed.* That last year with Naomi had been tough. *That woman and her temper.* But before that hard last year, their trips together around the world had been marvelous. Especially while she was still grieving for her deceased husband, Morris.

She shook herself slightly. In her mind, Morris had been a saint, and his passing not something to relive tonight. *No*, tonight, she wanted to be about the present. And in her present reality, there was the danger presented by Nadya's letter—what Margaret knew was the Cooper woman's interest in the Cooper-Rhodes legacy, and how that could affect Leiv.

In particular, *The Mojave-Stone.*

Margaret sighed and further thought, *I won't think about all that yet.* A few moments more enjoying the sunset with her cats were needed first. Still, *I wonder if Leiv understands how Nadya and her relatives view the world.* Again, she forcibly tried to banish thoughts about Leiv's cousin.

"I wish neither Naomi nor Everett had confided in me." She was aware only her cats were hearing her words, nonetheless, for some reason she thought they needed to be spoken into the world outside of her.

With Leiv's father Everett, the confidence was way-back-when in Chicago. *At a faculty cocktail party, no less.* Well, a fund-raiser actually for her beloved research. *No,* she had not been in the right place with Leiv's father—hearing secrets from an inebriate senior faculty member.

Again, Margaret tried forcing her thoughts back to the present, back to the beautifully forming sunset, back to Leiv. *The living.*

Another similarity she saw between herself and Leiv was their comfortableness being alone. But like their perches in the Shiné hills, once again coming from different directions. For her, an only child, and a widow, the peace and solitude of her own thoughts, desires, and actions were cherished, not bemoaned. While with Leiv, she was sure he was escaping. "Want to be alone these days after being so public for so long." he'd told her in a private moment. She knew it was more than that. Margaret reckoned losing Melissa had near killed him.

Probably regrets telling me now. Just like his father had regretted *his* revelations and subsequent actions so many years ago. *Seems like an eternity now.*

Yes, private time, especially now she was well into her sixties with a grown son close in age to Leiv, she was preferring her solitude more and more as the years passed. Her son Glover, Leiv, Pastor Apply, Samara and Silky—and now Dobie—were enough to populate her little world these days. Usually.

"A lot of the world we can do without," she said softly—mainly talking to herself, and partly to her cats and the world she was disparaging.

Still, there were times, like this evening, watching the sunset, when she wanted to share the moment with someone, a *human* someone. Moments like this, her fluffy black cats—Samara, nestled comfortably in her lap, and Silky stretched out on the deck at her feet futility trying to capture waning sunlight heat—were not enough. *Maybe I should have gone to Leiv's tonight,* she second guessed herself.

She felt in her smock pocket, her hand first finding her letter from Nadya, then her cellphone. *I brought it,* she thought, referring to the phone. But she didn't pull her fancy new Smartphone out to take a snapshot and send it zinging along the Internet to her surprisingly large number of online friends. *No,* electronic sharing was not enough either. She took a couple seconds to marvel anew, once she'd tiptoed online, students and teachers from over the years and past endeavors bombarded her with enthusiastic "friend" or "follow" requests. *A surprise, indeed.*

No, Margaret finally decided. She would keep this picture-perfect sunset to herself—with its brash golds, deep oranges, and burgundy-reds—all merging and morphing gloriously across her uniquely broad horizon. Her best friends Leiv and Pastor Lloyd Apply were probably missing it, comfortably sitting in front of the Rhodes Castle's massive fireplace, and she wondered if Leiv and Lloyd were able to enjoy their ritual Saturday night get-together without her. She smiled hearing her egotistic thought.

She'd begged off for some yet unclear reason. *An uneasiness about Nadya's letter, of course.* And her unwanted thoughts of her dear departed friend Naomi. She remembered that trip to Burma with Naomi, then Thailand—my had they *eaten* a lot. *Climbed* a lot of temple steps. *Seen* a lot of unique animals—she pushed away those happy yet unwanted memories because of the present day quandary they presented.

"They're probably talking about tomorrow's sermon over cordial glasses of sherry," she said, this time louder so her cats could surely hear. Neither seemed to be listening.

Margaret wondered if Lloyd would bring up Tucker's mental deterioration with Leiv? It was clear for anyone looking. Which was most of the population of Shiné. *Nosey bunch.* Margaret sighed loud enough for Samara to deign a look up in her direction. She gave her feline friend a reassuring stroke down her back.

And she would never actually say it, but suicide was possible. *Oh yes,* she mused, *suicide is an option for some.* "Poor Tucker," she said.

Saturday's sunset was disappearing rapidly across a typical Shiné winter horizon, leaving in its wake the gray and drab-feeling of dusk. Her view of the Shiné Mojave valley, she gratefully thought, was as good as the one from Rhodes Castle. *Better maybe.* Of course she didn't have a mountain in back of her; but Margaret fancied she liked the front and back openness better. Like now, it was a unique experience feeling the night encroach upon her from all sides.

She felt her phone vibrate in her pocket and pulled it out. *Glover.* Margaret answered immediately, "Dusty?"

"Just calling to check on you."

She smiled. "Are you going to church with me in the morning?" Asking the question caused her smile to disappear, but she only allowed herself a second to wonder why. Usually she enjoyed Sunday services.

"Yep," her son assured her. A few seconds passed before he asked, "Do I hear a cat purring? Are you at home, not at Leiv's?"

Margaret heard him take a deep breath, and her smile returned. "Not to worry, sweetheart. There's nothing wrong with me."

"You're sure?"

"Positive." She knew how lucky she was to have a son who gave-a-damn, but he was rather a worry-wart. Margaret knew in her heart, the main reason he took the job as Shiné's Chief of Police was to live close to her. He certainly had the *bona fides* to work at a top level in any law enforcement department he wanted. "I just didn't feel like going tonight." She rushed on before he could speak, "And don't ask me why. Don't know really."

"Okay."

After several goodnight exchanges, she was finally able to hang-up. And only then, with another sigh, Margaret allowed herself to face the real reason she hadn't gone.

Tucker. She didn't want to talk about Tucker being blamed for killing Naomi Hall. And what he might decide to do.

And should I tell what I know?

Margaret forcibly refocused her attention on the Shiné night developing before her. She could see the town below as it spread itself along Shiné's one main street, and she had a fading view of the Union Pacific rail-freight cut as it ran eastward. Tonight, few lights besides the one Shiné traffic light were coming alive in the darkness, and the tracks were silent.

The train schedules, even after all these years, still eluded her. But she considered the soothing clickity-clank of the slow moving cars a gift, no matter when they passed through. And if the weather was right, she could occasionally hear the Southwest Chief heading to Chicago from LA, making its way at that point on a section of track near Route 66. Shiné was farther north, and her usual soothing track noises came from the Union Pacific north of Shiné. Out toward Lookout Loop.

The evening was turning chilly—and though her diminutive frame was shrouded in a heavy wool-lined Native American jacket she'd purchase eons ago in Albuquerque—with the impending darkness, she felt a chill run down her back. She shook it off.

Nighttime chilliness?

No, fear of something quite unknown had already slipped tentacles into her psyche. And Tucker was in the center of it—pulling her and her friends into something yet unknown.

She pulled her jacket in tighter and hugged her arms around her torso. Then Margaret closed her eyes, her thoughts once again going backwards, this time, letting herself first fondly remember her friend and their travels. Then on the downside, remind herself Naomi was not a woman to be either trifled with or harassed.

Another reason why she hadn't gone to Rhodes Castle, enjoyable as those evening chats usually were; tonight she preferred to be alone with her memories, moral predicaments, and decision making quandary.

When Glover Deers decided to relax, he took it seriously.

This Saturday night was a "kick-back" night. He was stretched out in his favorite recliner, in front of his big screen television—at the minimum distance away for viewing—and tuned to a channel specializing in classic movies. Potato chips, a cold Dos Equis, and a bag of M&Ms were at hand. This was his idea of a perfect relaxation session.

Maybe my last one before the storm.

As to *why* he thought and felt a storm was coming eluded him. And it wasn't a weather-type storm he was anticipating. Glover knew he was a straightforward practical sort of guy, personally and professionally. So having a premonition sort of thing—if that's what you called what he was feeling—was a unique experience.

Everything was the way he wanted it—but for some reason, tonight was different. He was Shiné's Chief of Police for goodness' sakes. *Been in law enforcement all my life.* "And darned successful," he told his television, "if I do say so myself."

The TV movie host was giving a seemingly heartfelt promo for the upcoming movie. It was a World War II flick, one he'd seen and thought well made, but he didn't feel up to the carnage of world war battles tonight.

He was an unapologetic John Wayne and Gary Cooper kind of guy when it came to classic movies. Good guys were good, bad guys were bad, and that was that. No ambiguity in his fictional world of movies and books. Using his remote, Glover switched to movies he'd already recorded, and chose *High Noon*, one of his favorites. An admittedly more complicated movie than a cursory glance would indicate—but it had Gary Cooper, good versus bad, a highly dramatized ending, and Oscar-winning theme music. *What could be better?*

His movie selected, Glover could move on to worrying about his mother, Margaret. He wondered if she was at Leiv's for their regular Saturday night "philosophy gab." He could call her, see if she answered, but he didn't want her thinking he was keeping tabs. Of course, he was—and he figured she knew it. Nonetheless, he didn't want to be too obvious.

Tough being a son, sometimes.

Leaning back in his brown faux-leather recliner, he picked up his portable phone headset from its resting place on his prized IKEA side table—he'd assembled and stained it himself, then lugged it across country when moving back to Shiné. He would call his mother, and he'd probably end up going to church with her in the morning.

While he was dialing, a disconcerting and uncharacteristic shiver surprised him.

"Ain't it great?" Hester Miller had said into her cellphone. "Sunday, no later than Monday. It's gonna' be a new day."

"You're sure she's one of us?" her cousin Bersch had asked from his flat in Chicago's Lincoln Square.

"Yep. Known her family line before LC." *She's one of us on both sides.* Sometimes Bersch was dense as a two-by-four. "So do you." Hester held back an audible sigh. "She's a Cooper, remember?"

"What about her husband?"

"Treasure hunter, I'm thinking." *Why else would anyone want to marry Nadya?* She certainly didn't remember her as a dark-haired raving beauty. If not exactly homely, she certainly was plain. Hester had spent a few more minutes chatting with Bersch, then rang off.

Have to keep up family connections.

Her generous apartment was in the west-wing of Rhodes Castle, above the household kitchen. Her parlor—as she called it according to LC's wishes and passed on to her by her mother—was comfortably furnished in the same Edwardian styled furniture, rugs, and accoutrements LC procured with fervor for the entire house decades ago. *Viola,* the name popped into her mind for a second, and she smiled. *Another secret only I know.* Viola's influence on LC's purchasing decisions.

Not that Hester hadn't made her own mark in her piece of Rhodes Castle. *"Dull old Europe stuff,"* she occasionally mumbled. She bought colorful throws, pillows, hanging lamps—which oddly enough fit right in. In cahoots with her purchases, Hester often had a saucepan on the stove in her little personal kitchen with an herbal mixture she claimed came from her great-great-grandmother. Thinking about the herbs, she smiled again. She actually found the concoction on the Internet.

I have an image to uphold.

Indeed, no one but Hester knew her actual age, and she planned on keeping it that way. In truth, she was only a teenager in LC's time, but her mother, Hester Miller Sr. had taught her everything, and she quite purposefully dressed, spoke, and carried herself to give the impression there was only one Hester Miller—from the earliest days of Rhodes Castle to the present. *And there always will be someone like me to carry on the traditions LC so wanted to bury.* Unfortunately, Hester was childless.

Maybe the next someone will be called Nadya?

Sitting in front of her own fire in her own more modest fireplace—this Saturday night, Hester felt quite good, with her feet toasty warm in thick socks. She'd intercepted and read Nadya's letter of course, before giving it to clueless Leiv. Then she'd called Bersch to find out what he knew. Turned out, not much.

Her call now a memory, Hester reaffirmed aloud into her high ceilinged old-English parlor, "Someone who understands is coming. Someone who appreciates what we're duty bound to protect." She wasn't sure who she was talking to, but knew someone, somewhere back in time was listening.

"Soon the Mojave-Stone will be in good hands again."

Sydney Collins pulled his eyes off his wife Nadya for a few moments to take in the Las Vegas Strip, sparkling and alive many floors below. "Glad you asked for a tower room." *Lovely.* Both Nadya *and* the lights below. *Unbelievable, really.* This was a moment like so many previous moments, when he thanked his lucky stars Nadya loved him. *This fantastic creature, and she's all mine.* There was little he wouldn't do for her—going forward with their lives, or going back to fix the past. Though *going back* would be a bit complicated, and not just his decision alone.

They were standing shoulder-to-shoulder at their upscale Las Vegas styled and engineered-for-the-view window. She snuggled in closer, slid her arm around his waist, and said, "I knew you'd like the view."

He was about a foot taller than her, and Sydney thought their bodies fit together just perfect. He sighed happily, and didn't realize he had until he heard his expression of contentment himself. But who could ask for a better wife—and such a perfect moment in such a perfect place?

He hadn't really wanted to leave Chicago—a lot of paperwork—and fly out to the far reaches of the country. *The desert, no less. California, no less.* And just to visit a cousin in some strange town Nadya's grandfather had started. *Who starts a town in the desert anyway?* Though to be fair, when he called in, they hadn't cared. As long as he stuck to the rules. Rules he'd so far diligently followed. Then Nadya told him about the Mojave-Stone, and everything from his perspective changed.

Finally, he and Nadya actually landed in Vegas and settled in their hotel tower room facing the strip. And surprisingly, a tingle of excitement had edged its way into his emotions. *If you didn't count the airports and planes, this trip might turn out to be very interesting.* Fortunately, he had the best COO a man could ask far to run his box business back in Schiller Park, and Sydney figured he could take a couple months off without a problem.

"This will be fun," he said, his mind not only on Nadya, but also on what she'd told him about the desert, Shiné, her cousin Leiv, and the Mojave-Stone.

Nadya let her head fall against his chest and didn't say anything.

He took her cuddle of endearment as agreement, They were about to have an exciting adventure together. *Yep,* he was a happy man, and wished all moments of his life could be like this one.

Chapter Two

From LC's journal: *I'm having my altar, don't give a darn if
Reverend Armstrong has his britches all bunched up. Altars make a
church. And a church, a tavern, and sidewalks make a town. Viola
will prevail with the church and sidewalks...but I'm thinking...the
tavern is up to me.*

Sunday Morning

It was seldom Pastor Lloyd Apply missed the furtive
early leavings of his congregation members. *Furtive*, because
valid reason or not, leaving before service ended was
communally frowned upon. He wasn't sure if the censure was
due to a sense of politeness, or rather, an "If I have to stay, so
do you," attitude.

Most times, he saw them sneak out—more often
during his sermon than during group discussions—usually
with their eyes down, stealthy in movement, and quick to
cover the distance between pew and door. The side door was

favored, a darker and quieter spot, and less likely to run into late arrivers coming in the main door.

This Sunday morning, Lloyd watched Tucker stand up abruptly and walk determinedly toward the exit door at the side of the church's monstrous altar. Nothing secretive or abashed in his movements—more like a man set on a task he didn't want to be distracted from.

Good thing I didn't spend hours on my sermon, was Lloyd's first thought. He liked the fact Shiné Community Church—*my church*—was large, even though his congregation was small. An additional reason why a lengthy "walk-of-shame" from front to the massive double-entry doors behind them was seldom done. Indeed, as purposeful as Tucker's exit was, he hadn't headed to the main doors. Though Lloyd guessed it wasn't shame motivating Tucker this morning. *No,* Tucker's body movements indicated his hastily departing parishioner was in a hurry.

Lloyd wanted to sigh and make a face of displeasure. Of course he couldn't. Though, in what he thought a nonchalant movement, he turned slightly to watch Tucker better, angling his body more toward the large Catholic-religion-style and size altar behind him. *LC and his grandiose statements,* flitted through his mind. Indeed, the huge altar was inlaid around its edge with an eclectic selection of rocks, with one *exceedingly dull looking one,* Lloyd also thought, *and unfortunately in center position.*

But what caught everyone's eye and made the altar a majestic item and grandiose statement was the bronze relief sculpture spanning its entire front—telling the story of Jesus in three panels. Showing Him in Gethsemane, at the Crucifixion, and the moment when He appears to Mary Magdalene at his tomb. Lloyd knew LC stole the idea from a church in Chicago, and he could almost remember the original artist's name—but not quite. He'd yet to use the altar—their services did not require it—but Lloyd decided to talk about it a little today, asking what his congregation thought. Maybe they could plan an event around the history of its building. *A way maybe to get Tucker back into the community?* He eventually assessed his plan as feeble, but also hadn't come up with anything better.

Lloyd was just getting to the altar part in his sermon where he planned to segue into his group discussion where he'd hoped Tucker and the twenty so members gathered today would have a frank discussion. A *discussion* that would help Tucker get over his guilt. *No hope for that now. Tucker's fled.*

He didn't think Tucker's leaving had anything to do with his sermon, per se. Indeed, he tried to keep it upbeat, nothing to set anyone off. Since his desire to come up with some parabolic homily had not materialized, he instead decided to next talk about charitable giving in the modern world. *Then* he hoped to move to guilt associated with the crucifixion, *then* to the altar, *then* to the altar celebration, *then* back to guilt in general. *Won't happen now.* Still, maybe a discussion about guilt would materialize in their group without Tucker.

An impulse to run after Tucker surfaced for a moment, but like showing his disapproval, he couldn't follow him—service wasn't over yet, and he was the pastor for goodness' sake. Lloyd also wanted to glance down at his watch—but didn't do that either. *Has to be almost noon.*

Out of the blue, he thought he sensed a shared wave of emotion move through the group of parishioners facing him. An emotion he couldn't identify, not even label as malevolent or good. *Something to do with Tucker?* It was a happening he'd never experienced before. *Had his imagination run amok?* He also thought he heard a couple conspiratorial whispers, but didn't see any head leanings, facial expressions, or gestures. In fact, everyone seemed calm—just looking at him expectantly, waiting for him to continue.

Except for Margaret. He read her expression as worried alarm; which was disquieting. She was usually the fresh breath of happiness and good cheer beaming back at him. But what he saw in her eyes and the downturn of the corners of her lips was definitely not uplifting. He did notice her son, the Chief of Police, had joined her this morning. Good signal to the whole community.

High Noon. The two iconic words took hold of his consciousness—seemingly from nowhere—and obliterating any other thoughts. *What a strange moment, what a strange thought,* he almost said aloud.

With his head dropped back, his face looking upward, Tucker released his words to the sky, "At last."

It was a Mojave sun-baked high noon. *Perfect.* Didn't make any difference it was winter—it was still hot. Real hot. *Just Perfect.* He left church just at the right moment, then he'd taken the drink he'd prepared before driving back home. *A stolen drink from a woman I hated. Now dead.*

Tucker Oakes had made the special five foot diameter stone circle he now stood in three years earlier. It was his special spot—on a light rise in the earth, and right in the center of everything he claimed as his. A tall thin man, from this spot, he could see his alfalfa field surrounding him, his rows of pistachio trees in the distance to his right, and his nectarine orchard to his left. And behind him closer to the house, his recently plowed-under watermelon field. And behind him, were the mountains—*hills really.* A fleeting smile touched his lips. He was a Mojave farmer in the Shiné bowl. *More important than being Mayor.*

And on this *perfect* day, his alfalfa field surrounded him—once deeply colored, almost forest-green and vibrantly proliferated with bluish-purple flowers. But now, Tucker could *see* heat rising and rippling through the air—smell its burning parchment-like odor. Not like summer heat—*no,* winter heat had its own smell. Half an acre away, his circular pivot irrigation boom now stood idle—looking dejected as if water would never flow through its long and graceful boom ever again—even though surrounded by its children, so-to-speak. Of course his boom would water again. *But not by me. All Cal's now.*

High Noon. *Perfect.*

With a winter sun engulfing him, Tucker stood in the middle of his special circular place—his go-to-church jacket, tie, and shirt left in the car—now hatless, barefoot on pebbled sand, and dressed in a short sleeved T-shirt and the jeans he'd worn to church. And though an unseasonably hot winter day, it certainly was not as bright as a July day—allowing him to look straight up into the sky without protective glasses.

Tucker knew it was after twelve, but didn't now know how long he'd actually been standing in the heat, or remember the exact time when he'd left church. Had to be at least an hour ago.

All he knew was he wasn't sweating anymore, and his brow was dry. Hopefully, by now he was dehydrated. He hadn't allowed himself anything to drink last night and all this morning except for his special concoction stolen from Naomi Hall's garage.

I didn't really want her dead. Did I?

Never knew what *she* used it for, environmentalist she claimed to be, but the diminutive but bright red X on the bottom of the little bottle told him it was poison. *And a fancy bottle it was.* Antique, he'd guessed. A bottle he'd found skulking around—*trespassing actually*. Fitting he was using it now. *My end will be soon.*

He remembered this morning, while still sitting in church, already craving water, and Pastor Apply just wouldn't seem to stop talking. Endless it had seemed. Eventually he just got up and escaped. He prayed his collapse was imminent, while they were all chattering away without him. Possibly about him.

Perfect.

Running his dry tongue along his dry lips, Tucker could taste Mojave dust, and for some reason, it was sweet. If he brought his head back down, he could still see Lookout Loop in the distance in front of him, even though he faintly heard the very edge of railroad cars clanking along—from or to Barstow, he didn't know—for the tracks were at least ten miles away. *But if conditions are just right.* Tucker liked trains, and in the past he'd driven north and west to Kelso Station, built by the Union Pacific Railroad, in the twenties he thought—to see and feel the past. *I'll miss the trains.* Then he wondered if there were trains in heaven—*how silly.*

But all in all, he was glad his body was finally shutting down—actually reveling in the feeling of being inside an oven—baking from the inside out. *Yes,* he would die today. In fact, it was what he wanted—and it would be a just and farmer-like end. *Better than rotting in jail for a murder.* A murder he may or may not have committed.

Tucker wanted to cry out loud, tell the world, *I should have been nicer to her.* But he couldn't seem to make his voice or lips work; there didn't seem to be any saliva in his mouth. And for his sins, he would melt into the earth standing in the middle of his land—Oakes Ranch.

Finally, Tucker dropped his head all the way forward, his chin almost touching his chest, and closed his eyes. He caught his breath and heard a choking-like sound come from within. And he really didn't know if he was still standing.

Not much longer.

It had been a silly feud—a *feud* that now made him the prime suspect in her death. Everybody knew they were fighting over land boundaries, maybe even heading to court. But what was eating at him the most, was the fact he hadn't been nicer to "The Spinster Woman." He could have said a kind word to her, here and there.

She'd been alone, now hadn't she? Now she was dead—and he hadn't been there to stand at her gravesite. *Couldn't bear it.* Too ashamed. *Flat out drunk when she died. No idea what I actually did.* All he'd cared about was her obstructing his road.

His lack of kindness—plain old-time friendliness—spoke to what kind of man he was when it came to Naomi. It was not a man he could now tolerate being. Of course he recognized he wasn't Naomi's keeper; she was alone he suspected because of decisions *she'd* made.

Still.

At last. Tucker was beginning to feel faint. *I must still be standing,* he realized because his knees felt weak, like he was going to drop to the ground. A fitting end, dying of heat exhaustion in the middle of his precious Oakes Ranch. In the winter, at Mojave desert high-noon time.

He licked his lips again, they were even dryer, and this time he tasted salt. Tucker thought a slight smile flickered across his face for a second, though he couldn't feel his facial muscles move. This dust had turned from sweet to salty, and he wouldn't be able to tell his brother, Cal.

Cal. A gentle soul. He'd take care of Ida, a strong woman in her own right. *Funny,* he thought for the first time—

now that he was dying, *Cal will probably miss me more than Ida. Brothers, it was like that with brothers,* he vaguely supposed. His thinking was getting a bit fuzzy.

And slowly, but at last, he was losing his balance. Tucker looked back up, thought he saw a silent airplane gliding through the sky above. *Of course it couldn't be*—there were no flight patterns over Shiné at any altitude. An apparition? *Of course it was*—and a premonition of something about to happen? *Of course it was*—and there was nothing he could do to stop what he saw as the inevitable. His death. And it was what he wanted.

Better to die this day , rather than sitting on death row waiting for your turn in the gas chamber, or whatever California was planning on using next. Moratoriums didn't last forever. *Leaving now,* was a good decision. At my place, at my time of "execution."

"Tucker!" For a moment, the distraught male voice he heard from the distance was for him, the only sound in the world. "What the heck are you doing?" the voice continued, even louder.

Tucker finally dropped to his knees and clamped his hands over his ears to ward off his brother's yelling and the sound of feet running toward him. *No, no,* the words screamed inside his head. *Go home, Cal, go home. Let me die, let me die.*

Ida Oakes loved free-floating in her pool, and yes, it was *her* pool. Her husband Tucker only built it because she'd insisted, and rarely used it himself. *All the better,* she thought, her face down in the water, holding her breath with arms and legs stretched out—her body almost flat and riding near the surface. She was buoyant that way, and knew it had something to do with lung capacity, body type, bone structure, weight, fat—all that stuff. But she certainly couldn't say how it all fit together or worked. What she did know was she could float for ages, turning her head when she needed to get a breath of air. And it felt good.

She especially *loved* floating when Tucker was out and about, doing whatever he was doing—like trying to make stuff grow in this patch of desert-dirt she was stuck on. Or on a Sunday morning like this one, with Tucker and all the other Shiné yahoos in church—floating was even more delicious.

Here I escape, was Ida's first thought as she let her naked body relax and become a lithe leaf floating on the water's surface. Indeed, she could hold her breath for ages. It was her alone moments. Most of the time. Ida knew her brother-in-law, Calvin, did occasionally accidently-on-purpose walk by her glass enclosed pool. Catch her floating. Saw her nakedness. *Not much I miss, even while floating.* And even though her face was underwater, she smiled without breathing or opening her mouth. Tucker and Calvin.

Only I know the truth. And now, at last, she had the two brothers to herself. *And why not?* What else was there in this god-forsaken place? *Not much, now was there?* Ida thought she heard a siren even though her ears were below the water's surface. She brushed off the annoying intrusion as a volunteer fire department practice drill. Nothing to be concerned about.

Intent on enjoying her water escape, she continued to ignore the shrill wailings—even though for some strange reason, they seemed to be getting closer.

Leiv seldom attended his friend's Sunday services. The pastor had told him on several occasions he understood his absence, and didn't mind; but Leiv guessed Lloyd was actually disappointed. He was a wayward sheep Lloyd wished he could pull into the protection of the flock.

Consequently, after Sunday breakfasts, which he always prepared for himself, and while most of Shiné population spent Sunday mornings listening to Pastor Lloyd Apply's words of wisdom, Leiv took the time to reflect in private. Often in his library—like he was this Sunday morning. Sundays were indeed special, but no matter the day of the week, the question, *"Library or cupola?"* was often his first wide-awake thought.

From the start when he moved back to Shiné, Leiv insisted HM take Sundays off, and this morning, HM had requested Dobie hang out with her. He imagined Sunday mornings were a lonely time for HM since her mother died. For him, it was a long time after losing Melissa before he was free from fighting minute-by-minute depression. *It's still tough.*

Remembering Melissa, Leiv sighed, but refused to let himself mentally wander back to those horrible days, and pulled his mind back to his Sunday morning musings.

Even if it was Sunday and HM and Dobie considerations aside—*cupola or library*—had, as always, risen for consideration. Should he experience the sunrise from LC's five-sided cupola with its generous windows and window seats at the very top of Rhodes Castle, or from his old-world-comfortable and richly adorned library—most assuredly the heart of LC's monument. Leiv felt like he could reach out to his grandfather across the years from both places—though neither place had as strong a connection as LC's secret cave.

In the library, he could also touch his father. His grandfather LC started developing "The Library," and left his distinct imprint there. Then his father, Everett, built upon it, adding his own touches.

Now, it was his to enjoy and embellish. *Yes,* he looked fondly at the surrounding floor to ceiling glass-fronted bookcases—now jammed full of legal tomes. He'd shipped much of his law library to Shiné—some he'd given away. Many he would never read again, probably not even open. They were comfort-possessions. A piece of his life he could carry forward with him. Books he could feel, touch, smell— and know he was the same man, even though in a different spot on planet earth.

Further enhancing Leiv's pleasure, the library featured an attraction only a few Rhodes Castle rooms and the cupola possessed—large windows that were not stained glass like the entryway on the floor below. The library's one large window was plain and clear, looking east and allowing him to fully appreciate the *promise* that came with Shiné sunrises.

On Sunday mornings like this one, having enjoyed a Saturday night get together with Lloyd and Margaret, Leiv usually had several philosophical nuggets to ponder as he either sat at LC's desk, or lounged in his father's armchair while gazing outward through LC's clear window to the world.

Leiv occasionally wondered, *had the window been LC's sneaky way of keeping an eye on things from on-high, and unobserved?* A spot to see who was coming up his long, and to Leiv's mind, overstated circular driveway. An architectural design based on practical considerations, not aesthetics? This morning, Leiv's own thoughts were also on practical matters. He'd read Nadya's letter, and it had shaken him a bit. He was not yet sure why.

I need this time. And I need Grandfather's library to think.

Leiv liked his cousin Nadya in their younger days, and wondered how different she was now? But more importantly, *why* was she visiting *now? Of course.* She was married *now.* But that really shouldn't make a difference to him—though somehow, Leiv knew it did. She was bringing a new person, her husband, into the mix of his Shiné life. Again, that shouldn't make a difference, *should it?* An acceptable, or even clear answer eluded him.

Leiv's internal questioning did not last long. Abruptly, and without any precognitive forewarning, sirens in the distance broke through his library quiet.

"Oh no," he said aloud. *Our EMT ambulance?* At first, he thought so, and sounding as if they were heading farther east, out toward Tucker's place. *No,*not the local guys. The shrill noises were coming from the freeway, coming into town. *Damn,* meant something Shiné volunteer paramedics needed help with.

Without second thought he got up quickly and rushed out of the library without closing the door behind him. Once downstairs in front of the massive entry staircase that separated castle wings, he ran into Hester and Dobie peering through the front door's thick stained glass windows. They would have looked cute, or comical, or even sweet, if the feeling in the pit of his stomach wasn't so strong. He'd been forewarned last night. Whatever he was dreading and fearing had started. He'd had the same feeling before several horrendous cases that went on forever, full of gore, hyped by the media and ravenously eaten up by the public.

"I'm going to see what's going on with all those sirens," he said.

"Noise of the devil," Hester responded, with a noticeable touch of apprehension underneath her words that surprised Leiv.

He seldom used the monster double-door garage connected to the far end of Rhodes Castle LC had been so proud of—preferring to leave his dark-blue Ford pickup out front where it was easy to get to. Enough trauma just driving—didn't need the added aggravation of walking what seemed like half a mile to the end of the house, through the kitchen and pantry, and once there, struggling to open horse-drawn-carriage evocative doors, then closing them when he left.

Besides, he liked going out LC's front door. The stained glass always brought thoughts of his grandfather, and what he must have been thinking when the doors and windows were installed. LC's journal reflected excitement sometimes, and frustration occasionally. At the moment, he couldn't remember how the entry door installation went; his mind was on the sirens. Leiv did remember LC was very proud of them.

"Stay with Hester," Leiv admonished Dobie as he rushed outside to his truck. He was surprised how warm it was. Hot actually. But then again, it was in the middle of the day on a bright sunny winter afternoon.

High Noon flitted through his brain. He had no idea why.

Then Leiv straightened his back, tightened his jaw, breathed deeply, and whispered his mantra, almost inaudible except to his own ears. "I can drive, I will drive, I can drive, I will drive."

But that all-too-familiar little voice from the other side of his brain—*his amygdala*, Margaret had told him as if she knew—warned, *just stay in Shiné, stay in Shiné and you'll be okay.*

"This is not Chicago," Leiv whispered to himself.

* * * * *

As soon as Chief of Police Glover Deers heard sirens, he patted the knee of his mother sitting next to him, stood abruptly, then rushed to leave Shiné Community Church through the main double-doors in back. No slinking out for him. Sirens meant something was not good in Shiné, and he was in uniform, on duty. This was his bailiwick, his responsibility.

Truth was, he was pretty much always on duty and consequently often in uniform, including jacket—like this morning in church. Except, he always took his hat off in church, of course. *Mother would be mortified if I didn't.* Besides the dictates of good manners, Glover had chosen his own uniform, head to toe, and his three-inch brimmed "Smokey the Bear" Campaign hat—which he was quite fond of and paid dearly for—was a bit much for many. Especially inside.

Hatless or not, in church or not, a law enforcement officer needed to be prepared on all fronts. Especially if you were the only "it" guy. A small town like Shiné didn't need two cops sitting around twiddling their thumbs; while at the same time, sometimes it was a lot for one man to handle.

The few times something big came up, like when the motorcycle ruckus spilled over from Laughlin to Shiné a few years back, he'd deputized Tucker and his brother Calvin to help out. And there was always the San Bernardino County Sheriff's deputies to fall back on if he really needed help. In fact, his Shiné office, a storefront like most businesses in town, was a modest affair, with a cold-room out back, and in front, two desks, a bench, and a small break area. One desk was kept just for whatever public safety personnel might be visiting. He liked to think of it as a courtesy sitting-spot.

Within seconds of leaving church, Glover was on his portable radio. Then within another minute or so he was in his patrol car scanning his Mobile Data Terminal, checking his two-way, then his GSM communication system. Consequently, within a very few minutes Glover had all the information he needed to track down the sirens piercing what had previously been a tranquil Shiné Sunday morning.

He sighed and prepared himself to address what he now knew was a "Medical Emergency"—at Tucker Oakes's place.

Damn.

Leiv was aware his hands were squeezing the steering wheel tighter than they should be, but it was the best he could do—especially since what he really wanted to do was pull over.

"This is worse than most times," he told himself out loud.

Why so bad today?

He tried to make his hands relax. They refused to obey. *Stupid.* Beating up his hands wouldn't bring Melissa back.

The sirens were drawing him toward Tucker's place. "Jeez." Tucker was at the center of this. His senses started telling him he was heading to Tucker's a few miles back, but he hadn't yet wanted to face what his body and mind were telling him.

Avoiding the obvious—he'd seen a lot of that during his days on the bench. Defense and Prosecution both—*avoiding the obvious.*

Glover stood stiffly, hat in hand, next to Calvin Oakes, as they stared into the back of the ambulance where Tucker was stretched out on a gurney. Tucker looked lifeless to the Chief, but an IV tube was attached to his arm and an oxygen mask covered much of his face.

Still alive.

"We're taking him to Barstow immediately," Walker Johns, a Shiné voluntary paramedic said, climbing down out the ambulance. Then he closed the doors, cutting off their view. "Barstow might send him to Victorville, or maybe down below."

"I'm going with you," Calvin half demanded, half pleaded. "Isn't there a hospital closer?"

Glover put a hand on Calvin's arm, hoping to both calm and comfort. "You know Barstow is closer than Needles." *Not much,* he admitted to himself. "The faster he sees a doctor," he let his sentence fade to nothingness. Glover wanted Calvin to hang around, to fill him in on why Tucker evidently tried to kill himself; but he knew Calvin needed to go be with his brother. Turning to Walker, he asked, "Dehydration?"

"I'm not a doctor, but looks a little worse than that— he's not as responsive as you'd hope." Walker darted a quick look at Calvin. "We're treating him for shock. I'd say something else is going on too." He shook his head. Calvin turned away, and Walker took the opportunity to lean in closer to Glover. He said in a low voice, "I'm worried he's slipping into a coma." Then without further ado, Walker hurried to the side door of the ambulance, hand-signaled to the driver, and hopped in. Glover turned to talk to Calvin, but Tucker's brother was already getting into his yellow Focus, clearly planning on following the ambulance and his brother.

Soon the sun would begin its downward sweep across the western horizon—and Glover knew in winter, that afternoon descent was quick. Hopefully, they would make it into Barstow—or farther if need be—before the sun would be blazing into their eyes. *Well, can't worry about Cal.* He had enough on his own plate here in Shiné. It hadn't passed Glover's notice Calvin didn't mention Ida, leaving him the one stuck calling her, telling her about her husband.

Never liked the Ida Oakes woman.

Glover wasn't surprised by his spontaneous and callous thought. Indeed, he didn't consider himself the most fair-thinking of men—*as long as I apply the law fairly.* From first meeting Tucker's wife, he experienced a visceral dislike to her. He remained unsure why.

Glover sighed lightly, rubbed his chin, and clicked out the side of his mouth a couple times—taking a few moments to think about his next duty and options. He ended up pulling his cellphone out of his uniform jacket and pressing button number five. No answer, eventually going to voicemail, and he left a quick message for his mother. Next, he pressed button number six, while praying Margaret had talked to Ida before he had to.

His call to button number six was accepted, and Glover asked, "Leiv?"

"Yep."

"Can you meet me out at Tucker's place? Out in his field. Can't miss my cruiser."

"I'm already heading there."

Glover shook his head and realized his brow was wet. He took his hat off for a moment and swiped his forehead with his sleeved right arm, even though he was well aware leather wasn't the right material to conquer sweat. "You know it's illegal to drive while you're on your cellphone." He started to wiggle out of his jacket, but decided to wait until he'd rung off.

"I'm driving in Shiné," Leiv said. "What the hell am I going to hit?"

True enough. Glover rang off without answering Leiv's question aloud. He did think his friend's teasing tone quivered a tad, but that didn't fit the Leiv he knew, so he chalked it up to cellphone reception—which sucked in most of Shiné. There were too many surrounding hills, and they weren't close enough to either of the transmitters running along I-15 or I-40.

He was a Chief of Police, but Glover knew when he needed help. He would have turned to Tucker or Calvin, but both those options were obviously out. And Leiv Rhodes was the smartest person he knew. Besides, he liked Leiv, though he never really thought of him as a "cop type."

Glover realized he was suddenly getting really hot, *like Tucker must have been standing in that circle.* Leiv probably wouldn't be there for another ten minutes or so, so he pulled off his jacket to let his long-sleeved blue uniform shirt "breathe." Glover was in the camp of loose fitting attire covering as much of your body as possible. With a sigh, he walked over to his Crown Victoria, scraping the ground slightly with his feet—then caught himself. It was a habit from childhood, often used when things weren't going his way. Well, his childhood was long gone and Tucker Oakes had evidently tried to kill himself.

Unconsciously giving in to the discomfort he was feeling from the heat, Glover further rolled up his sleeves, revealing his Coleman look alike-tattoo. His mother had told him his father had a August "Cap" Coleman tattoo, and his grandfather a real one. He'd never noticed his father's, or met his grandfather; but in homage to both and Cap Coleman— and quite inebriated at the time—Glover had followed suit with a look-alike eagle. His way of touching all three men. Standing in the blazing sun this afternoon, hot as hell, Glover scoffed aloud, remembering the sentimentality and stupidity of that moment so long ago. Getting that tattoo had hurt like hell.

Nobody was left at the scene to complain about his dress code or stare at his tattoo anyway. Yet he was reluctant to leave, now intuitively wanting Leiv to also take a look at Tucker's suicide circle. Maybe see something he hadn't.

Sure, there was a lot of talk, but not enough for Tucker to want to kill himself. And Shiné's mayor never hit Glover as a coward, or weak in the face of adversity. *Maybe he was trying to protect someone else? But who?* No names popped up. Nor motives other than Tucker's personal feelings of guilt.

Guilt with a capital-G was a powerful motivator.

Before he dropped into the front seat of his cruiser to turn on the motor and the AC while he waited for Leiv, Glover found Ida Oakes in his directory, then pressed the dial button on his cell phone. *I need to do this myself.* Not much of a son, relying on his mother to do his dirty work. Hopefully he could next go over and tell her in person.

Informing someone their loved one was dead, was a terrible job. A task he'd performed too many times in the past in various jurisdictions.

Chief of Police Glover Deers sighed one more time— loud, plaintive, and resigned. He'd cooled off a bit and rolled his shirt sleeves back down.

Leiv wasn't sure what caught his eye, *maybe* a flash of sunlight on metal? *Maybe* just one of those hunches that aren't really explainable? He'd heard lawyers hundreds of times in the past trying to turn what he considered hunches into evidence, or at a minimum, logical deductions a jury could latch on to.

Today, there was the swirl of sand fueling his hunch, a "devil-tornado," he called them. This one was small by comparison, isolated, but an arrow-marker of sorts. *"There's something here,"* the devil-tornado said to Leiv. *"Come take a closer look."*

Leiv said, "Let's look over there." He pointed to the eastern edge of Tucker's field where he saw the flicker of light.

"Something caught your eye?" Glover asked.

"I think so." Leiv knew they were walking away from Tucker's circle—a circle a man had wanted to die in—*this very noon-time.* And from the way Glover described Tucker's condition, their mayor had possibly accomplished his desired deed. The thought made Leiv sad—almost sick to the stomach.

He brought his attention back to the *something* pulling at him, out in the distance, on the far edge of the alfalfa field near the road. Away from Tucker's circle of death, and toward *something* he feared was equally bad. Or possibly worse than Tucker's attempted suicide?

Hopefully just a stupid devil-tornado causing me to make a fool of myself.

He heard Glover say behind him, "Why were you coming out here to Tucker's anyway?"

"You called me."

"You were already on your way."

Leiv didn't answer. How could he explain to the Chief of Police he was both compelled and nosey, without Glover thinking him ridiculous. He liked Glover and considered his mother Margaret a close friend; but his own lifelong curiosity about other people's lives was something he thought best kept private. Curiosity was not the first trait that came to mind when thinking about a judge. But he knew from his own experience, it certainly had been part of why he'd kept at it—*maybe longer than I should have.*

Silently, Leiv led the way east toward a slight hillock he fancied was calling him—all the way there, very careful not to step on flowering alfalfa plants if possible. He found the small bluish-purple blossoms appealing—though not luxurious like other flowers he couldn't remember the names of. And with the summer crops, little yellow butterflies would flitter from flower to flower throughout the fields. There were no butterflies this time of year.

Melissa would know the butterfly's name. It seemed like his wife knew the names of every butterfly imaginable. Unconsciously, a slight smile of remembered fondness flickered across his face. *My Melissa died far too young.* He caught himself, and consciously pushed his developing train of thought away. *Not now.* Not the time for his personal sadness and regret. The present was far more compelling than waddling around in the past.

Turning his head slightly, Leiv said over his shoulder, "Just a little farther." *Probably making a fool of myself.*

His thoughts now firmly in the present, Leiv smiled fully thinking about Glover following him—solidly built and making quite a statement in his cowboy boots and uniform, his jacket slung over his shoulder, a slight swagger to his walk, and his three-inch brimmed Campaign Hat topping it off. They were of the same height, but Glover always seemed to Leiv as sturdy-looking, like a pillar of strength; while he pictured himself as more the lanky-looking type, even in judicial robes. In Leiv's mind, Glover was a perfect fit for Shiné's Police Chief. *And here he is, indulging me, following along on some stupid hunch.*

Leiv kept walking, and with a building and unexpected sense of urgency. In addition, a fear of the unknown had also seeped into his consciousness. Quite unnoticed until this moment. *Something bad had begun,* he previously thought, and now *felt.* What Leiv said was, "Suddenly turning cold." He shivered. "Don't you think?"

From his rear, Glover said, "It's winter, you know." Then he made a grumbling sound. "Personally, I'm hot as hell."

One of the things he liked about Glover was his chiding sense of humor. Similar to Margaret's. And for a second, Leiv wanted to laugh, but what he thought he was seeing wasn't humorous at all. Quickly he stretched his arm out to his side, and said, "Stop, don't go past me." All his instincts told Leiv the piece of weathered black leather with what looked like a zipper tab attached, sticking straight up out of the sand, and lightly moving with the ground level swirls of wind and sand was not innocent desert trash. "Damn," Leiv added, waiting for Glover to reach his side.

Once the Chief's gaze was also pointed to where Leiv's was, Glover said, "Is that what I think it is?"

He wasn't looking at Glover's face, but Leiv heard him sigh slow and long—a *sigh* seeped in what Leiv easily recognized as a *weariness* akin to his own when he'd finally left the bench. A *weariness* of criminals, death, and evil. *Now it's here in Shiné.*

Of course he had no way of knowing this wasn't the result of an accident. But he intuited murder—even before he was sure. Murder. *I can feel it, taste it.* Indeed, The Bench had "seasoned" him into perceptive shoe leather, as Melissa had been want to say when confronted with his too often negative perspective and predictions.

"We'd better make sure," Glover said.

A few more steps and Leiv was *sure.* And from the tone of Glover's second sigh, he figured the Chief was *sure* too.

Even though he still felt cold, Leiv watched as Glover took off his hat, swiped at his forehead with the back of his hand, then looked up toward the sky where the sun, though descending through the afternoon horizon, still hung fairly high.

"I need to notify the Sheriff's Dept and probably the State Police." Glover sighed yet again, this time, Leiv heard distaste and frustration also edging his weary tone. "More than I can handle on my own." Glover reached for his portable radio clipped on his hip. "Stay right here, will ya? Until I get backup or some Sheriff gets here?" Then he turned around back toward his car, mumbling, "We'll need a bus, a forensics team—"

Leiv stopped listening before Glover was out of earshot. His eyes and mind were now lasered-in on the weathered leather jacket sleeve encasing a dead person's arm, looking like it was trying to escape from the earth. *Indeed.* The human hand—dry, wrinkled, and mummified looking, was protruding out of the sleeve and reaching out in such a way as if trying to touch a beautiful Sunday afternoon desert sky.

Of course I'll stay here. How could he possibly leave? A person's body had been lying out there in the sand for who-knew-how-long—alone and unnoticed. But now he had been found, no one would leave him alone anymore. The living didn't always get the attention they deserved, but dead bodies, now that was something else. Another lesson from the bench.

After a deep refortifying breath, Leiv took a long moment to finally look around again. They were on the very edge of Tucker's property maybe, but it also could be they'd crossed over onto Naomi's property.

Naomi Hall. The source of Tucker's guilt ridden suicide.

He shook his head in the same manner he'd done so often in the past, in private moments when retreating to his chambers after a long and tiring session in the courtroom.

People and their seemingly serendipity connections. *Always amazing*, Leiv thought, and wondered where Tucker's attempted suicide, Naomi's death, and this John-Doe body would lead him. Rather, *them*—him and Glover.

Glover could see Leiv's back in his rear-view mirror. *Still standing there.* "Good," he said aloud to himself. "Thanks, Leiv."

Despite the circumstances, a smile flitted across his face as it often did looking at or thinking about LC's grandson. In his mind, rightly or wrongly, the name "Leiv" conjured up a tall sturdy Russian or Scandinavian image. Though his mother Margaret had pointed out there were also Hebrew and Vietnamese etymological connections with Leiv's name—with various spellings. And then there was the talk of his Gypsy lineage—through Chicago all the way back to Bosnia in the nineteen-hundreds. HM *talk* mostly. Bottom line, Leiv didn't look anything like any of the images his name conjured up in Glover's mind.

Glover remembered laughing when his mother pontificated on and on about names, their meanings, and origins. His name, she'd further elaborated, was old-English. Then in a rare moment, his mother also rather sheepishly admitted she'd chosen his name because the janitor in an apartment building she'd once lived in was enigmatically only referred to as "Mr. Glover."

An old lover, he'd guessed, but never confirmed. *One of her secrets.*

Still focusing on Leiv in his mirror, he was reminded how close in build he and Leiv were—yet so different. For one thing, Leiv didn't seem very solid. Never did, even as a child. *Egghead image.* True enough, he'd seen a picture of the man in a judicial robe—quite a different image from the jean and chambray shirt clad figure now capturing his thoughts. He'd also gone hiking with him in the Kelso Dunes, and knew he was stronger and sturdier than he might appear.

It was on one of those walks Leiv confided to him about his wife. How she'd died in an auto accident. How it had taken all the life out of him—and probably first instigated a psychological journey, then his real-world return to his family homestead.

He hadn't said much, just let Leiv talk. Truth was, he hadn't known what to say. Divorced himself, he knew how hard it was to lose a spouse, but not to death. All hope gone. Indeed, his divorce was a happy event in many respects, but like everyone else in the world, Glover wasn't a stranger to loss on other fronts.

That sharing of a confidence was a year back by now, but it seemed to him, the man was still grieving. Without doubt, his mother Margaret thought that was the case. "He'll never forget," she'd said. At the time Glover felt there was more behind her words than a comment on Leiv's grief, but he'd been too scared to pursue any hidden intent. Even at his age, his mother still intimidated him when it came to retaining her own secrets. He didn't mind that part of their relationship, and smiled at the thought of their unique mother-son closeness. *Lucky in that,* even though she had some secrets he figured he would never know.

By the time Glover pulled into one of three reserved spaces in front of the Shiné Police Department, he'd brought his thoughts and actions back full circle to the dead body on

Tucker's land. Or maybe Naomi's land? He wasn't sure if it mattered.

He needed a couple things from inside, things he should have been carrying in his cruiser—like markers, camera, and crime scene tape. Keeping the peace in Shiné was one thing; murder and crime-scene paraphernalia, quite another. *Usually no need to lug all that crap around.* Sure, there'd been other dead bodies found in the desert—several highly publicized—but never figured he'd be finding one, too.

Of course there had been the story about the gypsy supposedly disappearing—but everybody knew HM was making it all up.

Several hours later, Leiv was standing next to a heavy-breathing Glover on a spot just on the edge of Tucker's field. A hundred feet or more separated them from where they saw the arm—a marker, pointing to the sky.

In light of the spectacular discovery he and Glover had made, Leiv thought his desert world eerily quiet—and for a second or two, the feel of that silence took him back in time to the Midwest, during tornado watches. *The quiet before the storm.* Yes, an ill wind was coming their way; he could feel it without knowing how, why, or what form it would take.

Not like my early days on the bench when I was constantly being blindsided. He'd survived—and learned a lot along the way.

"You want to come over for a drink when this is all over?" Leiv asked. *Glover must be tired,* he thought. "Or I can call HM. She could cook you something." *She'd probably complain, but she'd do it.* The thought of a grumbling HM cooking Glover's favorite snack, steak and eggs, uncharitably amused Leiv. HM was both a treasure *and* a nuisance in one sharp-tongued but hardworking package.

Glover didn't seem to hear him, and the silence was a strange note, given all the people around him were hard at work, doing what they were supposed to. Securing and dissecting an incident scene. It had seemed like hours, but the San Bernardino County forensics team arrived quickly, including a fully equipped forensics van. Especially, considering the distance from San Bernardino.

Also on scene, and first to arrive after Glover's calls for assistance was a Deputy Sheriff assigned to Needles who helped Glover mark off the crime scene. The two of them also completed some preliminary looks, more like searches, around the circular perimeter of Tucker's alfalfa field before the San Bernardino contingent arrived.

Leiv was impressed with the man. Indeed, he found something comforting about Deputy Brad Temper. Solid, like Glover. It wasn't he was a large man, or commanding in attitude or mannerisms. More like he exuded an aura of stability. Leiv almost laughed at himself—he'd squelched many similar feelings during his time on the bench. Auras, hunches, visceral likes and dislikes, were *not* evidence. And sometimes, in retrospect—quite wrong.

Admittedly, Leiv knew from his grandfather's journal, LC had made some big decisions with little more than a hunch to go on. *The opal stones for one.* Letting his mind wander a little more, he thought back over several memorable entries his grandfather made. *An opportunity to indulge myself.* Hold up and analyze yet again the emotional and intellectual vagrancies that had drawn him back to Shiné. Was it the lure of making decisions based on feelings like LC? *What a luxury.*

Not that easy. Indeed, Leiv knew his own return was not as easy as a one-liner explanation. LC on the other hand, certainly wrote his own experiences down as if they were easy; but Leiv was sure many of the happenings LC wrote about were more involved and iffy than his grandfather's hubris would allow him to put to paper.

None of the police or medical professionals working away on Tucker's land had bothered Leiv. Indeed, it felt natural, him standing there next to Glover, watching all the activity around him, even though he really didn't know what to think. Or what to feel. The only item he was certain of—he shouldn't insinuate himself into their crime-scene management.

The head of the San Bernardino Sheriff Department unit was a woman name Portia Sherman. She'd spoken to Glover, but barely acknowledged Leiv with the flimsiest of nods before proceeding to direct crime scene activities. Quite understandable. A body had been found—not a time for idle banter and glad-handing.

With that thought, more memories wanted to push themselves forward, but Leiv forced the accompanying pictures back to their synaptic hideouts. Many a crime scene had been verbally and pictorially reconstructed in his courtroom—sometimes well, sometimes not so well. Only once had he been at an actual murder crime scene, and once had been enough. Tape, powder, chalk markings—even blood splatter—he didn't like the look and smell of it. Charts in a courtroom were one thing. Real bodies *in situ* quite another.

Yet, here he was again, miles away from Illinois in California, in the Mojave, on a hot winter afternoon, standing and watching another body being preliminarily examined, then carefully bagged, put in the wagon, and hauled away. With seemingly hundred of pictures taken. Nonetheless, revolting or not, and hot or not—Leiv couldn't pull himself away from the scene.

Eventually a television crew arrived, all the way from LA according to the writing on the panel van's side and the equipment markings topside. A little over a three hour drive, Leiv estimated, and wondered how they knew so quickly? Someone had called, *but who*? Certainly not Glover or the San Bernardino Sheriff's department. *And why?*

What a way to spend a Sunday.

Leiv heard an airplane motor and looked up. A helicopter, a Boeing Vertol CH-46 maybe? Out of Twentynine Palms he guessed. Leiv couldn't seem to take his eyes off the big chopper as it got closer and closer. It felt like the thundering machine was heading directly over them, but it wasn't really. And without warning he was taken back to that horrible night when a helicopter came to airlift Melissa and him to the hospital.

He made his eyes close, wanted to bring his hands to his ears, but Leiv forced himself not to. *Not here. Not in front of Glover.*

Finally, he managed to divert his thoughts to a different type of airplane, commercial this time—and the arrival of his cousin in Vegas. Tomorrow Nadya and Sydney Collins would drive into Shiné. *Drive into my life.*

He sighed—and wasn't sure what prompted its depth, length , and edge of apprehension. The deceased, or Nadya, or his emotional uncertainty in general? Maybe just too much of the unexpected all of a sudden? Psychologically his world was probably still in the courtroom. Everything orderly, slow, and logical in its progression.

Shiné however was not a courtroom he controlled. *No,* Tucker tried to kill himself today, a half buried John Doe was found on Tucker's property, and his cousin Nadya was coming tomorrow to visit him out-of-the blue for reasons unknown. And on top of all that, his instincts told him Nadya

57

and her new husband's visit was very much tied into the Mojave-Stone.

That damn Mojave stone. Leiv heard himself sigh again, but when he looked around, no one was paying attention to him. Even the helicopter had moved on, westward toward the setting sun, and now barely in sight and taking the horrendous noise with it. Still, he shivered yet again in the winter heat—and hoped it also hadn't been noticed.

Glover was saying, "What the hell is that over there? You see it, Brad? Shining like it's brand new almost."

"A motorcycle?" Leiv thought he heard Deputy Brad Temper mumble.

Now there's a motorcycle, too?

One of the things Leiv had yet to get used to, let alone accept, was the late night silence that engulfed and permeated every corner of Rhodes Castle. No matter the evening's activity—such as after he'd done with evening TV watching, or Saturday entertaining, or just the ordinary non-eventful evenings when HM finally stopped skulking around and went to her quarters for the night. Without fail, a heavy silence seemed to close in, like fog settling in on a pound. Occasionally, Dobie would hear a perceived threat and bark and break through the heavy quiet, but that was seldom, and not long-lived.

Leiv had yet to decide whether the silence was good, or bad. *Sometimes* he would linger, eyes mostly closed, in his comfy chair in front of his grandfather's stone-monument of a fireplace. Half awake, half in dreamland—Dobie at his feet, usually snoring—enjoying the ambiance of total quiet. And *sometimes*, he found himself rushing off to his bedroom on the second floor, wanting to escape—rise above an ominous feeling associated with the quiet he felt "settling in" on the main floor.

Tonight, he felt like lingering in the parlor, the evening's fire down to embers barely visible behind the massive fireplace grate. Sometimes moments like this were often portals to memories of LC. But tonight there was more than his grandfather to ponder upon.

Margaret had called him almost immediately after he came home. He heard the phone's first ring walking in the front door—even before HM and Dobie knew he was home—and he'd answered the demanding ring in the foyer on the side of the stairs.

"What kind of motorcycle?" After a perfunctory greeting, Margaret didn't waste time getting to the point of her call.

Leiv knew nothing about motorcycles despite the fact he'd presided over several cases involving bikes. One, a four month long civil suit regarding a supposedly—per the defendant—malfunctioning Harley. "Glover says a Suzuki something or other. Found it smashed up about five hundred feet away, just off the dirt road running the perimeter of Tucker, or Naomi's land—depending on your point of view."

"Probably a Suzuki V-Strom 650," Margaret responded with surprising authority and knowledge.

Leiv thought their conversation strange, and quickly tried to get a mental footing on why Margaret called, and where she was going with her motorcycle question. "I gather you've talked to Glover, know about the body, and the fact a motorcycle was found half covered with sand not far away?"

"Yes, but he didn't tell me what kind."

Leiv was still rather lost. "And why does it matter what kind of bike?"

Margaret hesitated, like she'd revealed too much of *something.* "Oh, I don't know...just curious."

"If you were wondering if it was Naomi's bike that went missing awhile back," Leiv said, guessing at what concerned her, "I asked Glover that already, and he says, no, different kind."

"So, the dead man hadn't stolen her bike?" Margaret half asked, half stated.

Leiv was sure he heard relief in her voice. "No, not Naomi's bike," he assured her.

"Goodnight, Leiv." She hung up.

Not her style to hang up so abruptly, and once again Leiv thought about their conversation. His mind was used to parsing of words, and implied nuances hidden in questions — one of the staples of his working life — but he didn't feel comfortable he knew with certainty what Margaret was trying to figure out. His quick guess was, Margaret wanted to make sure *this* bike was not tied to Naomi. But why would it be? *Very peculiar.*

After Margaret's call, Leiv finally got settled in LC's withdrawing room — some cheese and crackers courtesy of a grumbling HM, a cordial glass of Harvey's Bristol Cream, and a sleepy Dobie in front of the hearth.

Finally, he'd felt he could relax a bit. Ponder.

Tucker Oakes tried to kill himself, and Leiv had a suspicion all the pieces of his life, and maybe several others were about to be tossed in the air — jumbled, mixed, and confused. An unavoidable happening started by Tucker's attempted suicide. Hopefully, when this hodge-podge fell back to earth, it would be in a pattern he could comprehend. And live with. *Yes,* the wallpaper of his life was about to change — and he hadn't a clue how to stop the inevitable. Or even if he should attempt controlling fate.

Most disconcerting was—there were no legal precedents, no authority or powerful connections to make things go his way. This was *real life*, not courtroom legal life or political-bubble patronage. He'd come to Shiné to get away from that world; but could he handle this Mojave one?

Admittedly, up to now it certainly hadn't been all bad—on many levels. A need for *something* had called him back to Shiné, and he would be very naïve indeed if he didn't think change would be a big part of his life. The comfortableness he'd felt so far in his return to Shiné, he realized this night, was based upon past connections and friendship. *LC's legacies.*

Before Leiv could go farther back in time, drift off to familiar events laid out in LC's journal, the phone rang again, this time a different phone—the one on the table at the end of the settee where Margaret invariably sat. A phone that seldom rang because HM usually answered the first line before it switched over to this one with a message device. So unexpected and startling was its impact, Leiv jumped dramatically.

He reached to answer—the phone was an out-of-date and heavy twenty year old black model—but in the couple moments it took him to get up and go over to the phone, he felt an intense emotion sweep through him.

"What the hell was that I just felt?" he asked Dobie who was sleeping and not listening. For a long moment, Leiv found himself eyeing the phone suspiciously. Usually, he would have just answered it immediately—this time, however, something turned this ordinary act to an emotional experience. *Fear? Or* was it just the freaky nighttime silence of Rhodes Castle? *Or* a intuitive dread tied to this call in particular? Maybe all?

Leiv certainly didn't consider himself a macho-hero type, but at the same time, not a man much motivated by fear. *No*, you couldn't be a judge and a "Fraidy Cat." For the briefest of seconds, he smiled at his cartoonish cat imagery. A child-like image he'd picked up and retained from another very un-childish lawyer years earlier. But the real world non-cartoonish fact was—threats were common in his former life. Only on a few occasions had he been actually afraid. And that was because the police told him he should be.

He took a deep breath and answered the phone. "Hello," he said with his stock nondescript telephone voice. Truth was, in the past, even though his Illinois number was unlisted, he never knew what crank would get hold of his home number. It was a tone-of-voice grounded in caution. Lloyd had complained several times Leiv's phone-answering voice was off-putting; even Margaret had quipped, he sounded like someone trying to avoid bill collectors. Then she'd added the practical advice, "Get caller-ID, for goodness' sake." When she'd seen the actual phone, she'd modified her advice. "Get a modern phone and answering system, for goodness' sake."

"Cuz Leiv?" a tentative female voice asked.

He hadn't heard the salutation "Cuz," a term common in Chicago among his and Melissa's relatives, for years. "Nadya?" he asked in a softer voice.

"Glad you're home."

"Not many places to go in Shiné." Maybe they'd change their mind. *Too dull for them.* Go back to Chicago.

Contrarily, she sounded genuinely eager to come to Shiné. "After Chicago, the peace and quiet'll be wonderful. We're leaving Vegas first thing in the morning. Everyone says traffic sucks on Sunday afternoon on, so we're waiting until in the morning."

"Great." Leiv hoped he sounded enthusiastic. "Takes less than two hours—"

"We have a GPS. We'll find you."

He smiled. More than one had relied on a GPS in the desert—to their eventual dismay. "You have my number, call if you get lost." Then he gave her his cell number. "Just in case," he explained.

Leiv replaced the receiver in its old solid cradle—allowing Rhodes Castle to return to total silence.

As was her ingrained want and unconscious habit, admittedly learned from her mother the senior HM, Hester listened at the door after bringing a snack to see if she could figure out what clueless-Leiv was doing. Nothing gained there.

But now back in the kitchen—purposely letting the call go to the second line so clueless Leiv would think she'd gone to bed—while actually listening on the extension as Leiv talked to Nadya, Hester thought—*at last*. An heir to LC's legacy. *The Mojave-Stone will soon be safe in Romani hands.*

Chapter Three

From LC's journal:*...three times now, and I helped find out about those "incidents." Not good business sense my friend Doc Rhodes would say, to have locals involved in murder and misadventure. And truth was, it was usually them outside interests influencing us residents. That's why we need to stick together. Still, guess we do need a town flatfoot. Like with a church and a tavern. Ain't real otherwise.*

Monday

    Cupola or library? As always, Leiv's ritual morning decision. Experience the sunrise from his open pentagon to the world, or from his comfortable library. Both places, LC held his hand across the years. This morning he'd chosen neither.

    HM will just have to babysit Nadya and Sydney. Leiv's thought was in response to twitches of guilt nagging his conscience—pulling him in two directions. Tucker or Nadya?

    His sense of good manners dictated he should be at Rhodes Castle to greet his cousin; but he was doing what he had to do this morning—venturing out into the world where he needed to go. *Where I need to be.* Tucker was a friend. In addition, another demand from his heart was nagging his conscience—*fix this.*

Tucker was important on more than one level, and key to more than one issue that needed to be aired or solved. Leiv just hadn't yet sorted out what those issues were. Regardless, in his mind, Tucker was a good guy, caught in some bad circumstances. *No,* he didn't think Shiné's mayor was a murderer.

His overnight rest helped Leiv sort out this tiny little bit—he needed to go see Tucker. And through last night, and continuing into this morning, instinct or experience continued to tell him there was an unraveling of things happening around him needing his attention. Sometimes court cases had been cut and dry; but more often than not, they were more like untidy and poorly wound skeins of multicolored yard needing to be unwound, straightened, and then rewound in an orderly and understandable fashion.

This morning, the Tucker-colored thread was pulling Leiv. And fortunately, Glover, in his official capacity as Shiné's Chief of Police, offered to let him ride down with him in his cruiser to St. Mary's in Victorville. A two-hour plus drive at the speed limit, and a lot of it through what Leiv considered intimidating desert. *Glover will probably speed. But I won't have to worry about driving.*

Glover's plan was to check in on Tucker at the hospital, *then* hookup with some San Bernardino County Deputy out of San Bernardino, *then* come back by way of Apple Valley with the deputy to personally talk to a Mrs. Tonia Potter. DMV registration for the bike and ID found in the jacket indicated one Martin Potter as the John Doe in Tucker's field. Tonia was his wife, and she hadn't yet been informed.

"You got that information fast," Leiv said when Glover called him early that morning—barely after he finished a slender breakfast—eggs, toast, and tea. No juice, no potatoes, no bacon. Of course he didn't need all that, but Hester usually piled it on, except when she was distracted—or scheming. *Something's up with her,* he'd fleetingly thought at the time.

Glover had bragged, "I'm in 'the loop,' you know."

"What 'loop'?" he teased back.

In truth, Leiv was glad—heck, everybody in Shiné was glad Glover was so experienced and turned out to be such a good Chief of Police. Nationally well respected, from what Lloyd told him. The kind of person you were glad to have-your-back and your town's interest at heart.

Leiv ended up leaving Rhodes Castle quickly, promising a seemingly unconcerned Dobie a walk when he got back. He wasn't worried about her, knew she'd spend most of the day laying around and getting treats in the kitchen from HM.

The moment he stepped out of the house, Glover pulled up. Once safely in the passenger seat, and after one glance at Rhodes Castle in his side view mirror, Leiv said, "Damn, I meant to grab some waters."

"Got a small chest in the trunk with ice blocks and more than enough for all day."

"All day?" Leiv hadn't yet thought about how long the trip was there and back, and of course spending time with Tucker. Actually, he hadn't thought about logistics at all, just trustingly followed Glover's lead.

"Why are you meeting this Deputy anyway? Is this your case?" Part of him wanted Glover to be in charge so he'd know everything as it happened, though a little cautionary light was blinking—running things meant headaches. Being in the middle of things wasn't necessarily the best place to be when trying to figure something out.

"It's a joint team. Me, her, and Brad from Needles."

Her?

Glover must have read his mind. "Don't be such a chauvinist. It makes you an old man."

"I'm not a chauvinist," he protested, while feeling his face warm. This moment and this circumstance were not the time and place to explain to Glover how hard it was to interact with woman of a certain age. A certain age he guessed this deputy was in. *How can I explain I keep seeing Melissa's face on their faces? How can I explain how crazy I am when it comes to women after our accident?* He couldn't of course, at least not today.

"You met her in Tucker's field," Glover said.

The deputy that ignored me. "Oh yes, I remember her."

As it turned out, they ended up having to drive all the way down to Loma Linda where Tucker was transferred to from St. Marys. No one at the Victorville hospital would tell them anything conclusive about Tucker's condition, and Leiv knew this was not a good thing. *Loma Linda* meant specialists. *Loma Linda* meant a patient in trouble.

All in all, though, with all his various concerns occupying his thoughts—mainly Tucker—the drive went faster than Leiv expected. He was mostly silent, clinching his jaw often, not looking around much, just trying to survive this particular "riding in the car ordeal." Glover hadn't seemed to mind or even notice. *Tied up in his own thoughts,* Leiv guessed.

Glover did point out in passing through Oak Hills, "That's the restaurant where we're meeting Deputy Portia Sherman for lunch." He'd tsked and added, "I need to call her, push the time later."

"Did that sign say something about Ostriches?"

"Yep."

Time also passed quickly partly because Glover pushed his "cop-in-a-cruiser" speed on several occasions. Though Leiv never saw Shiné's Chief of Police turn on his strobes or hear his sirens.

Once safely at the hospital and in Tucker's room— having navigated reception, endless nondescript halls, wards of poor sick people, open doors you're scared to look into, the universal hospital smell, all the things that make hospitals hard to endure. Leiv tried to relax a tad, though, he still wasn't sure which was worse, having to endure the lengthy drive, or actually being in a hospital.

Prime example, his current reality-hell was *being* in Tucker's room—where he wanted to be. But Shiné's mayor was in bed looking like he was dead, leaving him with Tucker's brother, Calvin Oakes—a so far reluctant talking companion.

Glover had escaped to take a call, consequently for the moment, Leiv was free to indulge his psychological discomfort, leading him to further wonder if *anyone* liked being in a hospital. Particularly, in a patient's room. In fact, he thought he sensed—but wouldn't swear—Glover was glad to leave for a few moments.

Hospital rooms—the look, the emotion, the sound of beeping machines, and the smell of sickness trying to be masked by disinfectant. Of course doctors and nurses had to endure all that, if not actually like it.

This was their home away from home.

Then, for the first time in his life, Leiv considered the possibility there might be people who didn't like being in government buildings—courthouses and courtrooms in particular. Yet, he loved them. Those buildings and those rooms had been his home-away-from-home. *The look, the smell, the emotion.* He almost laughed at himself, but didn't. Couldn't. Not here, not now.

Leiv held to his bias anyway; hospitals sucked and courthouses didn't. He also knowingly allowed himself the smug and self-righteous pleasure of would-be intellectuals—having an idea, examining it, and retaining his biased position in the light of supposed rational examination. He wanted to smile again, but forced it down. There was a very sick man in the bed only feet from where he stood.

He wasn't, however, able to continue pondering, for almost simultaneous with Glover stepping outside, events inside Tucker's room deteriorated as Calvin suddenly became upset. Glover had clearly been a calming influence, maybe a valve of some sort?

Calvin was definitely more agitated—*maybe no longer in full control of his emotions?* He started hurriedly pacing back and forth between window and door in a room barely ten by ten square, and wringing his hands in a manner reminiscent of a dramatic parody skit. Leiv also noted an odd expression on his face, the way his head seemed to be wobbling around on his neck, and rapid sigh-like breaths. Calvin looked to Leiv like a man suddenly in distress. Possibly near some kind of breakdown.

Maybe I should go find Glover?

But he wasn't comfortable leaving Calvin alone for even a few seconds. *At least we're in a hospital if he collapses or goes bonkers.* Leiv wasn't sure what he should do besides call a nurse from the station down the hall. At least he was here, trying to help, not meeting and greeting Nadya at Rhodes Castle. Family intrigue suddenly paled in significance. Leiv took a couple steps to the left, closer to Tucker, though he wasn't sure why. Doubted Calvin would intentionally hurt his brother.

Leiv's mind again flitted back across the years to his judicial days—landing squarely on two defendants indelibly imprinted on his brain. Both had mental breakdowns in his courtroom, right in front of his eyes. Not pleasant, horrible in fact, even though guards had quickly taken them away. *But people could have gotten hurt.*

A flash of shame washed over him. *Shame* he'd never bothered finding out what happened to those two men. He's *assumed* at the time they'd been taken to Elgin for evaluation. *Assumed.* He almost said out loud, *I should have checked.*

Calvin stopped at the window this time, turned to face Leiv without immediately heading back across the room.

He's a little calmer, maybe?

Tucker's brother forced his hands into the pockets of his rumpled blue-jeans. His shirt, the same one he was wearing yesterday, was wrinkled and dirt stained across the chest, and didn't look much better than his pants. "You've got to help Tucker," he pleaded. His eyes were opened inordinately wide, with an intense and unwavering stare boring in on Leiv. His body seemed calm, but the tenor of Calvin's voice was high, almost hysterical in its import. "You've just got to."

Then his shoulders slumped dramatically—deflated—and he turned his gaze to the hospital bed his comatose brother inhabited. A bed where machines rhythmically beeped Tucker's alive-but-in-limbo status.

Even though he'd stepped closer to Tucker, Leiv did not follow Calvin's lead to actually look at Shiné's mayor in his sick-bed. He was told by one of the attending physicians at the nurse's station Tucker was in an induced coma. Had to

71

stop the vomiting and there seemed to be esophageal swelling, maybe even tissue necrosis. They were waiting on tests.

Leiv had also—and all too vividly—seen the tubes, wires, and machines when he'd first entered the room. Seen Tucker's hands laying outside his sheet covers—rough, calloused, almost raw looking. And the impression of his tall thin body under white hospital bedding, looking more like a sheet draped skeleton, than the body of a young man many cared about. Shiné's Mayor, no less. Un-summoned mental pictures flashed once more—this time, back to the first time he met Tucker and shook his hand. *The hands of a working man, a farmer.* Nothing like his colleague's well-manicured-feeling handshakes back in Illinois—lawyers and politicians mostly.

Yes, when he'd entered this hospital room, Leiv had seen the look of nothingness on Tucker's face, and felt deep sadness this man tried to take his own life. He didn't want to see his face again.

In contrast to his previous pacing, Calvin now stood almost motionless. Leiv guessed his emotions had flat run dry, like a motor out of gas. Oddly, with his back to the window, a cheery winter-blue sky haloed Calvin's silhouette from behind, and the view of sky outside was almost like an ethereal glow, contrasting and mocking Calvin's miserable demeanor.

Amazing.

Still, Calvin wasn't completely wound down. He turned his head slightly, moving his stare from Tucker to Leiv. "Your grandfather would want you to help."

Leiv had to catch himself—control his voice, body motion, and expression. The young man's words weren't only a surprise, but quite disconcerting. Calvin couldn't possibly know about LC's journal. *No,* it was something else he was referring to. *Had to be.* He waited. *Stories going around Shiné?*

Despite Leiv's attempt not to give anything away, Calvin must have seen something in his face, for he turned his head quizzically, and said, "You really don't know how people think about you and Rhodes Castle?"

Leiv felt his face warm. "Pastor Apply has intimated." It was a dodge. Leiv wasn't really sure how townspeople viewed LC, his father, or himself. Truth was, he wasn't sure he wanted to know.

Fortunately, Calvin let Leiv loose from his intense scrutiny, and turned his attention back to his brother. "I've been with him since yesterday morning." Leiv was relieved Calvin's tone was calmer—but still, heavy with sadness. "He's gotten worse." Slowly, Calvin turned his back on Leiv and Tucker to look out the window. The words, "He must have been out there in that damn field longer than I thought," came from over Calvin's shoulder.

Leiv had also wanted to come to the hospital for his own reasons, regardless of Glover's professional duties and possible personal intentions of his own. Another call Leiv received in the early morning hours had been from Lloyd—relaying a request from Calvin to come to the hospital. Glover's ride invitation ended up being a most provident godsend.

In reality, being here with Calvin in Tucker's hospital room, feeling his pain, and despite what his mind told him he didn't want to do, it was hard *not* looking at Tucker. Especially since he liked the man.

All this was truly a horrible happening—from Tucker trying to kill himself, to his own reluctance, or maybe inability, to look at his comatose body hooked up to machines. But he has here now, and Calvin wanted him to help. He stared for a couple long moments at Calvin's back, thinking how devastated he must be. First Tucker's wife dead in a tragic accident barely a year ago—now this.

Oh Melissa.

Finally, after a long and slow deep breath, Leiv forced himself to look over at Tucker's lifeless-looking body. *Damn.* He really did like their mayor, and seeing him like this was wrenching. "What did the doctor say?" he asked, then walked the few feet to his bedside. He almost reached out to touch Tucker s hand—but held back.

"It's doctors," Calvin answered without turning around. "A team."

"That's why we're here in Loma Linda?" Leiv let his rhetorical question evaporate on silent air. Which was fine with him. *More time to think for him, and more calming down time for Calvin.* Hopefully Glover would return any second with information. Since they'd first gone to St. Mary's, then been directed down the hill to Loma Linda, Glover had appeared quite unhappy he didn't have up-to-date information on the dead body in the field.

On the Tucker front, Leiv wanted to know if he was going to survive, yet he was definitely *scared* to push Calvin, *scared* to hear the truth.

"Sorry I was gone so long," said Glover from the doorway. "I did get to talk to Tucker's doctors."

Leiv learned early on after his return to Shiné, to even guess at what the Chief of Police was really thinking, you had to look directly into his almost black eyes. Right now, they were not happy eyes.

Glover turned his head slightly, talking directly to Calvin, and in an official tone of voice, said, "I'm glad you're here. You can let the rest of your family know."

Calvin took a step back. "Know what?"

Whatever this is, must be bad, Leiv thought as he watched Glover seamlessly pull himself erect, broaden his stance, tilt his chin up a notch, then clear his throat. "Tucker has been charged with murder." He inclined his head toward a San Bernardino County Sheriff's deputy who had sneakily, Leiv thought, come in and was now standing in the doorway behind Shiné's Chief of Police.

Glover though, kept his eyes on Calvin.

"What, what?" Calvin stammered, and appearing to Leiv like he was about to pass out.

Without thinking, Leiv took the few steps necessary, then reached out and grabbed Calvin's arm while asking Glover, "Dusty, what the hell's going on?" Leiv next turned his head to the large substantial-looking deputy in the doorway and demanded, "Don't just stand there, call a doctor, or nurse, or somebody."

Glover came over quickly and grabbed Calvin's other arm, and in *sotto voce* said, "So now you're giving commands to County Deputies?"

"When did you find out about that guard by Tucker's door?" Leiv asked. "The one who snuck in behind you." He was sure the deputy wasn't there when they arrived. This was a new development. Though admittedly, when they first arrived, his attention was focused on surviving the through-the-hospital experience and seeing Tucker for the first time.

"That's what the call was about." Glover blew out a breath before continuing. "Deputy Sherman called to give me a heads up." He scoffed under his breath. "Barely minutes between her call and super-cop showing up."

They had found an alcove about fifty feet or so down the hallway from the nearest nurses station. Leiv was confused and surprised by the guard on Tucker. Clearly, there was more information now available about the body on Tucker's land. "They're pressing charges? Why so quick, and on what basis? It's only Monday—" It certainly felt longer, but it was just yesterday Tucker had tried killing himself.

Glover gave Leiv a slight look of surprise. "The body we found *was* on his land."

"The body could have been on Naomi's land," Leiv objected.

"And?"

A woman—a nurse or technician type based on her scrubs—passed and gave them a curious once over. But she kept walking.

Leiv lowered his voice, "It just seems strange—the rush I mean. There hasn't been an autopsy—no time for questions. And they haven't examined the bike yet." By his mind, there were quite a few unknowns out there. "It's only been a day." He ignored the fact he'd seen charges brought swifter than these. Depended on a lot of things—often, personalities. More often than not, politics.

I need to remain neutral. Or did he? Shiné was a different world, a different life. LC's world.

Glover gave Leiv one of his annoying incredulous looks, then turned his back to the corridor so only Leiv could see his face. "You're right about the rush. It's political. As usual." He lowered his voice even more and leaned in closer. "He's the prime murder suspect because he's their only suspect. And the press won't be able to get enough of 'a body buried in the desert.' This whole story might even go national. Probably has already." Glover tsked out the side of his mouth. "Or hadn't you realized?"

76

Damn, I hadn't. Still, he wasn't ready to give up. "Just because the body was on his land—" Leiv almost winced, his emotions still working on taking in Tucker's suicide, and now he additionally needed to consider Tucker as a suspect in a second murder. In what felt like a physical counterbalancing movement, Leiv leaned in closer to Glover. *Two conspirators in a hospital corridor.* "That doesn't mean anything. Does it? Not out in the desert. And not when there're city-day-trippers tramping around all the time. Trespassing. Most probably a stranger is who we're looking for."

"We're?" Glover smiled, though grimly. "And they found holes in his chest."

Leiv made a face of his own, one he hoped Glover understood. "Okay, *you're* looking for. And what do you mean, holes?"

Glover didn't answer immediately, just continued to look at Leiv a bit, an amused smile now officially pulling at the corners of his mouth. Then the potential of a smile vanished as quickly as it had come. "Bullet holes. Rifle bullet holes. Two of them. Twenty-two, long rifle."

"You know that already?" Leiv straightened, stepped back—closer to the alcove wall to his rear—and crossed his arms. "Hard to kill a person with a twenty-two, right?" A waft of hospital-odor hit him from nowhere. Nauseating. But he ignored it. "Who's leading the investigation?"

"Common misconception on the bullet caliber. And, I'm lead when it comes to the body," Glover said, with an inkling of a smile returning. "But, it's probably going to be a joint effort. I think I already told you that back in Shiné."

But time had passed. Things had already changed. Leiv was pleased Glover would be in the main loop, offering him the opportunity to stick his nose in the whole affair.

"I've told you before, your poker-face sucks," Glover said. "And yes, I'll keep you tied in." He smiled. "Can't believe you actually sat on 'The Bench.'"

Despite the circumstances and location, Leiv found himself also smiling. "A different life," he quipped. *A different life indeed.*

Tucker did have a Ruger rifle. He'd seen bullets on his garage shelf with his own eyes, with ".22lr" clearly marked on the side of the box.

Plain, plain, plain, Hester uncharitably reflected. Nadya hadn't changed since she last saw her in Chicago as a teenager, and earlier as a child here at Rhodes Castle. Admittedly, both times were years earlier. *A plain girl, a plain woman.* Still, there was *something* Hester thought she could see in her eyes. Romani eyes?

"Long time since you were in this kitchen," Hester said, letting a mild edge of accusation edge her words. She wasn't going to let this opportunity to get a measure of this young woman slip away. To annoy her would be a good test.

"Chicago's a lot different from Shiné," Nadya answered through a thin smile. "And a long way away."

"But connected." Hester had placed Nadya and Sydney across from her at the table in the middle of Rhodes Castle's huge kitchen. That way she could see both their faces at the same time. So far, all her strategy yielded was the opinion Sydney was a sap, stupidly gaga in love, while the object of his desire was plain as dirt.

Sydney cleared his throat. "Because of the family connections?"

Obviously. Sydney had interjected himself into the

78

conversation several times now, mostly saying something stupid, she thought, while she wanted to talk to Nadya, not him. He didn't matter, no blood line there.

Dobie, seemingly was of another mind set, and was lying on the floor at Sydney's feet, her head on his right foot. *And they say dogs can judge character.* Hester almost harrumphed out loud, but caught herself in time. *Just like the silly dog does with clueless Leigh-Everett.* She squinted her eyes and peered into Sydney's for a long minute. *Nothing*—no fire there. She turned back to Nadya, scrutinizing her in the same manner—and Hester thought she caught a glimpse of purpose there. *Maybe's there's fire behind that plainness?* She certainly hoped so, prayed so.

Hester then looked up toward the kitchen's high copper-tiled ceiling as if she was thinking. She wasn't—knew what she was going to say already. But when she brought her eyes back down to Nadya, Hester asked her in a tone suggesting she was trying to recall forgotten or uncertain information. "Your mother is Mary, right?"

Nadya smiled. A smile that started in the corner of her mouth, then slowly spread across her face. The result was charming and exuded a warmth Hester had not seen before. *But does she care about what I care about?* She would have to find out. "And married to André, Everett's brother, right?"

"Yes, Leiv is what my mother calls my first cousin. Leiv's father Everett was my uncle."

True blood in her veins. "LC's granddaughter." Hester wondered if Nadya knew her mother was also from a Cooper blood line.

*   *   *   *   *

79

Leiv needed to concentrate on keeping a neutral face as surprises kept coming his way. First off was The Summit Restaurant itself on old Route 66, atop Cajon Pass. From the minute Glover pulled into the parking lot "something" grabbed and pulled him back in time. He'd always had a fondness for the idea of Route 66, having lived in Chicago for awhile before Shiné—and now there was the Mojave and Cajon Pass connection.

"You want to share an ostrich omelet with me?" Glover was asking Deputy Portia Sherman.

Another surprise, ostrich omelets. He'd seen and asked about the sign driving down to see Tucker, but now the real-deal was presenting itself. Glover was sitting across from him in a bright red padded booth with chrome trim, near a drinks station with an old timey yellow gas pump behind them—the pump staring directly at Leiv, a wistful reminder of a bygone era. And the San Bernardino County Deputy was sitting next to Glover—and their body-language was clear. *Another surprise.* He could see her well this time, and several wafts of a mild but pleasant perfume floated his way.

"Had it before," Portia answered in the same tone she'd greeted him and Glover with in the parking area. It had been noisy outside, with all the I-15 traffic rushing by, but her tone had come through, loud and clear. On the terse side, but not sharp or smart-alec; no nonsense, but not gruff; business-like, but not completely lacking in charm.

And just like with The Summit Restaurant, from the moment he met her, his reaction was visceral. Deputy Sherman hit him as an enigma. An enigma Leiv was definitely interested in trying to figure out, which was *another surprise.*

Leiv was right behind her as they'd entered the restaurant. He thought her on the short-side for a cop, with a wiry frame. Not very imposing. *And wasn't there a height limit for cops and the military?* There had been ages ago, when he'd rubbed shoulders with JAG lawyers and their clients.

She'd taken off her Campaign-style hat and left it in her cruiser, revealing dark brown hair, a surprisingly pleasant face—given her speech mannerisms—with average features, clear and smooth skin without benefit of makeup it looked to him, dimples, and a fairly pleasant resting expression.

But the disconcerting part was her near smart alec, non-compromising, and rather gruff demeanor. He'd expected a "feminine angel-type"—*like Melissa. I'm clearly biased.* Consequently, he couldn't quite wrap his mind around this San Bernardino Deputy Sheriff. Of course she'd have to be smart, capable, and tough to get where she was as a lead detective. Fluff would be perceived as weakness.

Maybe I am the chauvinist Glover thinks I am. Leiv was sure he'd been fair on the bench—but in his personal life, was there a different story?

"Appreciate your getting together on such short notice," Portia said. Her words were directed at Glover, but she was ostensibly looking out the window toward her cruiser being driven out of the parking lot. "Deputy Greggs is taking my cruiser to Victorville. Would appreciate you dropping me there when this is over." Her posture and words didn't hide the fact Deputy Sherman was actually staring at the side of his face. Taking a considered measure of *him.*

Touché.

So far, he'd mainly watched, smiled, and nodded as appropriate. Leiv had seen public safety officers in action, and was familiar with their particular brand of camaraderie, and their sometimes reluctance to quickly accept outsiders. And he expected their luncheon to be the same.

Another surprise. This was different. Not only was Glover staring at Portia Sherman with adolescent-like

expressions he wouldn't have believed his friend capable of—
but Glover's object of adoration, Deputy Sherman, wasn't
looking at Glover. *No, she's scrutinizing me.*

"So you're *the* Leiv Rhodes out in Shiné. The Judge."

He had no idea what to make of her comment, much
less what to say or do. Fortunately an efficient looking
waitress arrived, took their orders for two coffees, a chocolate
shake for Portia, two burgers for him and Portia, and the
infamous ostrich omelet for Glover.

Leiv thought he needed to flip the scrutiny-table—
quickly. Go on offense. He turned toward her, as she'd done to
him. "Why are you interested in our dead body? And
Tucker?" Leiv refused to look at Glover, for the moment, not
wanting to know what he was thinking.

She gave Leiv a curious look, then shrugged her
shoulders and said simply, "I'm a cop."

Out of the blue, Leiv realized he wanted this woman as
an ally. "I did notice the uniform," Leiv said in as light a tone
he could, then laughed, and put on what he considered an
ingratiating face—one similar to the expression he'd reserved
for annoying trial lawyers.

"Leiv, Deputy Sherman—" Glover attempted to
redirect the conversation.

Leiv cut him off. "I was just surprised Tucker was
charged so fast."

"Politics," she said, unequivocally and without
hesitation. "And as to why I'm the county representative on
this case—I pulled the short straw."

"What does that mean?"

Glover forced his way into the conversation. "Because
nobody wants to drive out to Shiné."

Leiv opened his mouth to say something else to Portia,
but instead, clamped his lips tight, fell back against booth

padding, turned to Glover, and continued to be surprised. The expression on his friend's face was even sappier than before. It was indeed very weird watching Glover, the epitome of what he considered tough masculinity, turned to butter—or whatever the appropriate simile was.

Portia, however, was still looking at him intently, and successfully pulled Leiv's attention and gaze back to her. "You are a sly one. Must have been a tricky judge. Hard to get anything by you."

Once again, Leiv didn't know what she was talking about—guessing she was seeing something in his words, facial expression, or demeanor. Before he could comment, *her* demeanor and facial expression changed. Portia's tone was still all business—professional, but now with a touch of genuineness Leiv thought hadn't been there before. Or maybe it was a little warmth seeping through?

"I've gotten three Mojave assist calls in the last month," she said. "Barstow, Newberry Springs, and Daggett." Portia released Leiv from her piercing scrutiny, turned her head back to Glover, and narrowed her eyes. "Two of those were bodies found near I-40." She blew out a puff of air, quick short, and business like.

Glancing at Glover and seeing the expression of admiration on his face, Leiv thought anew. *Good grief, he certainly is smitten.*

"One was that body buried near the railroad tracks. I want to find out who did that dump, and if your body is connected." She leaned back. "I want to be the one to put it together."

"So you think the bodies are connected?"

"Doubt it. Nothing similar. Yet. But, I'm not leaving it to some other yahoo-deputy to make that call." She gave Glover an acknowledging nod. "And I've worked with Glover before. Know his methods." Left unsaid, but underlying her words Leiv thought, was the sentiment Portia thought Glover was good. And maybe something more? Using first names was definitely a clue. *Another surprise.*

Glover was smiling like a school boy.

Before Leiv could fully comprehend what was really going on in this one little red booth in this iconic restaurant, on this one little spot on Route 66—Portia turned back to him. "My grandfather and your grandfather, LC Rhodes, were friends." Her facial expression was unreadable as she asked, "Does the Mojave-Stone actually exist?"

Despite everything else whirling around in his brain and emotions, Leiv was ready for her, as he was for everyone who asked about the Mojave-Stone. He answered smoothly and with nary a second thought, chagrin, or smidgeon of guilt. "Of course not."

Deputy Sherman let the Mojave-Stone question drop, they finished eating in quiet, then left The Summit Restaurant to deal with tasks at hand. Leiv willingly offered to ride in the backseat for their trip to Apple Valley as they headed off to see the wife of the now deceased Martin Potter. *Not an appealing duty,* Leiv thought.

It was an unique feeling being in back of a cruiser—behind bars sort of—even though Glover's cruiser didn't have steel and plastic transport barriers. Nonetheless, for a bit, he felt like a criminal being hauled in for questioning, or even worse, being arrested. On the plus side, his driving-anxiety was not as strong in back. Funny that—he and Melissa had been in the back seat of a limo the night she died. *I should feel worse.*

He couldn't hear everything going on up front with clarity, but the snatches he caught were about High Desert growth, accompanying crime, and population shifts. Law enforcement chitchat.

He thought he heard Deputy Sherman say Tonia Potter was a Graduate school teacher.

"Never get tired of this stretch," was the last thing Glover said that Leiv paid attention to. He came to fully recognize, even from the back, Glover was "different" around Deputy Portia Sherman. Leiv wanted to tell him to keep his eyes on the road, his attention on driving, and stop spooning. *Spooning.* A long gone word now, but LC used it in his journal. Leiv kept his mouth shut—wisely, he thought.

Turning his attention to I-15 desert scenery, Leiv noticed he could see a difference in terrains. *Been here too long,* he quipped mentally. At first, desert was desert. Now his aesthetic mind's eye could recognize items like whether there was more or less scrub vegetation, the amount of loose windblown sand, volcanic remnants—and even differences in what he'd first considered an all encompassing and monotonous dirty-tan landscape. He could now recognize variances in sand color. *Who would have thought?*

A black motorcycle passed them on the right, the rider hunkered down low and leaning forward. Glover was hogging the far left lane, with few drivers having the audacity to illegally pass him from the right lane. The motorcyclist was indeed a brave soul. The bike was shiny black, his helmet shiny black, and even his visor seemed black; though Leiv figured that was an optic trick produced by the sun and the almost face-covering tinted visor. He was also sure he caught the line of goggles underneath.

A safe rider. A smart rider.

Glover seemed to be entering something in his MDT console. Leiv leaned forward a bit.

Even though a bit of a drive, Glover occasionally headed out "down below." Usually, just for the heck of it. He liked the changing Mojave desert terrains. Although today he'd only gone as far as Cajon Pass to pick up Portia, he still liked seeing what changes were going on in the populated areas of the High Desert outside of Shiné—where in his mind, civilization stopped. That was the way he liked it, and was one of the main reasons he stayed out in Shiné.

On a practical level, at least once a month he did drive the distance into Barstow, sometimes going even farther to Victorville, for supplies, business, or an event. Or sometimes he'd head in the opposite direction toward Needles, then into Arizona.

With Shiné's gas station quickie-mart, online banking, and their locally owned hardware-cum-garden supply—most needs were taken care of at home. But for some things, like top quality butter, or a decent selection of wines and cheeses, he had to go farther afield. Being close to Route 66, there were several good restaurants in Needles if he wanted something different than what The Greasy Spoon in town had on their menu. Though Chef Jack, he thought, was the best.

Today's drive had nothing to do with supplies or checking out his desert environs. This trip was quite special on several fronts. He was investigating what he figured was going to be a high profile case. Dead bodies buried in the desert were irresistible fodder for the newspapers—and LA TV—and probably hit the national news. *Yep*, this trip would be good for the ego. As much as he liked Shiné and being the town's Police Chief, and as much as he also liked being close to his mother—it was podunk land as far as crime and accompanying publicity went.

Though, he re-thought, with Georgie Oakes's car accident last year, Naomi's accident around the same time, Tucker's attempted suicide, and this weekend-warrior death, there was a lot going on in his little policing-world. He was probably underestimating Shiné's crime rate. He almost said as much to Deputy Portia Sherman sitting next to him. He thought she was wearing perfume, though he didn't think cops did that.

Must be a rule against. She smelled luscious.

Yep, added to the high-profile aspect of this case, the specialness of this trip was revved up—sent into overdrive actually—by the presence of Deputy Portia Sherman. He stole a quick glance in his rearview mirror. He was glad Leiv was along, his presence keeping him from making a complete fool of himself with Portia.

Damn, does this woman kick my libido into high gear. Glover was also aware her presence made him act a little stupid. *Well, more like silly.*

But not completely silly, or stupid. He was still a cop, and had seen the black motorcycle pulling into the restaurant parking lot, then riding behind him in Hesperia, then passing him in Victorville. Somehow he'd gotten behind him again, and was passing on the right. A definite no-no. An alarm bell, albeit still a minor one went off, and he made sure his dash-cam was recording—plus, he entered the license plate number in his terminal.

* * * * *

The house Glover pulled up in front of was a large, rather new looking, California-styled one-story rambler with an oversized and impressive entry, and built on what at quick glance seemed like a several acre lot in a suburban feeling neighborhood. Leiv noted they'd approached the Potter residence via Apple Valley Road. Even from the backseat, he'd tried to pay attention to where they were going, taking in the look and feel of the entire Victor Valley area, mainly because he was awestruck.

Hard to believe all the growth from my days as a kid in Shiné.

He sighed quietly as Glover parked curbside—but not on account of growth in the area. Leiv also had time to internalize what they were doing on the drive to Apple Valley. He didn't envy Glover and Deputy Sherman their job. Tough stuff, informing next-of-kin—telling Tonia Potter her husband, Martin, was probably dead.

Indeed, Leiv hung back and behind as the three of them made their way up what seemed like an extraordinarily long concrete walkway to the Potter's front door. With his head down, averting his eyes away from what needed to be done, Leiv took in the Potter's front yard. White gravel and two big rocks. Nothing else. There was a message there in the Potter's landscaping, or lack of—but Leiv couldn't immediately put his finger on it. *Disconcerting at the least.*

He thought he heard Westminster Chimes from inside, followed by Tonia Potter answering her front door in less than a moment. Leiv looked up to directly face the current situation and spied Tonia through the space between Glover and Deputy Sherman. He couldn't believe his eyes. After Melissa, Tonia was the most beautiful woman he'd ever seen.

It wasn't make-up beauty like with movie or TV celebrities. It was natural, and unbelievably striking. Leiv

88

made a conscious effort to ensure his mouth was closed, so stunning was the deceased Martin Potter's wife. With his attention riveted on Tonia, Leiv barely heard Deputy Sherman make introductions. But when he saw Tonia's face cloud over, seemingly confused, he forced his mind, instead of his libido, to focus on why they were there.

"You're here about, Marty? But he's been gone for—" she brought both hands to her mouth, and Leiv now saw pain in her eyes. Barely audible, she said, "You've found him, right? More than a year. You've found him at last?"

It was hot, Leiv's posterior and back hurt from sitting in the car far too long, and they were delivering horrible news to a woman he guessed was still holding out hope her husband was alive—and his first and quite compelling thought was, *who is this beauty hiding out in Apple Valley?* His second thought—*my back hurts.*

Glover asked, "May we come in?"

Leiv clamped his jaw tight and pressed his teeth against his bottom lip until it hurt. Pain focusing his attention—a technique from his prior life to ensure a proper facial expression for the circumstance. Prior to these moments, Leiv had been mentally admonishing Glover for immature behavior in the presence of the opposite sex—and here he was, unable to think or act appropriately. Even during his youthful days, Leiv had never had such a discombobulating experience except one. *The day I met Melissa.*

Tonia didn't move, but she lowered her hands, and squinted curiously. "I thought you came about Marty's disappearance. He's not here, you know, on a trip, you know, gone for over a year, you know—"

She's trying to cope. Not understanding. Can't take it all in.

Her eyes went wide and pain was clearly visible again—along with confusion. "A long trip." She was moving

89

and flexing her hands as if she didn't know what to do with them. Abruptly and decisively she squeezed them together tightly in front of her.

"Mrs. Potter," Glover said, his voice now firm, sonorous, and authoritative, "we need to talk to you." He stepped forward and effortlessly slipped his hand under her right forearm. "It's important," he added in a softer voice, "what we have to tell you."

Tonia let out a wail, the likes of which Leiv had never heard before—even by the craziest of the craziest in his old courtrooms. Somewhere between a scream and a cry of anguish. She then more cried than said the words, "He's dead, isn't he? Marty's dead."

Leiv didn't know what to do to help, especially from his position behind Glover. But Deputy Sherman quickly stepped forward and took Tonia's other arm before she could start flailing them around—or maybe even collapse. Tonia had clearly lost control, and Deputy Sherman quite professionally mirrored Glover's directive, stance, and tone. "We need to go inside, Mrs. Potter."

Glover let go his support of Tonia, and somehow the deputy guided the grieving woman to turn around. "Maybe some water?" Deputy Sherman skillfully started leading Tonia Potter inside. "You're a professor and a counselor, right? Psychotherapy I was told?"

Tonia nodded, then looked *past* Deputy Sherman, and *past* Glover, directly at him, tears now streaming down her face. Leiv was amazed at his own reaction—a rush of excitement, not sexual exactly—but something he hadn't felt in years. *A powerful woman,* he thought.

* * * * *

"You can't be right. Marty'll be back tomorrow," Tonia insisted for what seemed like the hundredth time. It also felt to Leiv like her hundredth sniff and swipe at her eyes. Several times Tonia looked out through their front picture window as if Martin was about to appear and walk right up to the front door. "It was just a mini-vacation for him." She reached for the Kleenex box sitting conveniently on the end table next to the couch, then grabbed several more. After a long moment, and as if answering the question in Leiv's mind, she added, "Have to keep these around all the time. Allergies you know, especially this time of year."

He wondered if many people kept Kleenex boxes in their living rooms, especially in a sleek uncluttered one like this. But Leiv knew too well about sinus problems. He'd experienced several sinus infections since his arrival in Shiné, and Doc Walker had prescribed him a nose spray, an antihistamine, and on a couple occasions, an antibiotic. His sufferings were usually a late winter, early spring phenomenon. Apple Valley evidently had a different pollen producing eco-structure. Not surprising given what he'd experienced in the Mojave so far.

"And you say you'll do DNA tests on the body?" Tonia's voice sounded tiny and incredulous. "Like I explained, Marty's just still on vacation…"

Leiv certainly felt for her. At first it was near impossible to take in the reality Melissa was dead. *The mind doesn't want to accept.* Their little tableau felt to Leiv like a surreal movie scene—Felliniesque in import. He and Glover in armchairs facing Tonia, appearing slumped into the couch's cushions on one end, and Deputy Sherman sitting very close to her, turned slightly, as if ready to take action. What he was experiencing also felt staged in a way only Fellini could do. Indeed, it felt like he was looking in on something he was also part of. *Looking in and being in at the same time.*

Portia made the tea and settled them all in as if it were her house. *Portia?* Leiv realized he'd mentally moved to a first name basis, at least in his mind, with Glover's lady friend.

"We know this is a shock, Mrs. Potter, and we're sorry." Portia smiled most genuinely. She then opened the manila envelope she was carrying—carefully, and in slow-motion-like movements. While she did that, Glover officially broke the news the police thought her husband was a deceased John Doe they retrieved from Shiné, and Deputy Sherman needed to confirm their supposition with picture identification of the possessions found with the corpse.

Portia had told Glover and him in the car, the desiccated body in the morgue didn't look like anyone, and DNA tests weren't in yet.

With those depressing thoughts in mind, Leiv averted his gaze from the two women in front of him, looking at some spot in the far distance that looked like the family room of an open and flowing floor plan. For a moment, and out of the blue, he felt physically ill—with a wave of nausea unexpectedly overwhelming him. Quickly, Leiv took a deep breath, forced calm upon himself.

His nausea disappeared—gone as suddenly as it had come.

It wasn't he thought Portia had corpse pictures in the envelope, or that he hadn't seen his share of horrible, gut wrenching pictures in the courtroom—some, so terrible, he'd ordered them previewed first behind the closed doors of his chambers. Pictures, many of which still visited him in the wee-hours of the morning. Also, he had seen trauma, pain, loss, sadness, and grief in the eyes and words of victims and perpetrators. Somehow though, *this moment, this place, this woman has thrown me for a loop.*

Leiv did not like how he was feeling—the sense of loss of control, with his emotions ahead of his thoughts. Indeed, the atmosphere and his reactions seemed to be happening in some other dimension. *Ridiculous,* he chided himself.

Maybe it was the air inside, or lack of, combined with the angle of the afternoon light flowing through the picture window—highlighting brightly, and somewhat starkly the Potter's modern beige-colored decorating motif? *Even more ridiculous, lighting controlling my emotions.*

Or was it the lack of wind? Or because there was no greenery outside? Was it the smell of fear? Heartbreak? He didn't know what was going on, or what was sweeping over him—but the moment was "poignant," to use a word one of his law clerks had been fond of saying.

Leiv took a deep breath—consciously hidden by bringing his hand to his mouth.

Then looking around the living room again, trying to ignore feelings he couldn't figure out, while simultaneously attempting to listen to Glover, Portia, and Tonia without directly looking at them—Leiv felt like a neurotic child for a moment or two—trying to sort out and survive "the grownups" world. It was not a feeling he'd often experienced as an adult. Particularly not during his time on the bench.

Portia had shown Tonia the pictures of a watch, ring, and wallet, and as several tears found their way down Tonia's cheeks, the deputy was now saying, "I have a picture here you gave the investigating officer when Martin first disappeared. Do you have a recent one? And one of his motorcycle?"

Still seemingly in her own world, Tonia asked, almost like a child wanting to go to Disneyland, "Can I see his body?"

Leiv looked to the left of the living room, down what looked like a hall to bedrooms. *One of those bedrooms had been*

Portia and Martin's. He thought he heard the slightest bit of a cough—way down a hall that seemed endless.

Glover must have heard, or sensed something also. "Are you alone, Mrs. Potter? We have down you don't have children."

Tonia again looked confused. "No," she managed to answer. "Just me."

Just me. Sounded so sad.

"A picture?" Deputy Sherman nudged.

Tonia looked over toward a long thin side-table against the living room wall to her right. "There's one over there."

The table was cream colored, almost identical in shade to all the house walls Leiv had seen so far. Above the table hung a piece of modern art, cubist in feel, the shapes various shades of cream, with one dark tannish circle off-center. Lined up on the table proper was a row of tan framed pictures. Leiv wasn't close enough to make out details, but one looked like a man smiling proudly standing next to a motorcycle. Martin Potter, he guessed.

To this day, Leiv carried a picture of Melissa and himself, a photo-booth type snap in his wallet. He almost stood so he could reach into his Dockers pants pocket and pull it out. He caught himself, but the thought of how emotionally vulnerable he must still be when it came to Melissa caused his face to warm.

"Can I go see the body?" Tonia asked again.

He heard Glover sigh.

"Let's avoid going back through Victorville proper," Glover said after they both were back in his cruiser.

They'd just dropped Deputy Portia Sherman at the

Sheriff's office on Amargosa Road, and Glover had returned to the cruiser after walking her inside the station—an accompaniment, Leiv guessed—having nothing to do with investigation or cop-protocol.

While Glover was being gallant, Leiv moved from the rear seat to the front passenger seat.

"What did you think of Tonia Potter?" Leiv asked after they were both strapped in,

"Hiding or holding back on something," Glover said, apparently without need for forethought. "We'll go back home using Highway Eighteen, then Dale Evans Parkway." He gave Leiv a quick sideways glance before putting the key in the ignition. "You do know who Dale Evans is? Right?"

Leiv was surprised by Glover's quick and terse summation of their visit with Mrs. Potter. Nonetheless, after a good-natured sigh, he sang a bar of "Happy Trails." Leiv knew early on in grammar school he was monotone in the voice department, and tone-deaf in the ear department, so he didn't expect praise from Glover. He wasn't disappointed.

"Good grief." Glover's tone was incredulous. "Do you know how terrible you sound?"

"You want me to sing more?"

"No way." Glover backed out of his parking slot, and started maneuvering his way out of the lot. "Why did you ask me about the Potter woman?"

Leiv also didn't hesitate, he no longer needed to rely on rules of evidence, or listen to expert witnesses. He was free to rely on his gut. "I thought she was suffering from shock. Having just lost her husband and all."

"Could be."

"You see something duplicitous or phony about her?"

"Duplicitous?" Glover chided, then fell silent for a moment. "I'm not sure which is faster." He was clearly thinking about his route plan again. Finally, after a few more moments of silence, Glover said, "A feeling in my gut. At a minimum—and giving her the benefit-of-the-doubt, I'd say she knew, or had guessed Martin was dead."

"But how?" *Two guts, two different conclusions.*

"Good question."

Leiv fell thoughtful as Glover made his way back onto I-15, headed north until the Highway 18 east exit, drove east through the northern part of the old business section of Victorville, past the Route 66 museum, past the train station, then through a rather nice section of rocks to end up in Apple Valley again. But a different section from where the Potters lived.

"Isn't that the hospital where we first went looking for Tucker?"

"Yep."

"But the sign said Apple Valley. I thought we left Apple Valley."

"Thought we'd head back east this way, see some parts of the Mojave I'm betting you haven't seen."

Leiv was tired, with all his senses and emotions just wanting to go back to Shiné, Rhodes Castle, and bed. He wanted to collapse, ignore it all. What he said was, "Sounds good." And why not? All he had to do was sit back and let Glover drive. *What could be bad about that?*

Here she was, back to babysitting Sydney and Nadya. In a few minutes they'd be meeting her at the front door for a tour of Rhodes Castle—which actually wasn't that hard, and if pushed on the point, she'd have to admit she liked. And this time, well. this time she'd get an even better feel for the woman Nadya. Not exactly who she would pick, but so far, quite acceptable. And her birth line was perfect.

Sydney, however, she could do without. There was something lurking there, and at a different time she might have wanted to figure out what. Not now, not today. The Mojave-Stone and what Leiv and Glover were doing out there in the desert were more important. On top of all that, she couldn't shake the ominous card reading she had earlier, after she sent Sydney and Nadya off on their own for awhile.

A couple years back she'd spent what she considered a lot of money on a set of Russian Palekh-style fortune telling cards. The seller claimed they were authentic from nineteenth-century Russia. She guessed them to be knockoffs. Nonetheless, once in her possession, Hester thought the twenty-five cards beautiful, and the lacquer box they came in to her taste. Such lovely bright colors—quite a welcome contrast to Rhodes Castle. She'd also purchased an explanation book on Amazon when her set arrived. Clueless Leigh-Everett didn't know anything about what she considered her secret weapon against fate.

And I sure can't count on the cousins to do any modern Internet stuff. Not that she faulted them for that. *At least they kept traditions alive.* Well, she had her cards.

But she couldn't shake her reading from this morning. The same reading as Saturday and Sunday night. *Betrayal.* Were the cards chastising her, pointing a finger of guilt her way about her deceptive ways with clueless Leigh-Everett? Or as she thought, trying to tell her something else?

Hester sighed into her quiet kitchen, only Dobie to hear her. Well, it couldn't be helped. She had to betray LC's grandson, steal the Mojave-Stone. *If only he gave a damn about it.* Sadly, she was sure he didn't.

                              *   *   *   *   *

"Can I see what's in that envelope?" Leiv asked tapping a new clasp-type eight-and-a-half by eleven manilla envelope on the seat between them. He didn't give Glover time to respond before picking it up, but did stop short of actually opening it.

"Go ahead." Glover didn't take his eyes off the road. "I meant to show it to you anyway."

"From Deputy Sherman when you went in her office?"

"Yep."

In the envelope Leiv found several photos of Martin Potter. One from DMV, one that looked like a professional Christmas card type picture of Martin and Tonia together in "dress-up" clothes, and one of Martin straddling his motorcycle in a relaxed position, his helmet and goggles hanging from his right forearm, his gloved hands resting on the bike's steering bar. *Bet he even got a small tattoo to fit his biker image,* Leiv uncharitably mused. It was an article shot, and a caption was included on the photo page—Local Real Estate Developer is a Weekend Warrior. Attached to the photo were two pages of copy. One sheet of copy was a credit report that didn't look good. The real estate rollercoaster was at the bottom of the current housing prices hill.

The now dead man staring back at Leiv had been rather handsome in a straightforward way. Nothing quirky in his features nor expression—but a facial symmetry that couldn't be ignored. Leiv found himself rubbing his own rather large and not exactly straight nose.

The bike looked like other large motorcycles he'd seen. Except for one. A case where a man was assaulted at a bar because he was riding a small and colorful Japanese branded bike—a picture of which stuck with Leiv over the years. He found himself rubbing his nose again—one of the plaintiff's injuries was a broken nose.

For a second, a wave of sadness washed over Leiv—but different than earlier. It was a familiar sadness, from his early days, and came with dealing with crime and injustice. These days, even though these waves of sadness never stopped coming, the length and his ability to control this particular melancholy had matured. He could force it away, back into the recesses of his emotions. Like now, instead of dwelling, turning his thoughts forward to Shiné, his home and his inherited legacy.

After awhile, Glover said, "My mother says Everett was quite the puzzle solver."

"What?" Leiv was caught unawares, absorbed in his own thoughts of Shiné and why he desired so much to be home. Safe. *Funny that*, he'd fancied himself a *bon vivant* for so many years—years before Melissa. "Oh, you mean like chess?"

"Not exactly—"

"Grandfather's chess board in the library is quite nice." Leiv wasn't a chess player, but liked the wooden hand carved set, vintage unknown, except the pieces were probably carved in the early nineteen-hundreds. The set sat on an octagon shaped claw-footed chess table. The table's vintage and provenance were also uncertain. Could be a fake, for all Leiv knew. But he was fond of the table and its placement in the corner next to his cherished window and between two winged chairs. Pleasing to his eyes and emotions. The little tableau of table and chairs also sung to him of LC and Viola, battling wits. Indeed, there were several entries in LC's journal about those "chess events," as LC dubbed them.

"Like I said," Glover laughed lightly, "not exactly what I meant."

What then? Leiv tried doing a quick recap of his

grandfather's traits and accomplishments. Must be the stories—not repeated, only hinted at by HM—about Everett and Glover's predecessors cooperating on several incidents. *Hearsay stuff, magnified and embroidered over the years.* Leiv smiled and said, "Ha." Then he turned his head to look out the window. "That's nonsense, probably."

The area he was looking at certainly had grown—more strip mall type businesses, heavier traffic. Of course he hadn't been down Highway 18 for many a year.

Leiv added, "Though I have heard a couple things—a couple stories." Supposedly LC helped find a stolen horse in the early days, if he remembered correctly from his journal, and then a shed that was burned down. "Things are different now."

Glover said, "Might be in the blood, you know."

"What's in the blood?"

"Figuring stuff out. Keep your mind occupied."

"And what makes you think my mind needs occupying?" Despite his halfhearted umbrage over Glover's comment, Leiv did feel a slight twitch of excitement at hearing Glover's words. Indeed, several things were bothering him about the happenings of the last couple days. *But so vague.*

Reluctantly, he accepted, *yes*, he did want to figure out what was going on with Tucker's suicide attempt. And now a dead weekend-biker found on the border of Tucker and Naomi's properties. However, Leiv also knew he didn't have the interest in driving around, investigating, interviewing—*no*, he was not cut out to be a detective.

His desire for now—*to stay in Shiné.*

It was interesting though, driving through a big swatch of the Mojave on this trip with Glover. Especially in his cruiser. Everyone got out of their way. And now that they were leaving Lucerne Valley and heading in a roundabout but scenic way back home, it was pleasant. This part of California's desert was captivating. From its Joshua Tree prolific stretches, volcanic rock remnants, to its stark yet captivating Shiné valley.

All in all, he liked Glover's decision to change his mind from going back to I-15 via Dale Evans Parkway, and opted for this meandering slower route down Highway 18 over to Twentynine Palms, then heading back north to I-40. The sun would soon start its afternoon descent in the west to their rear, yet Leiv needed to pull his visor down for some reason. *All encompassing Mojave sun.* No matter what time of day it was.

On seeing a sign, Leiv asked, "Have you ever gone through Joshua Tree National Park?" He was sure Glover had, and realized for the first time, in his mind Glover needed to live up to a larger-than-life image. His friend, though quite smart, was also the "tough guy" to his "arbitrator" from the bench and mild-mannered thinking man.

"Professionally you mean? Like a crime happening there?"

"You know, I'm not sure what I meant." In his mind Glover represented all Policemen—city, sheriff's department, CHP, FBI—and further jurisdictional distinctions he couldn't think of at the moment. Especially if he considered all the federal agencies. *So much simpler when I started my carrier.* At the same time, Glover was also his friend, so he was interested in what he did on a personal level.

After a stretch of quiet thinking time, another sign caught Leiv's eye. It was welcoming them to Wonder Valley. "Is that a joke or a statement of something wonderful here?" he asked without thought.

Glover didn't answer right off, instead, drove for about ten minutes until they were in the middle of a unique piece of desert Leiv hadn't yet seen, or even imagined. Sure it was scrubby, sure it was vast, but trails—off road bikes he guessed—seemed to haphazardly appear, and very simple and small cabins dotted the landscape in what seemed like a helter-skelter arrangement. And there was an emotion riding on the desert air that filtered in even though they were in the protective cocoon of Glover's Crown Victoria. *This place is different.*

"Actually," Glover said, interrupting Leiv's musing on what to think about this new piece of the Mojave, "I do have an interesting story—" Glover slammed on the brakes, jerked the steering wheel to the right, causing his cruiser to hit the shoulder at far too high a speed. "Damn rear wheel drive," he cursed. "Shots." He kept control of his cruiser, and hissed to Leiv, "Sniper. As soon as I've fully stopped, slink down, slide out on to the ground through my side." He'd almost stopped the cruiser. "Follow me, squeeze under the steering wheel, just like me. Keep low." His tone was firm, commanding.

Leiv didn't think about what was going on, or what he was doing, just obeyed. Evidently Glover thought it better to stop than speed away. He trusted whatever Glover said. Instinctively, though, he felt in his pocket. His cell phone was there. *Thank goodness.* For Leiv did recognize something horrible was happening.

However, he didn't have time for considerations of any type or consequence. By the time he crawled across the front seat, to next literally roll out the driver-side door of Glover's cruiser, he heard a loud sharp pop, *then* another, *then* saw dirt fly within two-feet of where he landed on the ground. His thoughts raced—*such inconsequential sounds for something so deadly happening. Like a toy gun.* Leiv knew, however, what was happening to him and Glover was quite real.

Glover demanded, "Stay low. Flatten yourself against the car."

Without thought, Leiv obeyed as best he could. His

body and his mind needed to listen to Glover, do whatever he said. Shiné's Chief of Police was the expert—just like his guards in the courtroom had been. *Gun shots.* He was sure that's what was going on. *But why?*

"First shot hit on your side. The back door panel. SOB is out in those hills." Glover's voice was hard—all business. His 9mm Glock was in his right hand, while his left-hand held a Kenwood two-way he was calmly and succinctly repeating codes into.

I must be scared. I remember the invoice for that gun, that radio... Gun shots. He needed to think about how to help Glover. *And the computer was on the same invoice.* "Shut up," he whispered to his brain aloud. *Must be I'm really scared.* He needed to somehow help Glover, not think about silly stuff like what was on an invoice.

Another bullet hitting the ground inches in front of him and Glover, obliterated thoughts about anything except survival. Leiv realized he'd been scooting closer to Glover on his knees and using his elbows for propulsion. Both now burned like hell.

He knew Glover would get them out of this. *But gun shots?* He looked and saw Glover had his Glock firmly in both hands. Leiv couldn't see where the radio was. And strangely, other than the gun shots, the rest of the world had gone silent. No car sounds, no wind, no birds. It was them—and a sniper. The rest of the world no longer existed.

Another bullet pocked the dirt, only inches away from Glover's leg it seemed, and causing reality to finally penetrate his mind and emotions. *Somebody is really trying to kill us.* "What's going on, Dusty?"

Leiv could now feel his heart pounding in his throat and ears. He tried in his prior life to empathize with what victims went through. Trying to understand and feel was nowhere near this reality. "Who?" he heard himself ask. "Where?" Was someone from inside one of the several cabins to their right shooting at them? Or maybe from the one higher up? "Why?" His words were reduced to a mumble.

Glover gave Leiv a quick look. "Stay as close to the car as you can." He took a deep breath. "You got your cell?"

Leiv nodded. "Is he in those hills?" Had to be—not in the cabin. How else could those shots get over the the cruiser and hit the dirt near them. And a rifle maybe? Long rang give the sound? He knew a miniscule amount about guns gleaned from the courtroom.

"I've already called our situation in, but call nine-one-one if you have to later." Glover turned his head away, and Leiv thought he heard, "Can't be too high-powered, or we'd be dead already."

Later?

He watched as Glover tightened his arms and grip and took another deep, long breath. "Backup's on the way." Then he fully turned his back on Leiv, partially standing in the process and edged up closer to the front fender of his cruiser. But before he'd moved a foot, a bullet hit Glover in the chest and knocked him flat out, sprawled backward in the dirt. He'd evidently exposed his chest to the sniper—and now his friend was hit.

Oh my God, Leiv thought. *Is he dead? No, no...* Fear took over his emotions, then he saw Glover's leg move. *He's alive.* Unconsciously, Leiv took a deep breath, much like Glover had seconds earlier. *I have to get him protected, back here behind the door with me.* Without thought, Leiv crouched forward. He had to stay low, *but* he had to move. *Seconds before Glover's shot again.* Killed if he wasn't dead already.

In a milli-second, Leiv dropped even lower, to his knees, stretched flat out on his stomach, then scraped his body along the dirt and pebbles, this time using his stomach, hip muscles and elbows to move the foot or so necessary to reach Glover. He grabbed both his friend's feet and dragged Glover toward him, closer, closer, until he could grab him around the chest and rise up on his own knees enough to get him propped up against the entry into the cruiser's seat—the door a modest shield like it had been for him.

Blood covered Glover's chest, and a trickle of blood was dripping out the corner of his mouth. Then Leiv thought he heard a gurgling sound.

"No. No. No," Leiv demanded of the universe.

Next he heard the sirens. *So quick?* Then he remembered Twentynine Palms military base was just a few miles away.

Leiv pulled Glover's head to his chest, "The marines are coming, Dusty, the marines are coming." He thought he might be rocking, but wasn't sure. "Hang in there, hang in there. The marines are coming."

When Leiv finally had time to consider what was going on again, he was sitting in a hard plastic chair in the Emergency waiting area at Robert E. Bush Naval Hospital on Twentynine Palms Marine base—*waiting*. He was simultaneously *waiting* to hear if Glover was alive or dead and for Margaret to arrive. Seemed like hours he'd been *waiting, waiting.*

At least he wasn't hurting. After a quick initial assessment, they'd given him a few pills—pain and antibiotic he thought—to temporarily alleviate the pain from his scrapes and bruises. Glover was their first concern.

Up to now, Leiv hadn't been able to contemplate, much less accept the thought Glover could really be dead. He was prepared for a long stay of anxious and fearful moments— *waiting,* and not wanting to deal with the seriousness of Glover's injuries. Even though he'd seen the blood-saturated front of his light-blue uniform shirt. *Indelible.* Remembering their back and forth, especially the last couple days—Leiv almost cried out, caught himself in time. Then the memory of how they looked at countless catalogues, trying to decide on white, blue, or tan shirts for Shiné's police chief. Again, he had to hold his emotions in check. *Ironic how important the decision seemed at the time.*

Like the Mojave-Stone: for LC, a matter of bartering over a handful of rocks way-back-when, and now, crucial for HM.

The little things, the big things, the expensive things. Nits. All nits compared to Glover's survival. A seemingly unconnected memory surfaced—the mother who'd lost her son to a gang-banger over a pair of shoes and seeking justice in his courtroom. Fifteen or so years ago, but still with him; evidently, buried but not forgotten in his subconscious somewhere. Leiv's current thoughts on the color of Glover's shirt had somehow, after all these years, crystallized and internalized a mother's grief he'd seen in his courtroom so many years earlier. He could even now, still see her name on the court documents. *Lacey. Mrs. Lacey Johnson.*

Odd the memories we keep.

Leiv sighed loudly, then quickly looked around to see if anyone was in earshot. Only the nurse on duty—the other chairs-of-torture were empty. At least Glover wasn't vying for attention with other patients, having to be triaged with other traumas.

Funny, he hadn't noticed he was alone earlier—*waiting*. *Lost in my own thoughts.*

He'd already spent some time talking to Deputy Sherman. She'd just left, having stopped on her way to a cop-style "all-hands" meeting—all of them called into the manhunt for a sniper by the SBC Sheriff's Department.

Leiv looked around again, including taking a current time check on the large-handed wall clock above the nurses' station. This afternoon, the movement of time seemed at a snail's pace.

"Word is," Portia had explained hurriedly, "the Undersheriff and both Captains from Needles and Twentynine Palms have pulled out all stops on this one." She added, quite strongly, "It wasn't just *your* friend got shot, but one of *us*." She stared into his eyes for moment. "If you know what I mean." Then she gave him a more personal look. "You're not looking so good, yourself." Her eyes moved to his ripped shirt sleeves, torn Dockers, and what was visible of his underlying scrapes and bruises. "Possibility of infection, you know. Have to be careful."

"I do know," Leiv answered to both her questions. His arms and knees no longer burned like heck, and *yes*, the cop-brotherhood was strong. He'd seen it in action. "You're thinking he's still here in the area?"

Deputy Sherman's radio beeped, she nodded, then turned her back to him and walked over toward the nearest window. It sounded to Leiv like she was talking gibberish. Ten this, and ten that—but he knew it was a series of police codes.

As he stared at her uniformed back, late in the day sun was flooding the waiting area through her window, with some wayward rays of light seeming to bounce off and silhouette her torso. If radiant ambiance meant anything, it was a cheery place this time of day. Quite contradictory, if you were counting the minutes, waiting to see if your friends or loved ones would survive.

Which brought his mind around to Margaret. He'd called Glover's mother as soon as they arrived at the hospital, and she was on her way. Margaret was going to call Lloyd to drive her—if not she'd drive herself. And if she couldn't get hold of Lloyd, there were plenty others who would drive her.

The way LC wanted his town to turn out. Helping each other. One comforting thought in this whole ordeal.

Deputy Sherman was saying to him. "I'm gone. Call me as soon as you know about Glover."

As he watched her rushing out, Leiv doubted he could sit and wait much longer. Similar to what he guessed was going on with Portia, he wanted to *do* something. Help find the SOB who shot Glover.

But within seconds, a relieved-faced doctor came directly over to him. *Why is he smiling? Dare I believe?*

At first Leiv heard, but couldn't immediately absorb the doctor's words. The physician repeated a second time, "Police Chief Glover is stabilized. We've patched him up. We're watching him. And of course if his condition goes sideways we'll shoot him over to Loma Linda in a helicopter."

"He's going to live," Leiv heard himself mumble. He could hear how feeble his voice sounded, and he wanted to get up and shake the doctor's hand—even give him a hug. But his legs felt wobbly.

"We plan on doing our best to make sure he lives." The doctor, *Doctor Monroe,* Leiv thought he'd said when introducing himself, leaned in and down a little so he could pat Leiv on the shoulder. "Your friend will be alright."

Now Leiv really wanted to jump up, hug him, and thank him profusely. But somehow he couldn't. He'd been so worried, stunned sort of, and now, well now he was having a hard time just sitting up straight.

Doctor Monroe smiled, and something in his eyes told Leiv he understood what was going on inside him. Why he couldn't seem to talk, stand, communicate like a normal human being. He said, "Bit of a shock, these sudden events."

Thank goodness, Leiv thought. When he looked back up, the doctor was disappearing, a white coat fading into the bowels of whatever lay beyond the emergency waiting room.

Next, Leiv felt his head bobbing from someone shaking his shoulders, and heard Margaret's voice saying, "Where's Glover? Where's my son? Where's your...is he okay?"

It was becoming the longest-of-days. Nonetheless, with Leiv leading the way, they were trying to relax, ensconced in LC's "withdrawing room."

One of Doctor Monroe's assistants eventually cleaned, treated, and bandaged Leiv's scuffed up elbows, knees, and shins before sending him home. Still, Leiv was resting his arms quite gingerly on his padded chair arms, and had one leg elevated on a footstool. Nadya and Sydney seemed quite comfortable on the loveseat—seemingly with no concerns at all.

Night came none-too-soon for Leiv. And his frame of mind was leaning heavily toward disengagement from the world. Nevertheless, he had an obligation to be a good host. As a reminder of who he was, and what he needed to do, Leiv looked around the room quickly, his eyes finally resting on LC's huge fireplace, its rock face and center stone staring back at him. LC would want him to treat Nadya and her husband Sydney well, and with appropriate respect.

Leiv didn't initially tell his cousin and cousin-in-law everything about his day, and wasn't sure why. But over Beaujolais for them, Harvey's Bristol Cream for himself, and a plate of cheese HM prepared, Leiv did fill them in on the basic happenings of the last two days. *Maybe, I'm just too tired to go through the whole thing.*

Indeed, he'd spent a significant amount of time talking with Margaret after she arrived at the hospital, reassuring her Glover would be alright. Maybe reassuring himself more than her. Then he'd talked to Deputy Sherman again on the phone, telling her Glover was past the worst, and finding out from her about the manhunt. So far nothing and nobody. The sniper had disappeared into Mojave dust.

"I'm guessing hiding out in one of the homesteads," she'd said. "Maybe has help from a friend or family."

He asked if they were questioning everyone, and Portia assured him, "Damn straight, we are." She made a sound over the phone he couldn't quite interpret, but he did hear what he took to be the end of her statement, "Wonder Valley will wonder what hit 'em." Her words were jack-booted in intent if taken on their face, but her delivery, Leiv thought was cute—and he certainly understood how Portia felt. But no matter how her words sounded or her exact intent, a sniper had almost killed Glover and remained at large.

A long day.

In the silence they now sat in, Leiv took a moment to re-appraise Sydney Collins and his wife Nadya Rhodes-Collins. They seemed to fit perfectly in the leather loveseat to the right of Leiv's armchair—directly across from Margaret's loveseat. For some unconscious and unknown reason, he'd steered them there, as if Margaret's regular choice of seating was reserved for her alone. Leiv knew he preferred to turn to the left when talking to people—a fact he'd reminded himself of at many a dinner party. But tonight, he'd forced himself in the position of facing right. *So Margaret's loveseat won't be violated.*

"Seems like you've had a miserable day," Sydney said.

Leiv thought he sounded genuinely empathetic, and once again wondered at his initial reluctance to trust his cousin's new husband. Sydney's curiosity about the Mojave-Stone was not enough to doubt him—many were curious about that.

Sydney added, "Are you going to see your friends tomorrow?"

Without forethought, Leiv almost blurted out his auto-driving phobia, but caught himself. "Margaret is going to see Glover. Evidently, he's making a remarkable recovery." *The man's indestructible.* "Calvin is with Tucker still."

"So," Nadya said after a long sip of Beaujolais, "Shiné will be without a cop for awhile?"

Leiv thought it an odd question, but answered, "Doubt that." He smiled to himself imagining Glover sitting up in his hospital bed complaining, wanting to go home. "If I know our Chief of Police, he'll be back on duty as soon as possible. Even if he's in a body cast." He hoped his mental picture was not a fantasy—but a real prognostication. A slight smile came with this new picture of Glover bandaged from head to foot sitting behind his desk in his Shiné storefront office barking orders. Reality was, Glover had a chest wound. Whatever bandaging he left the hospital with probably wouldn't even be visible.

Sydney turned his head slightly and gave Leiv a curious look. "You must think a lot of him?"

"I do," Leiv admitted. "When it comes to tough and brave, Glover can't be beat."

"You know, Mr. Rhodes, I already heard about what happened today before you got back."

It was Leiv's turn to tilt his head with curiosity. "I thought we'd moved past the Mr. Rhodes stuff."

"Well Leiv," Sydney said, and put his glass on the antique mahogany side table between them and leaned forward slightly. "Ms. Miller said gossip travels fast in Shiné."

HM should know, Leiv mused, *being one of the main purveyors of said gossip.* Again, he wanted to smile, but willed his jaw line firm.

Sydney continued, "And what she heard was, you were the one who dragged Chief Deers out of harm's way." He picked his glass up and leaned back into his chair. "Saved his life, probably."

Leiv scoffed and made a face. "By the time I pulled Glover back toward me, the shooting had pretty much stopped."

"How many shots did you hear?"

"Two, maybe three."

Nadya chimed in, "Hester said there were fifteen shots."

Hester? Not HM. Leiv clicked out the side of his mouth, reminiscent of Glover, his father, and his grandfather. "And how would she know that?"

"From her cousin in Needles," Nadya said proudly. "Seems he's in deputy training there."

Leiv was incredulous on two fronts—Hester's cousin was a deputy, and fifteen shots were fired. "Can't be true. That many rifle shots?"

"Your adrenalin was going," Sydney said. "You don't know how brave you were today, Mr.—, I mean Leiv." Quickly clearing his throat, Sydney changed the subject. "I really like your house." He looked over to the unlit fireplace where Dobie was nonetheless stretched out. "And your beautiful dog." She was asleep and snoring lightly.

Thinking back, and unlike Dobie, Leiv had been on guard from the moment he got home and found his cousin and her husband waiting for him—and he still wasn't sure why the suspicious caution. Now relaxing and chatting with the two a bit, he was warming to these "intruders" into his Shiné sanctuary. Indeed, Sydney's appraisal of his home did sound genuine. "Glad you like LC's dream home." Maybe Dobie was right to be unconcerned. "And Dobie," he added.

"Actually," Nadya said, wiggling in closer to Sydney, half leaning on him, half snuggling into his shoulder, "it's not a house." She looked up into her husband's face. "It's called Rhodes Castle." Then she looked at Leiv, winked, and smiled.

Leiv smiled in return. "That was our grandfather, alright. Larger than life on many fronts." He remembered liking Nadya during their shared days at Rhodes Castle when he and his father had come back to Shiné to visit, then later after Nadya's father André died, and Nadya's mother Mary brought her and her sister Katey to Chicago when he was also there. Then there was the subsequent time they'd spent together while their family was also getting settled in the Windy City.

Still, Leiv didn't feel like he *knew* her. He certainly hadn't remembered her being as warm as she was with Sydney. *Love changes us all.*

He also hadn't remembered her being so pretty. *Or again, is it the glow of love and a happy marriage causing her to shine?* Indeed, she looked half-mesmerized, like he'd often felt in Melissa's presence. A lump rose in his throat. *Not tonight.* And before sighing aloud, Leiv caught himself in time and brought his hand to his mouth, masking his lingering inner sorrow.

Silence again fell over their little gathering as Sydney took a few moments to look around, reappraising probably—

including the high ceiling of the "withdrawing" room, the huge fireplace, stone floors, and cathedral style windows. "Well," he finally said, turning his attention to Leiv with a nod of the head, "does have that castle-like feel." Then he chuckled. "Though, I've never actually been in a castle." His gaze turned from Leiv down to Nadya, now completely snuggled into his chest. "Next year, I promise, sweetheart, we'll actually take that trip to Europe. See all the castles."

Leiv decided he liked the sound of Sydney's voice, deeper than his countenance and physical structure would lead one to expect. He also detected a genuineness and kindness in his tone and conversational demeanor that surprised him. *I need to rethink the Sydney and Nadya thing.*

Nadya smiled, then straightened up a bit and said to Leiv, "Do you remember how mother insisted on calling you Leigh-Everett, even though you told her hundreds of times you preferred to go by Leiv?"

"I sure do." His Aunt's face appeared in his mind's eye as vivid as if she was sitting next to him. "How is she?" He held his breath hoping they hadn't come to Shiné as bearers of bad news.

"She's doing grand. She and Katey are sharing a house."

Sydney squinted at him, again seemingly re-appraising. "Rhodes fits you. But Leiv doesn't." Then a wry looking smile curled the corner of his mouth. "Now that we've actually met, I remember seeing pictures of you in the Chicago Sun Times. And the Tribune. Some big trial in Southern Illinois I think." He chuckled. "A politician did something unethical most probably. If I remember, they always referred to you as Judge Rhodes." His chuckle turned into a tease. "Didn't know judges were allowed first names."

Leiv looked to Sydney, once more expanding his assessment of this new cousin-by-marriage. Besides his deeper than expected and congenial tone of voice, Sydney didn't seem bored with their family catch-up and talk from the past.

However, Illinois was a long way away in time and distance, and he didn't want to get distracted in his thoughts. On the other hand, he certainly didn't want to revisit his thoughts and worries about Glover lying in a hospital bed in Twentynine Palms.

"Well, Sydney," Leiv said hoping to turn the spotlight directly on his cousin. "What brings you and Nadya to Shiné? I'm guessing it's not just to avoid a Chicago winter." He nearly shivered remembering the freezing cold winds blowing in off Lake Michigan. Southern Illinois hadn't been as bad. But some weather conditions—like the Lake Michigan blasts—he would never forget.

"Syd, please." Sydney straightened a little, moving Nadya in the process, and leaned forward, turning more toward Leiv. "Everybody at the plant calls me that." Nadya, was forced to break her snuggle—pursing her lips slightly in the process—and sit up straight; allowing Sydney to look more directly at Leiv. He said, "I came to see the Mojave-Stone Nadya's been going on about."

Leiv had a lot of practice keeping a straight-face over his years of hearing the most outrageous accusations and defenses, so he was sure his jaw didn't literally drop, but he certainly felt like it.

While Leiv was recovering, Sydney added, "But now that I'm here, your suicidal alfalfa farmer, a dead body with an accompanying motorcycle, and a sniper attack on your Chief-of-Police are far more interesting." An unabashed eager expression speedily encompassed his face, as Sydney leaned in closer. "I think Ms. Miller has told us everything she can. But you were actually there." The excitement in his voice couldn't have been clearer.

Using his professional voice, Leiv said without a second thought, "On your first quest, I'm sorry to tell you, there is no Mojave-Stone." He shook his head to emphasize how ridiculous he thought the idea was of a gemstone hidden here at Rhodes Castle. To seal the deal, he gave Nadya a glance of dismay.

"But as to what I've been doing all day," Leiv continued, "I'll be glad to share more. I was just tired earlier, and none of it's secret." Quickly, he ran through the day's events in more detail than the first time. In conclusion, he said, "And you can bet money on the fact stories can really get distorted around Shiné." He was again thinking in particular about HM.

Leiv looked over at Dobie, still stretched out in front of the fireplace. Her legs were moving, *chasing something in her dreams.* And while watching Dobie's dream-chase, Leiv decided he definitely liked Sydney. So he spent the next half hour—further elaborating in the retelling—about his trip to St. Mary's, then Loma Linda, a sketchy account of lunch at The Summit Inn, with emphasis on the omelet—but leaving out what he considered "the enigma" of Deputy Portia Sherman.

He also skipped the "meeting," if that's what to call it, with Tonia Potter, figuring that was police business. Then there was the *wonder* of Wonder Valley. On the sniper attack, his retelling was still sketchy because he really didn't remember all those shots. *Fifteen?*

"And Chief Deers?" Sydney asked again, and sounding to Leiv like he was genuinely concerned. "I know Ms. Miller said you saved his life. But do you think he'll actually make it?"

"He damn well better," Leiv answered, surprising himself not with his words per se, profane or otherwise, or his tone—but with the depth of emotion he felt for Margaret's son. "I don't think Margaret could take another loss like that." Leiv inhaled. "Not after losing Naomi last year."

Hester decided Nadya's coming to Shiné was a godsend. Just like with Dobie. She really liked the mutt, a nice companion for a childless old woman. *"Arvah,"* she whispered, the Romani word for yes slipping out. She would keep the Doberman in her apartment all the time if Leiv didn't insist the poor dog stay with him. Truth be admitted, Dobie did spend many daytime hours with her.

At night, however, Dobie stuck with clueless Leiv. *Amazing to think the man once was a lawyer.* Definitely not made of the same stuff as his grandfather LC. *Not even up to his father Everett's standards.* College type. *Not a man's man.* "Wearing a silly eye mask at night like a vain woman," she scoffed aloud and shook her head.

Tonight, comfy in her own wingchair, and thinking about Dobie, Nadya, the Rhodes genealogy, her proud line, and as always, the Mojave-Stone—she nodded her head. With her feet toasty in multi-colored bright socks and looking back at her from a matching ottoman, it was easy and comfortable to indulge in familiar and comfortable thoughts; for the moment those thoughts were focused on Leiv.

Not just a lawyer, but a judge. A big time one, at that. One of Hester's Chicago relatives, the same cousin who crocheted the foot-warmers she was wearing, sent her several pictures of the man—Judge Rhodes he was called—in his robes surrounded by a lot of uppity-ups. And in his private life, *won't even go by Leigh-Everett,* his given name.

She wiggled her toes, bringing her attention back to her foot warmers. Hester liked looking at them—especially moving her toes around willy-nilly and making the bright colors dance. Unlike the long dead olden-times furnishing at Rhodes Castle, the thick socks seemed alive to her. Much like the throws and afghans she splashed around her apartment.

Hester closed her eyes and smiled. For the moment, despite her irritation over Leiv, she was comfortable and happy—especially now, with a possible heir actually here with her in Shiné. An intelligent and educated heir. She couldn't ask for more.

Hester ended up talking to the Collins couple at length earlier, subtly she thought, trying to gage Nadya's interest in protecting the stone and preserving the Romani interest in Rhodes Castle. She'd filled them in on the day's gossip, enhanced with information from her cousin in Needles, the wanna-be-cop. When she gave them the "castle tour," she'd left off Leiv's library. She was saving the hidey-hole to savor with Nadya alone.

Sydney had wanted to know more about the crest over the front door of all things. Like LC was royalty or something. All Hester knew was LC had the ugly dull thing especially made in England. Took ages to get it back. Then he'd done something to it in private that was supposed to make it uniquely a "Rhodes" crest. The nosey twit Sydney seemed interested, though.

Leigh-Everett came back right before sunset, ruining any further opportunities for talking and planning. She and Nadya had probably talked enough, though, and she'd looked into the woman's eyes, heard her voice. This young woman knew about *their* olden days, *their* olden traditions—mostly from her mother Mary. The change of name from Cooper to Rhodes hadn't made a difference with her either. She and Nadya were like-thinkers.

Her eyes were closed still, and Hester wiggled her toes some more, and smiled again, thinking about what she and Nadya were going to do.

Tonight, after she'd delivered a cheese platter and fresh bottle of Beaujolais to the withdrawing room, she'd listened from the door until Leigh-Everett finished telling Sydney-the-twit the part about the body they found on Tucker's land. When they started talking about desert weather she no longer found their conversation interesting and went off to tidy up the kitchen after sneaking a peek in the library, slipping a special envelope under Nadya's door, then finally retiring to her apartment and comfy armchair.

Hester opened her eyes and told her parlor, "Doesn't even know about wines. The schmuck." His daddy Everett always said, pick Italian. Never French.

Well, at least Sydney wasn't a *complete* schmuck, not believing the Mojave-Stone didn't exist like Leigh-Everett wanted him to. "Hah," Hester said. Though talking to herself out loud was not a habit she wanted to get into——not like her mother who used to do it all the time. *Keck*—she also liked the Romani word for no.

Quickly, she first blew out a breath, then symbolically clenched her teeth to keep her mouth shut. She needed to break both habits, talking to herself out loud, and using Romani terms. Didn't want to give Leigh-Everett any indication she was trying, like her mother, to keep the old ways alive.

Leigh-Everett was like his grandfather. Forgetting the Cooper line, embracing the Rhodes thing. Her mother never actually called LC a traitor, so neither had she. But others in

119

Chicago certainly had. Hester tried refocusing her thoughts. Old grievances were draining.

The body found at Tucker's yesterday *was* a surprise. There wasn't much she didn't know about, and she certainly hadn't heard about a body being dumped in Shiné. Not that bodies buried in the desert were a new thing, and she figured there were more of them still out there waiting to be found. Desert sands covered a lot of secrets. But her cousin Andreas Herne had disappeared, now hadn't he? More than a year ago, right before that Naomi woman had her accident. *Dearest Andreas.*

Hester once again focused her eyes on her feet, unconsciously enjoying the gaiety of her socks despite her new and unsettling line of thought about Andreas. Unconsciously her eyelids slowly lowered and Hester sunk into the cuddling-spell of her arm chair. She wanted to think more about today's events. *Maybe I should call my cousin Bersch?*

Half in the past, and half in the present, Hester's mind wandered for a bit around Rhodes Castle. Today's tour had brought back a lot of memories and considerations.

The "great-hall" had been LC's words. Everett, her mother, and she, just called the area "the entryway." Performing her duties during the day, she often passed by the twenty-feet tall double glass doors, overhead transits, and side-lites—all decorated with Edwardian styled dollops, vines, and tulip like flowers. Thinking about them again, and how LC had claimed all the stained glass had come from Europe. She certainly didn't like the rock design above it. Junk, just like that "thing" in the library André put together.

Still, she'd often stop and look out through the thick contorting glass, cut into off-shaped pieces by the leading, and giving a funny look to the world outside. She had stopped for such a moment tonight, on her way to her apartment for the night. It was dark, but with a full moon rising to her left. Hester loved full moons. Had something to do with her mother's blood line she was sure. And of course, blood lines always made her think about the Mojave-Stone.

Indeed, after her eavesdropping and before her kitchen stop, and knowing they were settled in LC's withdrawing room for awhile—Hester's library stop was because the Mojave-Stone was on her mind. It was easy to do, wagging around the dust rag she carried with her at all times. The rag was a prop, a ready excuse if found in an odd part of the castle at an odd time—performing a little late night dusting. She and her mother both had made it clear to the entire Rhodes lineage, when it came to housekeeping, especially dusting, there were no set hours.

Everett had said when revealing the secret-of-secrets to her, "No one knows about where it is, Hester, besides me. Not even your mother." He'd shown her where the stone was hidden—they'd been much alike in that respect. Both knowing how important things of this world were. Ensuring treasures—if not traditions—remained safe through the generations. Everett and André had carried it on, but she thought Leiv was an "outlier" when it came to treasure. Didn't care about lineage or the Mojave-Stone.

"I'll keep it safe," Hester had assured Everett many years earlier. And true enough, she periodically checked it was still there. Safely wrapped in its burgundy velvet cloth, and well hidden in a little safe behind André's silly rock relief plaque.

"The rock tree of life, guarding the stone," Everett had said. Of course she held her tongue that night about how ugly she thought the thing. Finding out where the Mojave-Stone was hidden was far more important.

Tonight, she hadn't turned on any of the library lights, but let the stars and full moon light finding its way through the tall and high library window guide her. Not that she needed any light. Hester could find it in the dark—and with her dust rag, she carried a trusty penlight in her smock pocket. *Never know.* She had a key to the old-style safe, of course. Hung around her neck at all times.

Once the stone was in her hands again this evening, she'd held it up high, letting a moonbeam catch its dark, almost black, brilliance.

Marvelous, she thought, *even at night.* Then after a few moments of pleasure, Hester reverently re-cradled the jewel in velvet and replaced it in its hidey-hole. A clear star-sprinkled night continued to shine through the plain-glass window above and to the right of Leiv's desk. *Night can't shine.* But it sure had felt like it. She figured it was the combination of the full moon and the Mojave-Stone.

Remembering those lovely library skulking moments earlier in the evening, the broadest smile of her evening spread across Hester Miller's face, still ensconced in her armchair—and her eyes again closing. Within a couple minutes she started dozing off, with her last thoughts of the evening circling around Sydney. Wondering if her cousin had come up with anything substantial about him. She still wasn't sure whether she should trust Nadya's husband or not. Hester was wise enough to know she could be completely wrong about him being a schmuck.

She hoped not, he might see the pictures she'd pushed under their bedroom door before Nadya, and figure a few things out on his own. She was old fashioned, but even she had a digital camera, computer, and printer.

Some of her cousins in Chicago were stuck in the old-days. Not her. Technology moved on, and she'd kept up. One good thing about clueless Leigh-Everett, he paid her well. She could get all the gadgets she wanted.

Among all the events of the day—*and there were many indeed*—Sydney Collins was also in Leiv's late night thoughts.

Better than thinking about Glover and Tucker.

It was quite late—even later in Chicago—but his friend Captain Herman was a night-owl and a wannabe-rake. Of course Hal was older now, but from the tidbits still filtering back Leiv's way, he hadn't changed that much.

Leiv was not yet officially ready for bed, but close. After he sent Sydney and Nadya off to their room on the second floor, he and Dobie headed to his library before retiring. He mind wasn't quite ready to shut down.

He smiled upon entering; the confined library air told him Hester had already visited for the night.

Without really thinking about it, he dialed Herman's number on the fake French antique rotary phone on the corner of LC's desk. When the phone company error message blasted in his ear, he remembered for long distance, he needed to use his cell phone.

Standing behind his desk, it felt like he could feel the night behind him through his large clear-glass window. Of course he couldn't, but Leiv turned to look anyway as he rummaged in his smoking jacket pocket for his cell phone. Surprisingly, that little muscle effort hurt. *Drugs wearing off.*

What he saw outside was the usual Mojave night sky, clear, black, and sprinkled with stars in constellations he never learned as a child. On the edge of the sky, a sizable and glorious full moon glowed.

Leiv knew he had rituals in life that kept him connected to what he considered essential to his current life. Sky or star gazing was not one of them; though a fill-in judging stint he did in rural Illinois opened his eyes to spectacular skies unmarred by city lights. Much like Shiné.

He sat down, found Hal in his contacts list and dialed.

Captain Hal Hermann answered after one ring. "Leiv, what the hell do you want now?" His tone was teasing, jovial.

"How did you know it was me? And I don't *always* call when I need something."

"Yes you do." Hal laughed. Loud and hearty-sounding even over a less than perfect cell connection.

Leiv had always found Hal's laugh infectious, impossible not to be caught up in, and felt a smile spread across his face. But the words he heard himself say were surprisingly serious—and overly sentimental. "You know, it's good to hear your voice. Brings back memories."

"Sure does." Hal laughed again, then in a more normal tone asked, "Have you done anything with that toxicity report I sent you?"

"Not yet." *Haven't a clue what it means yet.* "Don't know how it could possibly fit in with anything." He'd sent Naomi's blue bottle to Hal the day he'd first seen it in her garage. *Not sure why. A hunch?*

"Unusual stuff."

Leiv imagined he could see Hal shaking his head back in Chicago. Then he thought he caught music in the background? "Where are you anyway?"

"Dugan's."

"On Halsted?" *Still, a cop hangout.* "After all these years?"

"Some things don't change. So, Leiv, like I asked already, what do you want now?"

124

Indeed, he'd called, bothered Hal while he was out drinking, and for a moment a smidgen of doubt about his actions tried wiggling into his conscience. He brushed his doubt aside. "You think you could get a down-and-dirty background check on someone for me?"

Hal sighed. "Is that all?"

"I owe you."

"Of course you do. Now who do you want to know about? And do you want me to call in a Fed favor on this too."

"No, no," Leiv quickly qualified. He didn't want any potential agency alarm bells to go off. Not yet, at least. "Just statewide. Says he has a business in Illinois, a Chicago suburb actually."

"Name?"

"Sydney Collins."

After a couple more minutes of banter, Hal rang off with the excuse a "hottie" was headed his way.

Though near exhaustion, Leiv didn't abandon his library right away, but continued to sit in LC's sanctum, at LC's desk, ensconced in his father Everett's redone desk chair.

An unwanted but necessary task, he thought, was now done, and Leiv took a deep long breath—simultaneously expressing his relief at the deed done, and smelling even more distinctly the remnants of Hester's presence. She didn't wear perfume, but bathed with some god-awful soap that left a trail a mile long. *She's been in here tonight.* Most assuredly to caress her beloved Mojave-Stone. He did notice she'd also added a new afghan to the stack she'd been building over the last two years next to his father Everett's lounge chair in the corner. The new one, orange and yellow.

Dear Hester. In some ways he *was* fond of her.

Smiling to himself, he retrieved LC's duplicate journal from its secret hidey-hole drawer inside the leg space and opened it to its last page. The page his grandfather wrote before he couldn't physically write anymore.

Leiv took another slow breath, leaned back against the chair-back's padding, letting his body go, relaxing his muscles. Then he closed his eyes, put his hand on that last page, and connected—somehow, someway—like he'd done so often since his return to Shiné. Connected to Leigh Cooper Rhodes across the expanse of time. It was better in LC's cave with the original journal, but this would do for tonight.

His thoughts—bounding between the past and the present—a smile spread slowly across his face as he thought of Hester again, guarding what she considered the Mojave-Stone from his grandfather's era. Not her fault, of course, believing the gem in the safe behind him was the Mojave-Stone. Everett had thought it so, and now she did. Indeed, the opal in the safe *was* a glorious black opal, and high in value. But it had come from Australia, purchased by LC to keep idle, ritualistic, and avarice minds busy.

Yes, real fire opals were mined somewhere in Mexico or South America—and like no other. *Too bad father never read LC's journal.* But in his heart, Leiv knew LC's journal was for him to read, understand. Not his father Everett. Somehow he'd known they were especially connected when standing beside his grandfather's death bed—their eyes, then their minds somehow connecting.

Leiv opened his eyes. "And now Sydney wants to know about the Mojave-Stone," he told Dobie who was lying across the hearth of the closed doorway—not napping for once—short ears erect, as if she understood every word he was saying. Since the Doberman had arrived, Leiv found he liked talking to her. She was a sounding board of sorts—a sounding board that didn't talk back.

"Or is it Nadya pushing him?"

Dobie made a sound he took to say, "Unknowable yet, boss." Then she laid down and closed her eyes. *Nap time again.* Leiv smiled, leaned farther back in his desk chair. Then like Dobie, he closed his eyes again, seeing what he chose to see. And his smile broadened when Melissa's smiling face appeared, holding a Mojave-Stone fire opal up to catch a ray of sun.

But rudely, and quite dramatically, the visually brilliant and comforting picture of his wife and a Rhodes fire opal was pushed aside. First with the pervasive and unforgettable smell-of-hospital, quickly followed by a picture of Tucker's comatose-like body connected to what looked like endless tangled tubes.

That nightmarish vision was next pushed aside by the picture of a leather jacket clad arm and hand, with weathered wrist zipper-loops dancing in the wind—rising from desert sand, as if trying to touch the stars—with Tucker's center-pivot sprinkler wand visible in the distance.

The phone rang, startling Leiv enough he almost slid out of the chair, having to steady himself by grabbing the desk.

It was Margaret, asking if they could meet for breakfast, explaining she wanted to talk about Glover. Of course he agreed immediately, but before he could ask why or what about Glover, she hung up.

In two days, Sydney had fallen in love with Rhodes Castle. From the British royalty-evoking high ceilings, the meticulous stained glass windows, the extravagant square footage, the priceless, and he thought excellently chosen antiques—he felt at home the moment he stepped through the massive front entry doors.

And the bedroom Hester or Leiv, he didn't know which, selected for them was extravagant beyond what he could imagine. The huge four poster with a chest bed-seat spanning the bed's foot, several massive armoires, two armchairs—and gorgeous rugs. And an *en suite* bathroom.

"You know I could live here," he said to Nadya as she came out of the bathroom, a thick terry cloth robe wrapped around her body.

"I must say," her tone was one of surprise and admiration, "the water pressure is strong, the water hot, and this robe is marvelous." She was barefoot and had a towel turbaned around her damp hair. She came over and sat on the edge of the bed.

Sydney had already showered, and was now stretched out in the middle of the bed, enjoying feeling like gentry in a great mansion. "Yeah, good shower. Who would have guessed?"

"What's that?" Nadya asked pointing to a manila envelope at Sydney's feet.

"It was pushed under the door earlier I'm thinking." He yawned. "Don't know why we didn't see it before."

She picked up the envelope, pulled out several eight-and-a-half by eleven sheets of thick looking paper.

"What's in it?" he asked, closing his eyes as if about to fall off to dreamland any second.

"Oh, just a Joey Grey Soup recipe I asked Hester for earlier today."

He could hear her folding the paper, and softly padding barefoot across the room away from the bed. To her suitcase, he guessed. *Hiding the pictures.*

128

"Hope it's good," he said in as drowsy of a tone he could fake. "Is it like that stew you make?"

"Yep, same thing."

Sydney did in fact drift off to sleep quickly, but not before pondering the fact his wife was lying to him. *Just like I lied to her.* He'd opened the envelope when he'd spied it partially hidden under the throw rug at the bedroom door, then peered at the enclosed pictures for quite a few moments before realizing he was looking at shots of Leiv's library. Several were close-ups of a very ugly rock-collage hanging behind the library desk chair.

The hidey hole for the Mojave-Stone is behind that hideous thing. It was a guess, but Sydney was pretty sure he was right.

Chapter Four

From LC's journal: *Yep, have to stop a-frettin' — it's gonna be what it's gonna be. Either they'll come, or they won't. And sometimes, just touching something, any old thing...and you can end up knowing what's going to happen. Sometimes, even what's already happened. Kinda like you're inside their head.*

Tuesday

Ida Oakes woke up in the middle of the night, then again half an hour later, then again another half an hour later. Annoyed she couldn't sleep, and feeling as if it were still the middle of the night, she lifted her head up enough to see across her expansive bedroom and out the window. Still dark. No stars or moon-glow. Strange in that it was supposed to be a full moon night, and there wasn't a hint of a pre-dawn lightening sky.

Fitful, still annoyed, and tired, she forced herself out of

bed, and moving in zombie-like fashion, Ida headed out through the garage to their connected pool room. Ida slept in the nude and didn't bother clothing herself.

Besides, no one to see me in the middle of the night.

Tucker had willingly paid a large sum, by pool building standards, so everything was just the way she wanted it—including being able to walk from her bedroom to the pool, while still making it separate from the house proper. One of the things she liked about him—his adoration.

Once in the automatically monitored and controlled seventy-nine degree water—the temperature she preferred— Ida let herself float. First on her back for a few moments, then she turned over to her stomach, stretched her arms out wide, and letting her torso and legs relax.

She'd heard what she did in the water was called the "dead man's float." She called it her "thinking-time" float. Tonight, it would also be a sleeping tonic, she hoped. It didn't take long before she felt her muscles start to relax, first her feet which hung the lowest in the water, then all the way up through her body to her finger tips. This pool was her salvation, on several levels, and on several occasions.

Ida lifted her head and took a breath, though she could go for a very long time without one. As a child, she and her friends would have holding-their-breath contests in the public pool. That pool was gone now—just a fenced-in dirty concrete hole. *So sad.* Everett Rhodes should have spent the money to keep it going, fix it up.

And poor, poor, Georgie. They'd played together years ago, not exactly a lifetime in the past, but feeling like it was this morning. Childhood friend or not, some things you can't stop from happening. *Some things have to be done, and you just can't stop them. Or yourself.*

The community pool was also where she learned to

swim. Quite suddenly, Ida's childhood reminiscences where interrupted by the clear and unavoidable picture of Tucker's comatose-like face.

Oh God, do I love that man. The thought of losing Tucker was almost unbearable, and almost caused her to stand up from her floating position. Tucker and Calvin were her life-savers in the murky water of Shiné. *Oh to live on the ocean.* Maybe one day she would. Of course she would still have a pool no matter where she lived. *Can't imagine not having a pool.*

Even though not looking, Ida "felt" the sun rising. Another day in the making. And this day, she needed to figure out how to get Tucker out of trouble.

Cupola or library? Neither this morning. It was barely the touch of dawn when Leiv set out to meet Margaret at The Greasy Spoon against the backdrop of the coming-to-life horizon, a most striking shade of orange. An appealing color, and reminding Leiv of something he couldn't immediately identify.

TGS, as Shiné resident's dubbed the café in its early days, was the only restaurant in town. Nowadays, it was also a tavern at night, which Leiv had actually been to, entering through another entrance around the side, almost in back. Even the tavern had a quite ornate bar and rear bar wall with elaborate mirrors, complete with pedestal-like spindles and stone reliefs to add a desert-like feeling.

Oddly, even though TGS was next door to the only gas station in town, it was seldom full. Neither was it seldom empty. Chef Jack opened at six in the morning, and closed around eight in the evening, a couple hours after Nell opened the tavern. Limited bar-food was consequently available for a couple hours in the evening. Leiv heard, opening times, at both restaurant and bar, were sometimes a moving target.

He thought the place a treasure. Yet, he seldom came on his own. Meant driving into town from Rhodes Castle. Some of Chef Jack's lunch and dinner creations he also thought, were on par with anything he'd ever eaten. Even at some of the swanky places in Chicago or New York.

As was her wont, Margaret had already settled into, and disappeared from front door sight in the farthest away high-back booth—near the door to the restrooms—and with her back to the front door. She called it the "hideout booth." No one wanted to sit there, nor cared who did.

"Am I late?" he asked sliding into the booth across the table from her. Leiv hadn't actually seen Margaret from the door, but knew she was there. Clues—her car in the parking lot, and knowing her seating preference.

"No, I'm early." She told him, but before he could get settled past sitting down or say anything, she stretched her hands out across the table toward him. "Give me your hands, Leigh-Everett."

Surprised, and a little befuddled, he did as bid.

"I'm sorry," she said, "I hung-up on you so fast last night. But I wanted to say what I'm about to say, in person."

She sniffed inside a quick deep breath, and within those few seconds, Leiv blurted out unchecked, "Is this about Glover? No, no…he's not dead is he?" *Someone would have called me.*

She squeezed his hands, hard. "Leiv, I talked to him this morning." Her somber face turned into a smile. "Said he's ready to come home, doesn't know why they're keeping him." Evidently having seen something revealing in his own eyes, she added. "No, we haven't lost another cherished one."

He figured she was talking about Melissa—but on

second thought, maybe Naomi?

Margaret further reassured, "Glover is fine." She took another deep breath, slow this time, but still rushed to say her next words, "And he's okay because of you." Her eyes became moist. "I wanted to thank you in person for saving my son's life. Your—" She stopped herself, and refreshed her smile and usual composure. "Your quick action saved his life." She continued to hold his hands tightly.

Sydney had used the same reasoning. But Leiv didn't believe it; though he didn't reject Margaret's sentiment and accompanying statement. Too heartfelt to dismiss. Instead, his knack for diplomacy in the past came to the rescue. "Glover would have done the same." *Deflect, respond to an unasked question, side step.* Tools of politicians to avoid dealing with the heart-of-the-matter, and far too often, he'd had to be the politician, rather than just a judge.

In this case, Leiv was deflecting his personal pain at the possibility of losing Glover. At the same time, the memory of a contested primary election for Illinois Supreme Court surfaced. Leiv lost the election, and it had been political hell. *For me at least.* At the time, and to this day, he thought his opponent had relished the mudslinging.

Margaret squeezed his hands again, then released them slowly. Leiv was quite surprised by the emotion he felt despite his sidestepping.

Chef Pauley, the early morning short-order cook— Chef Jack called him a chef just like himself—appeared at the edge of their table and sat an orange juice and two waters on the table. "All I can carry and cook." He harrumphed emphatically. "Glow called in sick, *again.*" Then he was gone.

"I guess Pauley doesn't think he needs to take our orders," Leiv half complained. "Does Pauley have a last name?"

135

"Not that I know of, and he doesn't *need* to take your order. You've been here before for breakfast—he knows what you want."

Leiv felt like rolling his eyes like a irreverent teenager. *Never too old.* He smiled, though, and said, "Well if I get two eggs over medium with hash browns, white toast, with sides of salsa and sour cream, the man's a genius mind reader."

"Not what you ordered in the past?"

Leiv shook his head and said in a low voice, "You know, though, he's a damned good cook." He took a sip of freshly squeezed orange juice, then added, "And he knew I wanted orange juice."

Smiling and ignoring his food comments, Margaret said, "I want to say something else, Leigh-Everett."

Leiv felt his stomach muscles tighten, maybe even his throat constrict a little. Calling him Leigh-Everett—a throwback to his grandfather's day—didn't bode well for whatever Margaret was now about to spring on him.

"I really miss Naomi."

He let silence encompass their little booth, and smiled and nodded slightly. He understood. She and Naomi had been close friends, the kind of friends who shared secrets. The kind of secrets you don't share with anyone else.

Within a couple minutes, two eggs over medium with hash browns, white toast, and sides of salsa and sour cream appeared in front of him. For Margaret, Pauley brought pancakes, with an egg-over-easy on top.

Leiv shook his head in wonderment. *Pauley must have a secret way of knowing what his customers want.* A hidden microphone at the table? He found himself actually contemplating giving their booth a once over before stopping himself.

"Don't try figuring it out," Margaret said. "Everyone

has secrets."

Glover's mother had seemingly added reading his mind to her list of accomplishments.

He stopped for a moment, mentally, physically, and psychologically. *As if one can actually stop time.* "You can't actually stop time, take a break, now can you?"

"I know what you mean."

How could she? Margaret, even with all her considerable communication talents, couldn't possibly know what he was thinking—experiencing. Pull an aberrant and unanticipated thought out of the air.

"I really don't know how you could function as a judge," she continued with a smile on her face and in her tone. "We've never played poker. Maybe we should."

Leiv was momentarily speechless. For a second, he had the queerest feeling his friend's mother was looking into his soul.

Margaret leaned forward. "Though I've been told by reliable sources you were a very impassioned lawyer in your early days." She let her smile turn wry. "But," she hesitated for a millisecond tilting her head very slightly, "I'm also told in some quarters you were called 'Stone-Faced Rhodes.'" She laughed lightly. "Not the Leiv I know."

Leiv laughed without thought. Couldn't help it, remembering all the hours he sat alone in his quarters, or at night with sleep evading him—practicing the facial skill of not reacting. More like facial trick. For no matter what he showed the world, he'd never mastered controlling his emotions—disgust with his fellow man, and empathy for victims high on his wish-he-could-control list.

He started to speak, but Margaret raised her hands slightly in a gesture indicating she wasn't finished. "But to your 'time' question—no, you can't stop time." She leaned back, pulled her hands from the table, and patted her cheeks. "These wrinkles are testimony to that."

Once more, Leiv wasn't sure what to say. He wanted to tell her she looked great, and her wrinkles brought character to her face in a good way, but thought it would sound insincere—patronizing. *Aging, no good way to talk about that.*

"And before you tell me my wrinkles have given me gravitas," Margaret said, and getting close in Leiv's estimation to being an actual mind reader, "I wasn't fishing for a compliment." She cleared her throat. "Some moments, and you never know when they're going to pop up, make you want to take pause. Take a moment. Stop everything, and enjoy the moment. 'Smell the roses,' is the saying that used to be popular."

It was a strange sensation knowing Margaret understood his "moment," his desire to pause life for a moment. *Yes,* she'd understood exactly. *Amazing woman.*

She averted her eyes toward the women's restroom for a few seconds, then returned her attention to Leiv with a thoughtful but enigmatic expression on her face. "Your father, Everett, used that very expression sometimes."

And grandfather LC. In his diary. Claimed a famous golfer first said it. Evidently Margaret had known her father well. One day, not today, but one day he would press her for details. Another often regretted guilt journey was not spending enough time getting to know his mother or father better.

Leiv's eggs were delicious; with the salsa and sour cream adding just the right note—a real treat in that HM never mastered salsa, so he'd stopped requesting it. He and Margaret

138

ate in companionable silence for some moments, and he was about to wave his arm to get Pauley's attention and order a second glass of orange juice—another treat HM seldom bothered with—when he saw Ida Oakes, Tucker's wife, come in the front door.

He leaned forward, and asked *sotto voce*, "Does Ida know how serious Tucker's condition is?" He hadn't run into her at the hospital, but was sure she must have been there. Visited her husband. Talked to the doctors. He did remember Calvin hadn't mentioned her Monday morning in Tucker's room at Loma Linda.

"Why?"

"She just came in." Leiv realized Ida was heading straight toward them. "And she's heading back here." Not for the first time, his libido noticed what a striking woman she was. *Sexy, actually.* In truth, he didn't know what it was exactly, or what kind of label should be attached to what Ida exuded, but it was unmistakable and intense.

Leiv's earlier thought about managing and masking his real feelings returned as he remembered LouAnn Marcus, a defense attorney on par with Jackson Miller. He'd had both in his courts, more than once. While Jackson used charm and words to woo his jury, LouAnn sent out something—the something he couldn't put a name to—that was honey to male jurors. He'd commented once, quite inappropriately in hindsight, to his Judicial Assistant at the time, "I can almost see the male jurors drooling."

Leiv cleared his throat and straightened his back. He was mainly watching Ida's rapid approach, but he also caught an uncharacteristic scowl cross Margaret's face.

"Mr. Rhodes," Ida said before she was actually standing next to their booth, "I saw your car—" Clearly surprised to see Margaret even though her car was next to his,

Ida started, but recovered instantly. "Why Mrs. Deers," she said graciously, "how nice you're here, too."

Leiv watched as within a blink, Margaret's face turned her most gracious, and she offered, "Would you like to join us?" She made a motion indicating she was willing to slide over so Ida could sit next o her.

"I'd love to," Ida said without appearing to take a moment for thought.

While the two women situated themselves, including moving Margaret's place setting and remaining food—all done with help from a clearly mesmerized Pauley who ran over with a fresh place setting for Ida. Leiv waited patiently with what he hoped was a nondescript smile plastered across his face.

"No, no, Pauley," Ida said holding up a beautifully manicured slender-fingered hand in protest. "I'm not staying." His face, which Leiv couldn't see must have been crestfallen, because Ida added in a conciliatory sounding tone, "Well maybe a cup of tea, and one of those chocolate *Religieuse* you make."

"Fresh this morning," Pauley said with joy and headed off to the kitchen, or wherever he secreted away chocolate *Religieuse*. Leiv never heard of the pastry, nor been offered one himself. *Of course I'm not Ida.* Again, he had to refrain from smiling.

As soon as he was out of earshot, Ida said, "I won't keep you." She took a deep breath. "But when I saw your car, well, I had to stop."

Leiv looked to Margaret, who was looking directly at him, and with a face that clearly said, this has to do with you, Leigh-Everett, not me. He thought Margaret was probably right. *Now I'm reading minds.*

Before he could say anything, Ida continued, "Thank

you, Mr. Rhodes, for helping save Tucker's life."

He quickly demurred, "That was Calvin, Glover, and paramedic Walker Johns. I was late to the scene."

"But you visited him at the hospital. Cal and the nurses told me." She blinked and sniffed. "Means a lot."

"It was the least I could do." His words were meaningless, but what else could he say?

Ida sighed and blew out a breath. "And now they think he not only killed your friend, Naomi, but also a stranger." Her eyes teared over, and she grabbed the napkin Pauley had put at her place setting to swipe them, then her nose. She lifted her head, found Leiv's eyes, and stared at him for a few seconds. "Please, please, Mr. Rhodes, Tucker didn't kill your friend. He just couldn't do anything like that." She stopped and snatched a breath. "If anyone out here has the knowledge and power to help my husband, protect him, it's you." Her voice caught slightly at the end of her plea. Quickly, she slid out of the booth and stood up. "I left my purse in the car...," she explained teary-eyed.

Leiv wondered why Ida Oakes thought he had the ability or political sway to help Tucker, but part of him was definitely flattered she thought so. He started to slide over and stand himself, but she waved him back.

"As I've always thought—a gentleman," she murmured. "I'm sorry I disturbed you. I shouldn't have stopped."

Ida turned, and was gone as quickly as she'd appeared.

Leiv hoped Chef Pauley was still going to bring a chocolate *Religieuse* to the table.

Leiv was looking down while he walked, watching he

didn't trip while thinking and wondering about Tucker, Glover, Margaret, Naomi, motorcycles, mummified looking bodies, Tonia Potter's beauty, Ida's out-of-the-blue appearance at TGS—and how delicious *Religieuse* was. At least Chef Pauley's version.

For the walking part, he'd formerly thought of himself as a surefooted Midwesterner, but since his return to Shiné, Leiv too often stumbled on what seemed like mysterious desert objects appearing from nowhere. Invisible until he stumbled. And for visible hazards, desert rocks seemed to materialize out of thin air and appear in the middle of trails.

Consequently, with his eyes on the path, he almost ran into Sydney.

The expression on his cousin-in-law's face said he'd been watching Leiv approach, and indeed, he stepped to the side enough they didn't head-butt each other.

"Where's Dobie?" Sydney asked lightly before Leiv was able to completely take in the situation.

"Ah," he stammered, "with HM, helping with breakfast." Leiv didn't mention his own very early repast away from Rhodes Castle.

Sydney laughed. "She likes to eat, doesn't she?" He smiled. "Dobie, that is." His tone was not only light, but also infectious.

What a disarming young man, Leiv thought. And once again, Leiv was reminded of Jackson Miller, the defense attorney in Springfield who could charm birds out of trees. Very popular with the political class, and expensive.

But what the hell was Sydney doing out here? Too close to the entrance of LC's lair. An alarm bell rang loud and clear.

He didn't want to overact and maybe give away there was something to be known and seen. But if this young man was trying to follow him, looking for whatever—*the Mojave-*

Stone probably—he needed to be distracted, diverted. "You know, there's a place called Lookout Loop over there," he said, pointing to the East, "where you can see a lot of Shiné. But you'll have to drive." There was no way he wanted Sydney skulking around near the entrance to LC's little cave. *The place where LC kept his *real* diary, not the fake one left in the library for HM to discover and pick through. This secret hideaway, only LC, Viola, and now Leiv knew about.*

"I'd love to see Shiné from Lookout Loop." Sydney sounded eager and interested.

Again, Leiv rethought. Maybe his alarm bells were false? He hoped so, because he was really warming to Sydney. Something about him he liked. *Still,* Leiv knew he had yet to fit together Sydney's picture. Maybe tonight he'd hear back from Hal.

But just how did Sydney find this trail in back of Rhodes Castle? Following him, or exploring on his own?

He gave Sydney directions to Lookout Loop and bid him a safe drive.

When alive, Melissa was his best confidant, and now, Lloyd and Margaret were replacement treasures Leiv didn't think he could survive Shiné without. Nonetheless, *sometimes* he needed to confer with LC in his special lair.

Leiv often accomplished "talking" to his grandfather by telling HM he was going for a walk down the road, while actually taking himself to "their" special place out back on LC's mountain. He'd yet to take Dobie on these escapes—a fact Sydney commented on. *Maybe one day.*

Once inside LC's hidden lair, just a small cavern really, though LC had made it quite comfortable with a few accoutrements, Leiv felt the closest to LC. Especially when he stretched out in his grandfather's near fifty year old Eames Chair and closed his eyes—even though unnecessary, given the near pitch-blackness that engulfed the mountainside hideaway. He seldom lit one of the antique oil lamps. Originals from the nineteen-thirties he thought, but wasn't sure. And the air had a unique coolness to it—unusual, but pleasant.

And somehow, rather miraculously he thought, the temperature was usually moderate. Even on a winter day like this one.

It was so easy once ensconced in LC's lounger, to think about what it must have been like to live in the twenties, thirties, even forties, when his grandfather and father were making their marks in the world.

Funny how *sometimes* he preferred the warm and rich comfortableness of LC's library, and reread his entries in the journal copy there. *And sometimes* when in his study, Leiv would also look through his father Everett's boxes of papers, and pictures. He especially liked all the old mining maps— now safely, he hoped, protected in acid-free Mylar film. He was very careful with the actual documents, but occasionally, peeling back the Mylar, trying through touch to travel back through the years.

On one of those library occasions, and on one of those maps—he found this cave and LC's original diary.

HM also dusted the boxes routinely—a ready excuse he knew to sneak in and look around. Maybe even hold her precious Mojave-Stone. He knew though, she had yet to discover LC's cave, doubted she ever would—but also knew he couldn't put it past her.

All in my mind of course, going back in time. *Here, or in the library.* But it was a type of escapism Leiv had become rather fond of. Not into the world of a fiction author, and there were several he liked, but an escape back into his own heritage.

If he was in LC's cave-lair with the real-deal diary, Leiv would touch a page—and quite fanciful for a a man of his learning, experience, and sensibilities he knew—he felt a link back to LC and wondered if somehow, in some way, LC knew he'd touched his grandson. Leiv's memories from standing near to LC's deathbed were still strong.

He had yet to bring this silliness up with Lloyd. Figured he'd say it had something to God and life after death.

Leiv wiggled around in the lounger a bit, took a good deep breath, and forced his neck, shoulders, arms, and hands to relax. His breakfast with Margaret and subsequent walkabout had stirred up some emotions and confusions regarding Ida and Sydney. Mainly, their foe or friend status.

Leiv didn't *actually* notice when he fell asleep.

Sydney was amazed Leiv thought he could be fobbed-off so easily. Evidently Leiv didn't notice he'd *actually* only headed back for a short distance, then turned around instead of going back and driving out to Lookout Loop. Sydney then stealthily followed Leiv to the secret entrance to LC's lair.

It had taken him a few years of adjustment and practice, but Sydney was now a man used to keeping a low profile when he needed to. "Walk lightly," they had advised him.

"Well," he whispered watching Leiv seemingly disappear into the side of the hill. "Isn't that interesting?"

Quite pleased with himself, Sydney turned around and headed back toward Rhodes Castle and his rental car. Destination, Lookout Loop.

When Leiv woke up, a quick look at his cell phone told him an hour had passed. He was surprised, but felt refreshed. Energetic almost. And undoubtedly ready to tackle what was going on with Tucker and a dead body on his property. First off, he needed to check on Glover's medical status. On that front, and oddly in that he never wanted to drive, Leiv had the urge to visit the Shiné Sheriff's office. Didn't make any sense, but the urge was certainly there.

Sending Sydney off to Lookout Loop tickled an interest in him to revisit LC's own and private lookout point—a flat rock only a few more feet down the path. To his mind, it offered a better view than Lookout Loop vista point across the valley.

From LC's flat rock, there was a wide open unobstructed view, with the Shiné valley gently unfolding below him. This morning his grandfather's town was caught in the same orangish Mojave morning glow he noticed earlier, just not as bright; indeed, the orangish glow seemed to have permanently colored the horizon. Leiv even thought he heard a train whistle. But didn't see one. He also fancied Sydney was by now at Lookout Loop vista turnout, and peering back at him from across the valley.

"This spot makes me a crazy man." *Imagining Sydney was looking back at me.* Undeniably, he was a man of the law, *well, had been.* Definitely not whimsical nor imaginative by nature. He'd left behind any of that he once had, along with his romanticized world view and naïve idealism of youth, after several years of practice.

He also knew, but couldn't see from LC's flat rock, Kelso dunes or the Granite and Providence Mountains; but he knew they were out there. A part of his grandfather's Mojave world. And the trains. Unconsciously, Leiv shook his head in appreciation.

The country opened up with the Union Pacific line through the Mojave National Preserve, and the Atchison, Topeka and Santa Fe when he was a boy—now the Burlington Northern and Santa Fe around Amboy. That area was a trek away from Shiné, though children in Shiné almost had to go to school in Amboy back then. But just in time, Miss Marsha opened a one-room school in the back of Shiné's newly built Community Church.

Which reminded him of Tonia Potter. Before they'd left the Potter home in Apple Valley, Tonia or Portia had said. *What did she do? Something to do with schools.* A teacher, he thought. He certainly should have been paying better attention. *Was Tonia a college professor, maybe?* But what subject? He couldn't remember.

"Oh yeah," he said aloud. "Graduate school teacher. Psychotherapy." He remembered being impressed and thinking it must be online. No brick and mortar graduate schools out here. *Beauty, brains, and familiar with modern technology.*

Sunrises were an iffy experience with Hester. Sometimes she enjoyed them, sometimes not so much. Then there were those rare moments when colors and their juxtaposition in early light actually touched her heart—and what she called, her "Gypsy" soul.

147

This morning at first light, from the second floor window of her apartment wing, while she sneakily watched Leigh-Everett drive away toward town, the Eastern horizon grabbed her and held her attention—even overriding her curiosity about where he was going.

"Dreamsicle Orange," she said, and was immediately transported back to a favorite childhood memory—a visit to her cousin Bersch's family in Chicago. The Lovels.

A *childhood* summer, as only they can be. A sensory-laden memory of the wonderful ice cream truck musically going down their street most evenings during that visit. This morning's sunrise color was so perfect, she could almost taste the orange and vanilla ice cream.

Hester never forgot *that summer*. The summer she met Andreas. Such a beautiful child—turned into such an evil man. Her cousins had lived somewhere near a street called Lincoln, she thought. On the north side of Chicago. The family now lived in a different area, and she remembered her mother often saying, Chicago is always changing—shifting, she called it.

She sighed, then realized she'd almost missed seeing which way Leigh-Everett had turned at the end of the drive. She thought to the right, toward the silly woman Margaret's house. Probably for scones, or croissants, or something *frou-frou*—a phrase her cousin Kizzy Lovel liked to use. And tea, no doubt.

For a moment, her mind again left the present, once more flying back to that summer—and seeing through childhood eyes once again—Kizzy, Andreas, and Bersch. *That Kizzy, always trying to be "with-it," even as kids.* She also remembered how much Kizzy doted on Andreas—and for a second, Hester was surprised by tears wanting to come. *No,* Hester Miller never cried.

Along with unwanted emotions, a seed of suspicion again appeared in her conscious thoughts. *Odd that body.*

Seemingly not in her control, Hester's thoughts swung back to Leigh-Everett. There was no reason for him to turn left and go to town. *He must have gone to the right.* She made perfectly edible breakfasts right here at Rhodes Castle; far better than anything he could get in town.

Well, at least Sydney and Nadya had the decency to want to eat at home. For a second, Hester almost let herself take offense at Leigh-Everett's perceived slight, then she reminded herself she wasn't a sensitive sort. A point of pride with her.

But then again, out of character, and almost lost in thought, Hester lingered at the window a few more moments, watching her Dreamsicle Orange turn red, then yellow — touching her heart in a way she was unaccustomed to, and at a loss to explain. Here she was, reliving a childhood crush based on a sunrise silliness of some sort. Andreas Herne.

It was his looks, no doubt. The perfect little Romani boy.

Later, during breakfast with Nadya and Sydney in the kitchen, Hester decided Sydney wasn't worth wasting much more thinking time on. Not that it wasn't curious where he'd taken off to this morning. "A walkabout," he said, over a plate full of food. Why couldn't he just say *walk* like everyone else. Unconsciously, she shook her head at his pretentiousness. Fortunately Nadya seemed level headed. *Nadya I can trust.* People like Sydney, now that was a different story. Too complicated.

Although, he did seem to have a good appetite.

But now, sunrise behind her, spying on Leigh-Everett's early morning leave-taking, and breakfast with Nadya and Sydney also history, Hester stood at the front door wondering where the heck was clueless Leigh-Everett going now? He never went anywhere, and today he was rushing all around Shiné. Didn't really make any difference to her—*but somehow it's irritating me.*

Even though "Le Bric-à-Brac" was situated at the far end of town, if Mary Jones was standing in the right spot, and looking through the curve of her front window at just the correct angle, she could see the happenings on Shiné's Main Street all the way down to TGS at the southernmost point and start of the street.

True enough, she mused this morning, *not much of an accomplishment.*

She sighed, and stepped back a foot or so from her store front window—the most elaborate in town with its extended and curved corners, especially made to match ones she'd seen in New York. Mary had just watched Leiv Rhodes slowly drive down Main and stop at Chief Glover Deers office.

She liked Glover and his mother. They'd helped her with a lot of store details in the early days. In truth, Margaret in particular was a godsend when it came to the emotional aspects of adjusting to life in the Mojave. *She wasn't in La La Land anymore.*

Mary started walking around "Le Bric-à-Brac" slowly, making sure not only were her prized antiques displayed the way she wanted them—but also enjoying them. Their look, how they felt—smelled even. It was her way of visiting hundreds of lives—some gone, some still around—through their possessions.

But on the practical level, running a business was not the same as either experiencing antiques or *acting*. She'd bought an existing place of business for her escape from Los Angeles—*a second-rate second hand store*—with a dream of turning it into a genuine antique shop. A big challenge she freely admitted. Just wading through the rules, regulations, paperwork—then all the permits and fees. At times in the early days, she'd felt quite overwhelmed.

Remembering, Mary felt a little shiver surprise her. Quickly she banished the bad memories associated with starting-up her grand endeavor, preferring to look forward rather than backward, and ironically, returning her thoughts to Glover and Margaret. She didn't consider herself a religious sort, but last night she'd improvised a few prayers and sent them into the universe with the hope there was actually a God out there to hear them.

People died in her long-lived television series all the time. But often, and quite miraculously, they returned. *Not so in real life*. There was no coming back. "Get well, Glover," she whispered, hoping that same universe would somehow transport her wish to him in the hospital.

When it came to Leiv Rhodes, she'd met him a couple times, and there was something about the man that pulled at her. *Curious, that.* Main Street traffic this morning was light to nonexistent, requiring little urgency to get the daily dusting done, so Mary let herself indulge in a thoughtful reassessment of the man. She knew a little about his background—a nationally known judge and the legacy of being the town's owner, well, not owner really, but the direct heir of Shiné's founding father.

The stuff movies are made of. "Ha," she exclaimed aloud.

Inexplicably, she'd put Leiv on her good-guy list from the start. Probably because she saw in his eyes that he'd recognized her immediately at their first meeting. *Yes,* he knew who and what she was when not in Shiné. Yet, he'd only smiled, nodded very slightly, and said nothing. Adding to her appreciation of the man-inside. Leiv Rhodes, to Mary's knowledge and to this day, hadn't told another soul who she really was.

A quick look back out her storefront window in passing showed there still wasn't any traffic on Main Street. No cars vying for parking places out front.

"A slow day," she told the ballerina figurine on the display hutch she next walked over to.

In her mind's eye, almost like she was there again, Mary could see Leiv as clear as on that day some months previous. And most mysteriously, she felt like she was re-seeing those moments from inside *his* head, through *his* eyes. Not hers. It was a unique experience, and she didn't know what to make of it.

Leiv had visited her shop several times after the first time, walking over from the police station, she thought, just to talk a bit. Mary guessed he liked their back and forth banter. The day she was remembering, he'd made some pseudo-philosophical comment about the past, and how objects can carry "something" on into the future.

He didn't look like a fanciful man, indeed how could he be? A judge and all. But, *what a chord he struck with me.* Like he'd been inside her head that morning—similar to what she was feeling now.

Then there was his curious looking and astonished face as she said, "We're only here on earth for a millisecond of a millisecond in time." He'd seemed to understand completely.

The next thing Mary remembered well was lifting the little crater-pocked blue bottle into the air. It was a strikingly memorable moment—a stream of wayward sunlight somehow finding its way from her storefront glass window to touch the little bottle just so. And even stranger, the light seemed to further bounce around her shop as it were alive. She'd offered at the time, "It's a hobnail Penny Perfume Bottle, I think."

The more she thought about that morning, and now with the clarity of hindsight, Mary was even more awestruck by the magical feel to those moments.

"Is the one you're holding part of a set?"

Mary remembered smiling, and she smiled again now. "Naomi has its sister," she'd said. Mary could even see again their reflection in the mirrored back sideboard they were standing at—admiring the perfume bottle.

Naomi's accident was soon after that.

Still marveling at that visit, Mary's smile turned into a sigh—not sure from pleasure or from confusion. She had connected to Leiv in some special way, but she was still trying to wrap her mind around the event. She thought it had to do with touching items—items she knew a little about—but that wasn't the whole story. And there were flashes of memory which weren't really memories. *Reliving through another person's eyes.* Craziness, no matter how you tried to explain it.

Her sigh was a precursor to another shiver, this time laced with a touch of fear.

Fear based on the fact she'd touched Naomi's little sister bottle when talking to Leiv, and "known" what had happened. Well not really known, but guessed at something she hadn't dared tell anyone. *Never will either.*

Reluctantly, Mary pulled herself from her memories, and finishing her store walk-about—musing about Glover, his mother Margaret, secrets, and the enigmatic Leiv Rhodes—she returned to her front window intent on getting down to opening for business. Nonetheless, she noticed Leiv's car was parked at Glover's office. She hadn't actually seen him park and get out, but it was the only explanation.

Think I'll just take a walk down there, see what's going on. Mary didn't really want to *go in,* just peek through the window.

That decided, she felt more connected to the current real world, and when thinking of Glover again, this time, lying in a hospital bed, she wished there was something she could touch to give her answers when she needed them. But sadly, these strange "understandings" didn't seem to work that way.

Doing their own bidding, her hands were toying with another one of her "treasures" on the same hutch, next to her ballerina figurine.

Mary looked down—her fingers were idly rubbing the smooth surface of a small shining black obsidian, very nicely polished, and set into the top of a keepsake box. Her ballerina figurine and the box were an odd couple—the ballerina, light and whimsical, while the keepsake box, rather masculine for that type of item, was dark and mysterious.

She was immediately reminded of the Rhodes Mojave-Stone. She'd asked Leiv if it existed. He'd answered seemingly without giving her question a second thought, "Of course not."

Then out of the blue and not really based on any of her mental meanderings so far this morning, Mary thought—*no, I feel*—Leiv Rhodes will figure this whole thing out. Make everything right.

How odd.

Reluctantly, she pulled her hand away from the obsidian stone. Her walk down Main Street awaited.

*   *   *   *   *

Leiv ran his hand over the stainless steel table, and in an instant, it was a year ago. Even imagining he could hear Glover in the background out in the main office—of course he couldn't—his friend was in the hospital in Twentynine Palms. Shiné's police station was not the same without him, and Leiv wasn't sure why he'd driven back to town. Some kind of symbolism he couldn't articulate. As always, to drive had been unpleasant, but fortunately, the trip was quick and uneventful.

Muffled voices out in the outer office interrupted his thoughts—Doctor Walker and Walker Johns, EMT, paramedic actually, who'd been on the scene with Tucker, trying to keep Shiné's mayor in this world. For a passing moment, Leiv half wondered what they were discussing. Something about Glover's condition, or the weekend warrior body they'd found? *Martin Potter most probably.*

But Leiv's mind wouldn't let him stay with Doc and Wally. Simply touching the steel table unwillingly took him back to Chicago, to the Congress Expressway underneath the main Post Office. He couldn't make himself *not* be there again. His rational self searched for an explanation of why he wasn't in control. Not an experience he relished, or had a lot of experience with.

Lingering grief was the best explanation he could come up with. Leiv had seen it in others and in many manifestations. And guilt. *Oh yes, I know about guilt alright.* He heard himself also whisper, "Must be how Tucker felt Sunday morning. Standing there in the noonday sun." Leiv doubted the Doc and Walker were close enough to hear him.

Fortunately, whatever was controlling his mind—grief, guilt, or something he hadn't thought of—his remembrances, though still in the past, moved back to a more recent time. *To* right where he was standing now. *To* one miserable day just about a year ago. The station cold-room was seldom used, but that day, there were two bodies waiting for the "meat wagon" from Needles.

Two female bodies. Two females he knew.

In an instant Leiv was in that moment again—including holding back the nausea, the weakness in his knees, the shots of pain in his temples. He looked down at his hand, still touching the steel table. He thought he saw a tremble, but wasn't sure.

Then with the flip of some spastic time-travel memory switch, he was back in Chicago, hearing Melissa—her sweet words. "What a lovely evening." Her voice lilting and harmonic—a little bit of song always there.

Leiv forced his eyes closed. Maybe he was experiencing some kind of brain fever? At least there was a doctor and a paramedic in the other room—a thought Leiv found sobering and slightly humorous. Evidently, not sobering enough to bring his thoughts directly back to current day Shiné.

Chicago. Hundreds of thousands of cars drove on I-290 as it—miraculously it seemed—went under the Chicago Post Office. *Yes,* they were on the "Ike" that night, or the Congress Freeway depending on your generation. He and Melissa knew it as the quickest way to head west and get out of the city.

It was Fall, had rained all day, and an overcast night was engulfing the city. He was tired, and figured Melissa was too. Hence a driver.

Even now, the back of their limousine driver's head was outlined in hyper-contrast crystal clarity in his memory. It was dark—outside and inside the limousine—still he could see the back of the driver's head. The front interior light must have been on, and for the first time his curiosity asked, *why?*

Leiv didn't actually feel the impact, but the experience

in Glover's cold-room, was darned near close.

Then waking up in the hospital after a week in a coma. No memories until a moment in time when Melissa's sobbing sister told him she was dead. Then she'd slapped him, cursed him forever for meeting her sister. Indelible on his mind. He would never forget. *I should have been driving. Not called for a car.* Melissa had suggested he drive. She *knew*, even if he hadn't.

Another wave of coldness emanating from the steel table brought him back, at least for the moment, and Leiv finally pulled his hand away and looked around.

He was still alone.

But, even though he'd snatched his hand back from the table—Naomi and Georgie's bloodless bodies wouldn't leave his mind's eye. Neither could he shake a sensation of wrongness about all their deaths. Not just three good lives were gone, but *something else*? Unfortunately, what that *something else* might be, did not come. Melissa was *still dead* from a traffic accident he should have prevented, Naomi was *still dead*, murdered. And Georgie was *still dead* in a tragic swimming accident.

"You look like you've seen a ghost." The substantial and comforting looking figure of Doctor William Walker was standing in the doorway cradling a steaming mug with both hands.

"Not a real ghost, but damn near close," Leiv said calmly. He'd been startled, but didn't jump in surprise, not that he hadn't wanted to. His startle-response was a personality aspect he'd worked on controlling over the years. Judges needed to display poker faces as much as possible. "I was just remembering that day last year when we were back here." Then surprising himself even more, Leiv's voice caught. He recovered immediately. "It was cold."

William also seemed jarred by his own momentary thoughts, not answering immediately, and turning his body slightly away from Leiv. After a barely audible sigh, he finally said, ""Yeah." Then he turned quickly in the doorway, returning to the main office.

Leiv heard Wally ask the doctor, "Is Mr. Rhodes okay?"

And Doc Walker answering, "I really don't know with certainty." As always his enunciation was proper and precise. "Morgues, or just cold-rooms like ours are funny kind of places. Takes the mind in all kinds of directions."

Leiv liked the doctor. In looks, Shiné's doctor was the epitome of an archetypical country doctor, with savvy old-time wisdom and experience, combined with current day technical expertise. A comforting friend, and indeed, Leiv's idea had been to stop by William's office before he drove back to Rhodes Castle. Fortuitously, he appeared in person without any effort on his part—though Leiv wasn't sure why Doc stopped by. He did know Williams and Glover were gabbing buddies, often having breakfast or lunch together at TGS—but the doctor must know Glover was in the hospital. And Wally, well, he often stopped by and gabbed too. But why today?

Of course. If they came here like nothing had happened, Glover would be alright. He immediately understood their behavior. *Probably mine too.*

Thinking about Wally and Doc, Leiv's past pains slithered on back into their memory cave, releasing him to move forward into the present. With a fortifying deep breath he walked away from the table without looking back—*daring* not to look back.

As Leiv stepped through the open door frame, he forced a smile. "You really like that tea, don't you?" he said in as cheery a voice he could summon, while nodding toward the mug William was still holding. The tea was a guess based on insider information from Glover.

The doctor made a dismissive sound, took another long and loud sip, then smiled.

"Can't stand the stuff myself," Wally said from his position in the chair in front of Glover's desk.

His tone sounded rather grumpy for the usually agreeable young man. Leiv guessed it was the chair—not thoughts about Glover. Leiv had sat in that chair in the past, a hardback monstrosity he considered one of the most uncomfortable chairs he ever sat in. The only chairs he thought worse—an entire line of them—were in Illinois Chief Justice Jimmy LaCour's anteroom. The room where aspiring law clerks and seasoned lawyers alike counted the minutes for meetings. Leiv once quipped to his own law clerk, "Those chairs go all the way back to the beginning Illinois Supreme Court days in eighteen eighteen."

Remembering, Leiv smiled, and said about the tea, "Glover ordered it especially for you, Doc." He didn't mention he was the one who suggested to Glover he could order quality tea of all types online. Leiv wasn't that fond of the stuff either, but he could nonetheless appreciate the aroma when Glover or Doc would steep a fresh pot in the break-area. Not the aroma of coffee, but nice in its own right.

Glover better come through this alright. Leiv looked over at the break-area, with its mismatched cups and flea-market tea pot—the area Glover had squeezed in for Doctor Walker wasn't the most elegant; but Leiv always thought the doctor appreciated the rearranging Glover went though just for him.

Leiv walked over and grabbed two chairs from the break-area, pulled them over near Wally, sat down in one, and motioned for the doctor to take the other. But when he looked directly at him, William's face had clouded over, and in an instant Leiv felt the emotional wave of three men thinking, remembering, and grieving anew from past hurts—combined with concern for their friend in the present.

"I often think about the little things in life we take for granted after viewing a dead body." The doctor lifted his cup. "Like this cup of tea." Then he sighed and turned his head to look out toward Main Street through the front window. "Georgie and Naomi will never savor and sip another cup of tea."

Yes, Leiv now remembered, both women were tea drinkers. As immune to ordinary thoughts of death as Leiv thought he was, something in Doc Walker's voice brought a lump to his throat and caused him to likewise turn away— look out the front window.

No more now, Leiv demanded of himself. He needed to take an emotional breath, and after a moment, he attempted to lighten things up a bit. "Too many 'Ws' when I'm around you guys, Wally." He looked to the paramedic for a second, then switched his gaze, "And you, William."

"I know." A smile appeared as the doctor evidently took Leiv's hint about mood-lightening and pulled the offered chair to where he could look at Wally and Leiv, then sat down. "Especially if you throw my nickname into the mix."

Leiv gave him a questioning look. "Which is?"

"'Will,' of course," Wally answered for the doctor.

Leiv said, "So what we have here," he said, and looked to the paramedic, "is "Walker 'Wally' Johns." He turned to the doctor. "And William 'Will' Walker."

Wally and the doctor nodded. Leiv had to restrain himself from laughing. For a second, he thought of Mary Jones and her using a Shiné alias, and his smile wanted to broaden. *If folks only knew how famous she actually is. Names.*

160

From there, Leiv's reflections jutted off and landed on his own name. Re-considering his name decision for the first time since he'd started consistently introducing himself as Leiv. It had seemed natural at first, but had it been? Leiv or Leigh-Everett—what difference did it make? *Evidently it made a big difference to me back then.*

An easy silence amongst the three men followed, and Leiv was pulled from his little personal name detour back to Naomi and Georgie—and this morning's episode in the cold-room. Quite clearly, something in him couldn't let go regarding Naomi and Georgie, even though he wanted to. *Maybe there's something there I need to pay attention to?*

Briefly, he looked back at the door to Glover's cold-room. "You know I was there that day." *Of course they know.*

"Yeah," Wally said, clearly knowing what Leiv was referring to. "Naomi and Georgie." He shook his head, and the look Leiv saw on Wally's face was far too sad for someone so young. Indeed, he wouldn't call Wally baby-faced, but he did have one of those countenances that would look youthful for many a year down the road. It was also a face usually tending toward a smile. *He's probably seen a lot of sadness as a paramedic,* Leiv reminded himself. More than most.

Wally continued, "You know, from what I've heard, we've never had two DOAs here at the same time." He shook his head again, this time accompanied by a sigh. "Nothing like that before or after here in Shiné."

Silence fell again, and Leiv belatedly realized, he had some questions about that day, about the bodies—and wondered why he hadn't been more curious earlier. He stood and leaned uncomfortably against the edge of Glover's huge wooden desk, close to where Wally continued to restlessly search for a comfortable spot in a chair that offered none. Doctor Walker also stood up, but turned away and headed across the room to the break area. Leiv guessed he needed a tea refill.

We're all fidgety. "Doc," Leiv said, "did you get to examine the bodies before they were sent to the coroner?"

"Ha," the doctor said without turning to address Leiv directly. Tea refill was clearly his number one mission. "I *was* the coroner." His face wasn't visible, but Leiv heard him make a sigh-like sound. "At least I was the *first* coroner."

Leiv patiently waited while Doc Walker went through his tea-ritual—knowing from past experience everything had to be just right, and couldn't be rushed. Neither the process nor order of adding ingredients.

Finally, the doctor returned to the main part of the office where he and Wally were waiting, then he sat this time in the middle of the bench almost spanning the storefront window—a refilled mug of steaming brew in hand. The high-backed bench, probably equally aged as Wally's chair, had been mercifully updated with a nice thick burgundy bench-seat pillow.

From what Leiv could see through the window, outside had become another winter Mojave day. His magical-orange sky had finally faded away. Now it was clear as a bell, and getting hot, he guessed.

The doctor and Wally had parked in the back, and he'd pulled up out front, but parked out of window view. So what Leiv now saw was a frameable snapshot of a desolate looking desert town's main street. Doc was slightly off center in his window picture and in shadow; while in the brightness of daylight outside, the storefront directly across the street was vacant with an 'available for lease' sign hanging crookedly in its front window.

For a second, Leiv had a flash of what his grandfather LC might have seen when planning out Shiné. Indeed, he

162

remembered his scrawl, *"...either they'll come, or they won't."* LC was also fond of saying, *"It ain't over until it's over."* Leiv wondered, and again only for a second, when "over" should be proclaimed.

Doc Walker said, "San Bernardino was backed up, and so was Needles." He shook his head and an expression of sadness similar to Wally's washed across his face. "They've asked me to do them before," he said. "And I have. But I sure as heck don't like cutting open dead people." His expression turned uncharacteristically sour. "Then they had the nerve to still do their own look-over—using my records and specimens. If they didn't trust me to do it right," he finished in a grumble, "why ask me in the first place?"

"But, Doc, why autopsies at all?" Leiv asked. He didn't think they were required. "Was there a suspicion Naomi or Georgie's deaths weren't accidents?"

"Well, yes, and no."

Leiv wanted to sigh himself and roll his eyes—or something like that. Instead, he held his breath and waited.

Annoyingly, the doctor took a long sip of tea before continuing, "Both deaths were following accidents, and drowning is specifically called out in the regs. No problem if deaths are natural, and a physician certifies cause of death."

"No criminal act suspected?" Leiv figured there must be something the rumors about Tucker were based on.

"Nothing substantial, or prompting an extended investigation." This time he took a hefty swallow of tea.

Wally said, "There was the fact there weren't any skid marks. It was like Naomi just drove straight off Lookout Loop."

"And that would indicate?"

"That the brakes were tampered with."

"Of course," Leiv said. "And were they?"

"Not determinable." Wally evidently couldn't take Glover's inquisition-chair any longer and stood up, stretching and twisting his back and neck in the process. "Her car was towed and examined by SBC SID."

Leiv guessed his expression betrayed confusion because William offered, "San Bernardino County Scientific Investigations Department."

Always acronyms. "So nothing strange about Naomi's death?"

"Died of a broken neck, causing asphyxiation. Lot of broken bones. But she wouldn't have felt any pain," Williams said.

"Tox screens?"

"Don't know, but guessing the regular for drugs and alcohol," Wally said.

Leiv recognized a niggling feeling somewhere in his brain. But nothing more, nothing specific; yet somehow from that minor mental nudge, several more puzzle pieces might fit together. *Maybe with Hal's tox-screen from the little bottle?* He hated when that happened. He had such experiences in the past—the idea there was a missing puzzle piece in the evidence prosecutors were presenting—or for that matter, defense attorneys. Some piece of information they were holding back unless forced to reveal. And here his own brain was doing it—*holding back.* Nudging, not outright clarifying.

Again he looked out into the street beyond where William sat framed in a metaphorical picture post card. The inimitable Mary Jones from "Le Bric-à-Brac" was walking by—then she stopped about in the center of the window, circled her eyes from the sun's glare and peered into the office. An oversized Route 66 T-shirt was swaddling and flowing from her body, looking more like a shawl than a shirt, and where she stood in relation to Doc Walker inside and the lighting at that moment, was priceless. Edward Hopper would have been proud to paint such a picture. And with that picture, his niggling piece of puzzle made itself clear, then fit right into place. *Oh Naomi,* he almost cried aloud.

"And Georgie," he asked, "did her autopsy show anything unusual?"

"Nothing." The corner of William's mouth twitched ever so slightly, as if he wanted to smile, but thought better of it. "Death from asphyxia caused by a liquid entering the lungs and preventing the absorption of oxygen leading to cerebral hypoxia and cardiac arrest."

Leiv squinted his eyes and made a face.

The doctor did allow himself the levity of a wink. "AKA, she drowned."

"Where? The public pool's been closed for a few years."

"Tucker and Ida have a pool. Covered." Doc Walker drained his mug. "That was good."

Wally offered, "Their pool is nice. One of those pools you swim back and forth, back and forth."

"A lap pool," Leiv murmured. Then louder, and directed at the doctor, he asked, "Was she alone?"

"Yeah, poor thing. Ida found her, called nine-one-one, then jumped in fully clothed to pull her sister-in-law out."

"They tell you, never go swimming alone," Wally said in a wise tone. "Ida said they usually swam together, didn't even know Georgie had come over, much less decided to swim alone."

"So they were close?"

Wally looked to William for confirmation before answering, "That's what everyone says. Like sisters."

"How many towels were around?"

"Interesting question." Wally closed his eyes for a long moment, evidently remembering. "Just one. Sure of it." He nodded his head. "Yep, she was alone when she drowned. Terrible, terrible accident." Then he turned his head to the side, clearly trying to wish the memory away.

Leiv knew the feeling well.

Glover thought he was doing quite well, considering. He certainly didn't need to stay in the hospital another minute. Yet, when he tried actually moving his limbs to get up, or reach over and pull the darn tubes out of his arm, nothing responded as it should. Drugs. he figured, were keeping him immobile. Next time the doctor, who looked like he was twelve, came around, Glover was going to make sure he understood, no more drugs. But he wasn't complaining. *Care is excellent.* He thought. He was alive, wasn't he?

But I need to get out of here and find out who did this.

Deputy Sherman—*Portia*—was competent enough. But he was the one who'd been shot. He had *real* motivation to get this guy. Somehow Glover knew it was a man taking pot-shots at him. Not rational, not based on evidence. *I just know.* And Leiv, well he wasn't a police professional, now was he? Yet, when he needed to act, Leiv had been there.

Probably saved my life. His mother Margaret had pretty much said the same. He thought she might still be there in the hospital, maybe in the room? But he didn't want to open his eyes. Not at the moment. *Need time to think a bit*—about several things.

First off, why had he suddenly become a target? Sure, he was a cop, and sure he'd made some enemies along the way. But a sniper ambush?

Portia said an APB had been put out—and that made him feel good. The cop brotherhood had his back. Glover's mind returned to the key fact though—*he'd* been shot, and the motivation had to be with him. Somewhere in his brain was the answer. He needed to mull it over, maybe another few hours, then get out of here and go talk things out with Leiv. Use his friend's brain.

Which brought him back around to Leiv saving his life. Since Leiv's return to Shiné, he hadn't really thought Everett's son tough enough for the desert. He certainly acted different from Everett, and talked different than everyone. And sometimes he thought he didn't really want to be here. So why come back?

Running away of course. Just like he'd done when returning to Shiné. *Running away.* Saying it was because of his mother—though admittedly partly true. He loved her dearly. *But Mother isn't exactly doddering, now is she?* Undoubtedly an excuse.

He'd come back right after getting his tattoo. He wanted to reach over and rub his arm, but couldn't. And he still didn't want to open his eyes, look to see what kind of needle, or even sling contraption he might be hooked up in. That damn tattoo had hurt more than any pain he felt now after being shot.

He thought of Leiv again, how smart he was, how he'd left a fantastic career as an Appellate Judge. "To come back here to Shiné," he said aloud, and was very surprised to hear the sound of his own voice.

Then Glover sighed, and heard that also. *Well,* he was going to get the hell out of there—tomorrow morning at the latest. This was ridiculous him trapped here, drugged up in a hospital bed when he needed to be out finding the miserable SOB who'd thought he could take pot shots at him.

"I heard you speak and sigh," a soft and lovely-sounding female voice said. "You can open your eyes. I know you're awake."

Portia. Sweet and smart-alecky in one enticing package.

"This is a nice spot," Sydney said, after lightly touching the glass in front of him, then quickly pulling his hand back as if the massive window had startled him.

The thick window made a wall from ceiling to window seat level, and was one of five in the pentagon that sat atop Rhodes Castle. "LC built this Cupola special," Leiv said, and smiled knowing they were taking in the desert sky in one of LC's few detours into design originality. *And a good detour indeed.* "Doesn't really fit with my grandfather's massive manor vision, or his jumbled Edwardian and Victorian styles." Leiv found himself also touching the thick glass in front of him. It was cold, and copycat to Sydney, he removed his hand immediately.

They were standing so close together, Leiv felt he was just at the edge of his cousin-in-law's personal space—the minimum distance required between their shoulders. A concept he hadn't thought of in ages. It was a big thing when he had to do the cocktail circuit, way back-in-the-day. Invariably during campaign fund raising times. Remembering, he almost shuddered, but caught himself in time. *A new life now.*

"Regardless of style incongruity, it's a great spot to watch the stars," Sydney said after a couple minutes of silence.

"You can get pictures of the constellations and their positions in the sky. Hour by hour—all night. One website even accounts for your own position."

He felt Sydney smile before hearing him say, "Cool."

In that moment, Leiv *realized* he liked Nadya's husband. *Realized* he was lucky and happy to have him as a relative. *Nadya could have done a lot worse.* He also thought he wasn't a threat to him or the Mojave-Stone.

"There's been a happening." Hester didn't what to get Bersch all worked up, but she also wanted to make sure he understood the seriousness of what had happened. "A body." *That should get his attention.*

"A body?" Bersch asked, his voice sounding tinny through the corded rotary phone in her parlor.

Hester also thought her cousin sounded genuinely perplexed. "At least a year dead is what I've heard."

An exasperated sigh came across the line. "If I'm following you, they've found a dead body in the desert where you are. And somehow you think it's important to *us?*"

Hester had always considered Bersch a little slow, maybe even dim, so decided she needed to be patient. Take it slow. Though, he certainly should know what she was talking about—shouldn't have to spell it all out. She held back on a sigh. "Do you remember last year when Andreas headed out to California from Chicago?"

"Yeah."

"And he never made it here?" She waited a moment to make sure he was following her. "And he never returned to Chicago?"

Bersch's voice sounded like he was catching on. And interested. "You think that's Andreas? The dead body you're talking about?"

Hester was sitting in her regular and favorite

armchair—tonight facing a quiet fireplace. She scooted her butt around, burrowing in deeper into the chair's deep cushions. "Exactly."

Bersch whistled before saying, "So you're thinking Andreas is dead, and that's his body."

You've said it twice now, for goodness' sakes. Bersch fell silent and Hester waited. She allowed her gaze to move to the window beside the fireplace. The night was Mojave black, winter clear, and start-studded. *Poor Andreas laying out there in the desert for a whole year.*

"So," Bersch said, evidently still processing the information, "you really think the body is Andreas?"

"Yes." *Now the hard part.* "And I think you know who murdered him."

"Me?" his tone was incredulous and his voice loud.

Hester moved the phone away from her ear for a second or two. *Maybe he doesn't know?* "I think your sister Kizzy killed him."

Hester sat for awhile after hanging up, going down what she called memory-lane. Her thoughts, rolling around in flashes of memories from one very special summer.

My summer of romance. Andreas Herne, tall, handsome, swaggering. Even now, years later, she almost sighed like the young girl she'd been then. He seemed like a god then, and now, more like a lovely apparition from a time long gone.

Then that thuggy Jack Coppersmith, claiming Andreas was a criminal. Putting out he should be ostracized, causing her lover to disappear—leaving her alone.

My one and only love.

Talking to Bersch on the phone brought it all back. She

probably shouldn't haven't called him. *But it's done now.* Hester touched her phone as if she could undo her call. Then stroked the receiver several times before realizing what she was doing. Quickly and determinedly she pulled her hand away. Then Hester made herself think about meals for tomorrow, about cleaning the front stained glass doors, about talking to Nadya again, and about stealing the Mojave-Stone.

Hal Herman answered after two rings. "You actually got my message, huh?"

Leiv looked down at the paper message Hester left him on the hallway phone table. "HM wasn't her usual friendly self?" He smiled to himself. Over the last several years he learned to decipher HM's intention. Clearly from her tight and precise printing of only Hal's name and phone, no explanation—he knew she was PO'd at the time.

"Nosy," Hal elaborated. "Don't forget I've actually talked to her before. So I knew what to suspect. A grilling. Which of course I couldn't allow." He laughed. "Are we okay to talk?"

Leiv thought for a moment, then said, "I'll call you back using my cell." It didn't take long for him to hang up and call back using his cell phone from the library. The connection wasn't that great, but hearable. And unless HM had her ear plastered to his libraries door frame, they'd be safe from prying ears. But, he didn't put it past her.

"Okay," Leiv said, once reconnected with his old friend and eager to hear his findings. Nonetheless, he kept his voice low. "What did you come up with?" He was surprised how interested he was in satisfying his curiosity regarding

Sydney Collins. He guessed it was he decided he liked the young man, but was scared of being made a fool of.

"Nothing."

"Nothing?" *Hal must be kidding.* He'd never known him to fail on digging up information when his mind was set. The Captain Hal Herman he used to know was a bulldog.

"Well," Hal said, "nothing in this case might be 'something.'"

Leiv waited.

"There aren't many scenarios where you get nothing."

"Like no school records, social, DMV?"

"Oh no, all that's there. You don't arouse attention by not building a backstory, a life having been led." He made a sound Leiv couldn't quite interpret, especially because he couldn't see his friend's face and scratchy reception. "But Sydney Collin's background is too neat, too pat—well, hell, Leiv, anybody with any background check experience would know it's fake without a second glance."

"So my cousin-in-law is who or what he wants me to think."

"Or what someone else wants you to think." He laughed wryly. "And I bet you can guess who that might be."

His cold eye mask felt perfect. Leiv kept three of the masks intended to help with sinus problems in the portable refrigerator-freezer under his bedside night stand. He hadn't been affected badly yet—late winter he expected them to start acting up. But the masks just felt darned good, any time of year. He also kept some chilled water bottles and a couple snacks in the refrigerator section so he didn't have to trudge half-a-mile, it seemed, to the kitchen.

Occasionally he'd put one of the masks on the back of his neck. That also felt good, and helped relax aching neck muscles. He'd been clued-in to the specially shaped icepacks by a court reporter. They were filled with some kind of modern-miracle gel that could be frozen, or microwaved. He wasn't sure if the contraptions had side effects—he just knew it felt good.

Thinking about microwave appliances and freezers, a couple of the items he couldn't imagine the modern world without—*Melissa loved her microwave*—Leiv's mind not only wandered back to Melissa, but much farther back to LC, and what it must have been like when his grandfather arrived in the Mojave. No magic jell, no fancy freezers, no microwaves, spotty electricity, if any. Some places, no phone.

Then he remembered, sort of, Viola putting what looked like a damp folded towel on LC's forehead at his deathbed. Refrigerator cold, most probably. Even for LC, life changed a lot during his years on the planet. He was in his twenties when LC died, and though caught up in his own life and activities as only a twenty-something year old can be, he still remembered that day vividly.

Tonight, Leiv's modern-day eye mask was doing the trick. He took a long slow deep breath, then another, then another. Felt his muscles slowly relax, felt his mind start to float amongst memories from his life. He could also feel the first beginnings of the mental loginess signaling he was falling asleep—soon. He stretched his arms out sideways in his double bed, and wiggled his back around a little, then his toes.

Tonight. He wanted to forget Tucker, murdered motorcyclists, cousins with suspect motives when it came to the Mojave-Stone, a far too attractive grieving widow, Glover in the hospital—a loop of thoughts not respecting his desire for sleep.

When arriving at Rhodes Castle several years back—*was it two or three years,* for the moment he couldn't remember—Leiv chose this seldom used guest bedroom as his own. Not only had he not wanted to sleep in the room LC died in—with its indelible memories—but he also didn't find LC's master-suite aesthetically appealing. Especially its monster four-poster bed.

He adjusted his mask, and the touching took him to a piece of information he'd so far missed. "Dunce," he admonished himself out loud.

Last he looked before donning his mask, Dobie was stretched out across his bedroom door threshold, snoring away. *No wonder I can't sleep.* He half smiled, and made himself refocus his mind. His eye mask was doing its job on several fronts. Helping him drift off, and helping him fit puzzle pieces together. Admittedly, almost fabricated from whole cloth—*well,* more like taking what seemed like a minor item at the time—then letting his fancy take flight.

Yep, there were no goggles found at the motorcycle murder site. *Helmet either.*

Leiv touched his mask again, then drifted off to sleep.

Chapter Five

From LC's journal: *Had steak and eggs today, my son Everett's favorite meal. Viola fixed them. She does so much. Even with Hester around to help, we'd be lost without Viola.*

Wednesday

Just Wednesday morning, and so much has happened. Leiv was lingering over a third cup of English Breakfast tea in Rhodes Castle's cavernous dining room. *English Breakfast — so much better than that stuff Doc Walker drinks.*

Since his return to Shiné and Rhodes Castle, Leiv had become fond of looking down the long dining room table, seeing no one, and enjoying a splendor that touched back to royal and class privilege in old Europe.

He heard the phone ringing out in the hall, but purposefully ignored it. HM would eagerly answer. So when she appeared at the dining room door closest to the kitchen he wasn't surprised.

"You want to take this now? Or should I take a

message?" She had a modern cordless receiver in her hand.

"Sure," he said, starting to get up.

"Sit," she said bringing him the phone, then turning and leaving with unusual alacrity.

No time wasted in chitchat. Leiv smiled, knowing she was in a hurry to get to the closest extension, probably in the hall, and pick up. Giving her time, he waited a couple seconds before saying, "Hello?"

"Mr. Rhodes, this is Deputy Martin," a male voice said in a rapid and staccato tone. "Deputy Sherman asked me to call you immediately. Something about your Chief of Police was not available?" He didn't wait for a reply from Leiv. "We've found another body. She says you know the case and should come right away. I'm on my way there too. There's another motorcycle involved." Deputy Martin caught his breath and added, "They're at the lookout vista."

Leiv felt his heart jump, then race. He stood up and demanded, "Where?" He couldn't mean Kelbaker Road at Main Street on the way to I-15? He knew where that was—sort of. Further north, but not more than twenty miles on paved road. *Maybe I can drive that without freaking.*

"Lookout Loop," the deputy said. "The first turnout."

He was relieved—wouldn't have to drive far up a winding road. *I can get there.*

It turned out fairly easy and fast to get Dobie situated with Hester, rush to his pickup parked out front, drive down Rhodes Castle's lengthy Pindo Palm-lined driveway, then merge onto the paved road that would eventually turn into Shiné's Main Street.

In fact, within about ten minutes, he was on Main Street in early morning quiet hours, and felt surprisingly comfortable. Indeed, after several deep breaths, he took stock of his physical condition—his hands on the wheel weren't clenched, his right leg wasn't twitching, and his shoulder muscles didn't feel unduly tight. All his stress reactions were in abeyance.

Maybe this isn't going to be that bad.

Undoubtedly, he missed not having Glover at his side, and hoped he'd be released from the hospital soon. *Glover would know what to do.* He sent Shiné's Chief of Police a thought of get-well encouragement.

"In the meantime, I'll do what I can." Leiv wasn't surprised he was attempting to talk to Glover as if he were in the car with him, not in the hospital.

Dobie's influence. He *knew* she was a dog, but he acted like she was a person. Leiv also figured if you got in the habit of talking to your pets, you eventually end up talking to yourself. "Clearly, I was right." Leiv chuckled lightly.

Even though he wasn't as stressed as he'd expected, Leiv *took another moment* to breathe deeply again, this time like he'd learned in a yoga class Melissa had dragged him to. Starting way at the bottom of what felt like his stomach. Leiv hadn't been fond of the postures, but retained the breathing concepts and relaxing exercises. Even sitting.

He *took another moment* to take in the blossoming day, in particular the sky was now an unusual pale color. There was a hazy yellowish tint still hanging around on the eastern horizon line, instead of the bright, sometimes even blinding white or light blue glow he was used to. Or the unique orange tint from yesterday. It didn't seem darker or hazier than usual for this admittedly early time of morning. *No,* it was a lovely bright morning. Not a morning to look once again into the face of a corpse.

As he drove through town, Leiv noticed Chef Jack pulling into the side driveway of TGS. Inside the already well-lit restaurant, he thought he saw the outlines of early-bird customers having breakfast. Leiv smiled slightly, Chef Jack started early he knew, but Pauley got things started even earlier. He'd heard opening times were variable—meaning if Pauley decided he'd rather be cooking than at home doing something else—you might get lucky and enjoy breakfast at 4 A.M. And even though Leiv had eaten a substantial HM breakfast—making up for yesterday's slight—and consumed several cups of tea, for a few seconds his mouth watered thinking about TGS's food. Especially the fresh squeezed orange juice.

Quickly, his mind moved on from food to the phone call he'd received. A second dead body found in the Mojave. In Glover's purview. *Not a good thing*.

Nadya was in the bathroom, *en suite*, a lovely and surprising happening Sydney once again thought. Not what he expected in Rhodes Castle. Must have cost a fortune, and he guessed top of the line for the time. From everything he'd heard, Nadya's grandfather was quite a man.

"Not many like him these days," he said aloud, forgetting Nadya wasn't in hearing distance. He figured she wouldn't have appreciated his thoughts anyway about the olden more rugged days. So far, she seemed a modern woman on all fronts.

The fortitude, guts, and determination it must have taken to build this home, he mused. "And to start a town." A feat nearly unfathomable to him. He wouldn't even know where to start—and he ran a business of his own. Of course in "homesteader" days, you just landed, built, and did.

Sydney walked over to the window in their front-facing bedroom and looked out. The view was grand, by city-standards. From Rhodes Castle's circular driveway, to Shiné in the valley below, to the far hills across the valley. Especially this morning with the sun on the eastern horizon to his left, touching it all in a pale yellow, almost white glow. Not a cloud in sight. *Must be the difference,* he thought, *between yesterday and today.* Clouds. Though he didn't remember any clouds injecting themselves into what he'd considered a Creamsicle orange color. Yesterday morning's sky had taken him back a bit, remembering the ice-cream truck driving through the neighborhood on hot summer days. Or were they called Dreamsicles? *Something else* he wasn't sure about.

He smiled to himself, almost mesmerized by the view, caught in his thoughts.

Or was it atmospheric pressure? Or humidity? Something else he didn't know about, besides the cost and bother of *en suite* bathrooms in the thirties and forties, and what to call yesterday's orange sunrise.

Sydney's smile broadened, and he almost turned from the window to speak to Nadya before he remembered she was in the bathroom. He wanted to ask her about the name of the delicious orange treat—indeed he was beginning to salivate.

He sighed, and thanked his lucky stars. No "sicles" of any type in jail or six feet under. He'd escaped, and was surviving.

Sydney also wanted to confront his wife about the pictures. Find out what she and Hester were really up to. But he was scared to push it. *Do I really want to be certain about the truth?*

Movement in the driveway below caught Sydney's eye. Leiv? Getting in his car and driving himself somewhere. Didn't fit the narratives both Hester and Nadya had told him.

Nadya called from the bathroom, "Syd, I'm going to take a shower and wash my hair."

There was also something about the way Leiv was hurrying.

A sense of urgency. *Yes,* that was it. *Something* was happening.

His desire for orange and vanilla ice cream treats was immediately replaced with a sense of excitement. He knew exactly where he'd left his keys — on the dresser near the door, and he grabbed them on his way out. Absently, Sydney slammed the door behind him, vaguely hearing Nadya calling him; but his mind was on Leiv.

Main Street was almost empty, Leiv noticing only a big rig and two white pickups coming toward him, then passing. On his side of the road, going his way, he was passed by one in-a-hurry motorcyclist, *probably off to work at this time of the morning.*

Leiv felt himself relax a little more. Maybe he should be forcing himself to drive more instead of always relying on Lloyd or Glover to chauffeur him. When he first arrived back in Shiné, he considered hiring someone to drive him around. Quickly though, he realized he'd be setting himself up for being called elitist, *or* having to explain his trepidation when it came to driving, *or* even worse — his lingering pain and grief from losing Melissa. Paying attention to his driving right now, however, didn't allow Leiv the distraction of wallowing in self pity, or admiring the scenic drive out of Shiné.

He could, however, prepare himself for the sight of another body. Last night, Leiv thought his deductive mind, combined with fancy, had come up with some possible scenarios of events so far. *But things have changed this morning.* One good thing out of the horribly bad event of another body appearing—was its happening while Tucker was in the hospital. *Should take the spotlight off him. He couldn't have committed this murder.* As if a murder could be considered a good happening. *Of course, if the body has been out in the desert awhile.*

Another motorcycle passed, looking almost identical to the earlier one passing him in town. The motorcycle jerked Leiv back to the task at hand—driving—and the curiosity of this bike in particular. This time, there seemed to be something familiar about the motorcycle and rider—but he couldn't quite put his finger on it. Unfortunately, all black-leather clad silhouettes sitting hunched over two wheels looked the same as they speed by. *Crazy.* A case he'd actually forgotten resurfaced. He shuddered. In this particular case there were motorcycle accident pictures—a civil suit he'd presided over early in his judicial career. That case had almost made him quit the bench. Leiv quickly shut down the memories and banished the pictures from his mind's eye.

As it kept happening, he instead saw for the hundredth time a smashed up limousine. *Even a full-size beefed-up limousine hadn't protected my Melissa.*

Leiv wondered how old this latest corpse was. Glancing at his speedometer, he allowed himself to edge up to sixty miles-per-hour. *If* these bodies were connected and recent—Tucker would be vindicated. For the next five miles, Leiv's thoughts bounced around from Tucker to Naomi, to Deputy Sherman and Glover, to motorcycle accoutrements, to Tonia Potter.

After another mile or so, he slowed down. Leiv wasn't sure the exact spot where Lookout Loop Road came in, but did remember the sign was small, non-assuming. It wasn't state or federal land, so nobody much cared about "announcements." Locals knew where it was, and that was all that mattered.

Surprisingly, he saw the sign without any trouble.

"Well, I'll be," he said. It looked like a local had taken it upon himself to repaint and re-letter the small sign, even add an arrow that wasn't needed. The road only went one way. West, and up. There was still a little turnout by the sign, and for some reason, a picture from his past, right after his father's funeral, caused him to pull off after turning, and stop for a moment.

This body could wait a couple more minutes on the scale of infinity.

Without thought, Leiv looked eastward and north — toward I-15. It wasn't you could actually see the interstate, too far away, but the sun was just at the right height to catch metallic paint, chrome, and glass in its reflective powers, dispersing moving jewel-like sparkles of light along the roadway. But no sound of cars, trucks — just complete desert silence. It was an amazing and unique experience. One of those experiences he thought, that made you want to say "Wow." But just as sensory joy touched him — he was overcome for a few seconds with an overwhelming and body-encompassing flush of apprehension and dread. *Another dead body.*

Leiv had experienced similar apprehensions a couple times previous — both experiences occurred when he was preparing to go back into the courtroom for a jury verdict. A jury verdict he guessed was a wrong one. *Both times,* he knew a guilty man would be walking away free.

Like the sun's magical-like touching of I-15 — both experiences touched opposite ends of his emotional spectrum. Unnerving, but he forced his thoughts back to what he was doing, where he was headed.

Another dead body, and no Glover to hold his psychological hand or drive him up a winding narrow road.

Leiv decided this dead body would be the worst part. Sure, he'd been to several mandatory morgue walk-throughs, in several jurisdictions. He'd seen dead bodies, even touched several back-in-the-day. And it had been different out there in Tucker's field. Different too, that day in Glover's "cold-room," with Naomi and Georgie Oakes—their lifeless bodies waiting for the coroner's van. *Another image I don't want to deal with again.*

Leiv wished he could just shut his darn brain and emotions off for a few minutes. Make time stop like he'd tried explaining to Margaret. *She'd understood.* This, however, was not a stop and smell the roses moment.

Lookout Loop Road seemed better paved and wider than he remembered from childhood on the several times his father brought him up here when visiting LC. Then after his father and mother, Everett and Sophie, moved back to Shiné themselves, he'd come to visit several times with Melissa. But Lookout Loop hadn't been on the agenda.

Though his stomach had calmed down, Leiv couldn't ignore feeling his heart pounding in his chest, or hear it pounding in his ears. Surprisingly, it only took five minutes or so to drive up the steep winding road. The Shiné Mountains, rather high hills actually, gave a great view of the valley below, including the town of Shiné, both sets of railroad tracks, and a peek at the dunes. In truth, it didn't take much elevation to accomplish all those feats. Once there though, he remembered the view as being quite grand. At least to a kid's eye. *But not as grand as from LC's flat rock across this very valley.*

Once the beginning of the lookout guard rail came into sight, Leiv took another deep breath, preparing himself for reality. He didn't see a cruiser right off, but he did see a uniformed officer who he guessed was Deputy Martin, leaning forward slightly and looking down below over the modest guard rail of Lookout Loop's actual lookout pullout. Once again, and quite amazingly, some industrious soul had given the two-rowed wooden-plank guard rail a fresh coat of white paint.

The body must be lying below the road. Yet, eager as he was to see what had happened, before getting out of his truck, Leiv took another deep breath to calm himself.

He'd pulled up on the shoulder across road from the pullout where Deputy Martin stood peering below, and got out of his truck. Even from there, at that angle, Leiv could see out across the deep and expansive valley that separated Lookout Loop and Shiné. In a second, he visually and emotionally took in the view, his little piece of the world. All the way across to the hills above Shiné where Rhodes Castle stood like a desert mirage.

It was a grand sight, even to a man like himself who'd seen, done, and traveled a lot of the world.

And *for the first time* since his return to Shiné, Leiv realized what it meant to be the grandson of the man who started a town. What LC did, how he made history and changed the geographical face of what is the United States. LC had made a place for people to move to, live in, and grow their lives. Indeed, *for the very first time,* he understood deep within what his grandfather had done, and in that moment of insight and commitment, Leiv internalized and accepted the responsibility to continue LC's legacy.

Okay, in the past he was Leiv Rhodes, lawyer, judge, all that stuff—but now he was Leigh-Everett Rhodes, and everything that statement entailed. The magnitude of that responsibility? Still unknown.

What a time to realize this, he thought.

And then it happened.

A shot struck and pierced Leiv's right arm, then another in his right side—slamming him back against his pickup in a brutal sideways action—while simultaneously sending a shockwave of pain through his arm, down his back, and all the way into his leg. Leiv grabbed his injured right arm with his left hand, then jerked it away immediately when he felt the sticky warmth of blood.

My blood.

Leiv cursed, but for some reason couldn't seem to hear his own words.

In another second, he *couldn't* speak, *couldn't* even cry out. He felt himself drop to the ground, banging his still already sore, and now injured and bloody arm against something very hard. *Car? Rock?*

After hitting the ground, quickly and seemingly in silence, Leiv rolled to the right, but his truck's front wheel was there. *Couldn't have have rolled to the right. To the left? No,* that would be toward the shooter. Confusion overtook him. Except for the rational question; why would Deputy Martin shoot him?

He could feel his breathing, rapid and shallow, and he tried to make himself pause, breath slower, take in what was happening. *Yoga class, yoga class* his mind said—a mind he knew wasn't functioning correctly. But he couldn't seem to calm his breathing, on top of struggling to understand what was going on. Everything was taking place in seconds, maybe less—but it also felt like slow-motion minutes.

"You can't escape." Deputy Martin's voice was loud. Harsh. And unafraid.

A tenor, Leiv thought apropos of nothing that was happening. He felt for his cell phone in his jacket pocket. *I'm not wearing a jacket.* But he remembered grabbing his phone off the foyer table when he left Rhodes Castle. *Must be in the truck.* He wondered how much he was bleeding. *Need to stop it.*

"You might as well give up." The deputy's voice sounded closer.

He's coming forward. To finish the job. Leiv ran his hand over his stomach. Blood. *Too much* blood. *Fresh, warm, and sticky.* His life was flowing away—into his clothes, and on— *no,* into the Mojave sand. He had to stop this man, *and* stop his own bleeding.

I'm going to die, a tiny part of Leiv's mind said. But his body refused to listen and reacted without thought. Somehow, he not only stood, but also forced himself to rush forward toward Martin, taking every ounce of strength he still possessed—slamming into him and pushing the armed fake-deputy flat on his back against roadway pavement.

Leiv thought he heard a woman yell something, but doubted he was right.

He had to move fast before Deputy Martin realized a twice-shot man had slammed into him. Partly on top of the Deputy and still using reserves he didn't know he had, Leiv pulled himself up again, stumbling, causing shockwaves of pain to shoot through his entire body.

I only have seconds. A part of his brain knew his surge of adrenalin strength had limits. Nonetheless, additional untapped strength came, and Leiv rushed forward, towards Rhodes Castle in his mind, then stumbled, actually more like *propelled* himself over the low roadside retaining fence— hitting creosote, then sagebrush, then a rock, then rolling down, down, down.

*   *   *   *   *

Once on Main Street, Sydney didn't see Leiv's pickup anywhere. *But he must be in town somewhere.* He'd have to start at the beginning of town—at the gas station. Maybe the attendant there saw him go by. What else could he do? But he wasn't going to give up. This was important. *I just know it.*

"Now, now, Mrs. Miller," Lloyd said, his voice respectful and measured as was his way. "I'm not by any means intimating you snoop, but you must have an idea where Leiv went?"

Margaret saw Hester raise a critical eyelid at Lloyd's use of the word "intimating." It was a skill raising only one eyelid, *well,* more like a trick—and Hester pulled it off expertly. For herself, Margaret just wanted to shake the silly woman by the shoulders and get an answer. Maybe even slap her if she had to. But she would wait for Lloyd to do his gentle-Pastor thing. *Then I'll throttle her.* She knew her reaction was over the top, but she had an awful yet indefinable feeling that needed addressing. *A forewarning,* and Leiv was at the center of whatever it was.

When Margaret first recognized an uneasiness in the pit of her stomach this morning, she'd immediately known she was experiencing a harbinger of something bad in the making. Her first concern was for her son, Glover; but a hurried call to the hospital confirmed he was just fine. "Taking a little nap right now? Can I give him a message?" a helpful nurse asked.

After that call, she knew it was Leiv setting her stomach off. Yet, just in case her instincts were wrong, Margaret telephoned Loma Linda to see if Tucker was okay. "Being watched, and under guard. No deterioration in his condition."

At this point she felt sure Leiv was in trouble. But how could he be? The man hardly left Rhodes Castle unless prodded, pushed, or pulled—much like she'd had to do yesterday morning.

Hester was explaining, ever so innocently, "Well I'm not sure exactly where he was going." A mystified looked overtook her face. "All I know is he left in a hurry."

Enough, already. "Which way did he turn? Toward my house, or toward town?"

"Oh, towards town, he—" Hester caught herself, her eyes admitting she'd given away more than intended.

The three of them were standing in a huddle in the foyer of Rhodes Castle, streaming light tickling LC's stained glass double doors—mocking the task at hand. Hester had her arms crossed. *Like she knows so much*—Margaret also caught herself—she was letting her emotions and visceral distaste for Hester take control of her actions, and most importantly, her logical thinking processes. *But darn it*, her sense of apprehension was steadily growing.

"Did he say anything?" Lloyd's voice echoed Margaret's concern.

Hester shook her head.

Margaret wasn't satisfied, and pressed, "Did he get a call before he left?"

Hester quickly shook her head again, but Margaret had seen the tiniest bit of guilt flicker for a millisecond in her dark eyes.

"Who was it?" Margaret demanded. She knew she was speaking louder than she should, and with unladylike harshness, but she needed to know. Now. And Leiv had mentioned several times he knew Hester listened in on his landline calls. That knowledge had prompted her to call his cell if she wanted privacy.

"Deputy Martin," Hester blurted out. "Lookout Loop, another body."

Finally, Margaret saw Hester's true feelings in her now wide eyes. *HM is also worried.*

And winter or not, it was forecasted to be another hot Mojave day.

This is not good.

Leiv couldn't see. Everything was black. Nonetheless, he was coming around to consciousness—but in a jolt of confusion, physical, mental, and emotional. His first words were simple, "What happened?" He thought he'd delivered those two words into the world quite vehemently and loudly. What he heard was the feeblest of whispers.

He tried to raise his head in an attempt to actually sit up; instead his head seemed to move only a millimeter, slowly, and causing great pain to shoot down his back. The rest of his body was coming back, but in convulsive movements and an inexplicable order not under his control. His feet were first—not his torso, or arms, or hands. He couldn't see the length of his body, but it felt like coming alive meant twitching uncontrollably. Leiv tried to take control, make his hands work by bringing his right hand to his face. More pain—intense and all-encompassing.

Nonetheless, even with the pain, Leiv did manage a quick touch to his face. Cold and clammy. Yet at the same time, the rest of his body felt like he was sweating, his breathing was rapid, high in his chest, and another source of pain.

"I'm having a seizure." He couldn't hear his voice—not even the feeblest of whispers this time.

"I'm alive." *Where did I fall to?* "Where am I?" *Oh no,* "Maybe this is death?"

Leiv sensed there was no one around to hear him. But he had to speak, try to take back control of his mind and body. If he wasn't dead, he wanted to be alive for real.

He thought he shook his head to rattle his brain around—but he wasn't sure if his head actually moved. Leiv tried again, and finally, it felt like he was able to think a little. *My brain starting to work?*

Still, he couldn't see. He couldn't seem to make his eyelids move. Painful as it was, he brought his hand up to his eyes. *They're open.* "I'm blind." This time he heard his voice loud and clear. With an inch more of movement, his hand found a piece of desert trash, seemingly lodged in the branches of the creosote bush above, and covering his face. Belatedly he realized it was cardboard. A windblown, sand-whipped Coor's six pack packaging. *I'm not blind.*

Unbelievably—and as horrible as the time, place, setting, and circumstances were—and despite his pain and predicament, for a moment Leiv's mind and emotions marveled at the desert beauty around him.

I must be dying. And an instant of perceived blindness had brought into crystalline clarity what he'd miss. Mojave sunrises—red, orange, and blue in infinite mixtures above a jutting hills horizon line, and unparalleled in all his travels. Followed by clear blue skies all day, all season—culminating in sunsets that Margaret proclaimed made her heart miss a beat.

A unique world. LC's world.

Sharp pain shot up his side and philosophical meanderings vanished in a puff—replaced with his current reality. Someone claiming to be a Deputy Martin had shot him, and he was bleeding to death somewhere in scrub desert below Lookout Loop vista.

Leiv made his left hand lay flat against the ground. The scrabble-sand and rocks were getting warm. He couldn't see the position of the sun through the bush almost touching his face, but he could feel the direct heat from its rays.

He thought of Tucker, *standing in the noonday sun*. So despondent, he wanted to kill himself. A rush of familiar sadness flooded through him, not for himself, and not just for Tucker, but for all the sufferers of the world. *Oh yes*, he'd seen his share parading through, dragged through, and sometimes rushed through his various court rooms—from traffic court, to appellate. Always sufferers.

Stop, his mind demanded. *Stop*. Leiv didn't like the melancholy path he was starting down. If he was going to wallow in the past for survival inspiration, he needed to focus on the survivors, the winners, the triumphant ones—*not the victims*.

Though feeling he was now on the right mental path, Leiv still found it difficult to wrap his mind around what had happened, and what possible outcomes were in the cards for him. In response to his thoughts, his reflexes tried to move both his hands—only his left moved, but he managed to bring it to his chest. Again he felt for blood.

Dry? A wisp of optimism tried to surface. "My wound is drying up." He didn't hear his words, but Leiv prayed he was thinking right, beginning to interpret his surroundings and circumstances.

I want to live.

* * * * *

"Did you call nine-one-one?" Margaret asked again, barely able to stop shifting around in the front seat of Lloyd's Volvo station wagon.

"Yes, Margaret." his voice was calm and patient. *Almost to the point of infuriating,* Margaret thought, then immediately chastised herself for thinking so meanly of her pastor.

"You saw me. You heard me do it," he added.

She blew out a long stream of frustrated air. "Drive faster, can't you?"

"I'm going seventy."

Reining her emotions in a bit, she apologized in a softer voice, "I'm sorry. It's just—" She left the rest unsaid.

"It's just you're scared to death our friend is dead."

"Yes." She looked out her side window. "And it's getting hotter already. *And,* I haven't heard any sirens yet."

The pale yellow-white of the sunrise was fast fading, replaced with blue, and a recognizable sun-orb. Already, the desert landscape outside her window looked hotter. Not like in summer, where she fancied she often saw waves of rising heat. Winter in the Mojave was a little more subtle; but a killer nonetheless. For a second her mind and heart went out to Tucker.

Should I say something about Naomi now?

Quickly, Margaret brought herself back to the present circumstance, back with what she perceived as a life and death crisis.

Leiv knew he was still alive; for his mind was still working, but in a way Leiv had never before experienced.

Whatever constituted Leigh-Everett Rhodes was functioning on some kind of fugue-plateau. He had no control, his thoughts drifting and shifting, here and there, from the past, into the present, and vice versa. All dreamlike in nature. And though on the verge of he knew-not-what, death or survival—some part of his brain—*frontal lobe? Neocortex?* There was a brain-damaged teenager trial so very long ago—pieces of which would never leave him. Whatever it was called and whatever the brain location, some processes were still trying to figure out, *why would this Deputy Martin character want to shoot me?*

Then a few bits and pieces in the present started falling into place. Slowly, but assuredly. *Who would believe me?* Despite being in disconnected dreamland—Leiv tried to laugh. His inner ear heard it more like a gurgle, and he wanted to laugh even louder.

No goggles, no helmet, why not? More bits and pieces fell into place. Leiv was both sure, and not so sure. He whispered to the world, "Oh Deputy Martin, you sly conniving SOB." Causing Leiv to want to laugh even louder.

He'd seen Glover type the motorcycle license number into his cruiser console and he was sure what the results would show. Glover will put this together too. *Even if I'm not around.*

His mind floated on though, now wanting to visit, yet again, his most vulnerable emotional tender-spot. In a millisecond he was back in Chicago. Once again touching the limousine door handle, feeling and tasting sharp, crisp, and cutting Chicago night air.

The same remembrance, imagery, guilt, and grief returned he'd experienced yesterday in Glover's office with Wally and Doctor Walker. A cold-room table with two dead bodies. Now his own death. *Grief*, however, he'd seen take many manifestations. And guilt. *Oh yes, I'm guilty alright*. The same thoughts he'd had yesterday.

I wonder if it's getting near noon? It certainly feels hot enough.

Leiv tried whispering some more. Barely conscious or not, he figured if he could whisper, it proved he was still alive. "So Guilty. Must be how Tucker felt Sunday morning. Standing there in the noonday sun." He heard his own voice this time. All was not lost, and he thought he felt a tear run down his face. Couldn't be. If anything, he was dehydrated.

In a snap, Leiv was in a completely different place and time—a yoga class, Melissa at his side, both stretched out on matching mats—in touching distance of each other. It was the end of class he remembered most poignantly, relaxation time, recognizing every part of his body, loosening his joints and organs, from the tip of his head to the very end of his toes. Not very manly based on the standards he grew up with, but feeling extraordinarily good.

The instructor was guiding the class in her soft lyrical voice, explaining how to make the relaxation-journey. Leiv once again *felt* his breathing that summer night in Chicago, a warm breeze bathing them. Hearing Melissa's breathing next to him.

Soul mates—and Leiv's heart ached from across the years to this moment as he lay near death in the Mojave desert. It was in that particular class, on that particular night, Melissa lost yet another gold wedding band. *Three before her death*. In his mind, he smiled. One of her idiosyncrasies—to lose things.

Another piece of his mind recognized he wasn't back in Chicago in the comforting confines of Friends of Yoga's posture room, with twenty or so like minded yoga enthusiasts, but laying splayed in the desert, barely able to move—the sun getting hotter, the air on his face considerably warmer, the ground below him harder, the micro-sounds of what he imagined were desert critters getting louder. *How can I hear critters?* He fancied he could. Many more serious than ubiquitous ants, spiders, and beetles. Toxic guys like scorpions, vinegaroons, and black-widows. And of course, rattlers, sidewinders and the venomous Mojave Green pit-vipers. He was at their mercy. This was their territory—he, an immobile interloper.

The words *pit-viper* flitted through his mind again—but before he could further internalize the hazards around him— Leiv was back with Melissa and yoga, and he whispered to the desert, "'What a lovely evening,' she told me." He remembered her exact phrasing, lilting and harmonic. A little bit of a song in her words. *Yes*, he was back in Chicago, back in the safe emotional embrace of Melissa and her friends.

She took his hand. Leiv's eyes were closed, and he next saw and felt his grandfather LC take his other hand. Both there to show him the way.

No, I'm not ready yet.

Lloyd slowed down, eyes squinting at first, then reflecting his relief. "Someone's repainted the sign." He took his right hand off the wheel for a second to push his spectacles even tighter against the bridge of his nose.

Margaret caught herself before admonishing him to keep his hands on the wheel before addressing the sign. "Naomi," she said. No reason to either act like a harridan just because she was nervous and scared to death, or to keep secrets that didn't matter anymore. "She did it in memory of Burtie." Her tone reflected her sadness. How much she'd

195

wanted happiness for her friend Naomi. *All in all, though, more sadness than happiness,* she thought. "He put up the original sign."

Lloyd made the turn sharply, his wheels squealing slightly.

After they were solidly on Lookout Loop Road, Lloyd said, "Burtie?"

"Burton Hanson. You remember him, don't you? He and Naomi went places together."

"Oh yeah." Out of nowhere, a rabbit ran across the road, and he slowed. "But I didn't realize about him and Naomi." He took a deep breath that sounded to Margaret more like a sigh. "You know he was a Deacon. So sad about his cancer."

No need to go into details with her pastor about Naomi and Burtie's late-in-life affair. Rather torrid to blandly discuss with Lloyd. *A little more than going places together.* Margaret turned her head to look out her window at the hillside's rugged climbing rock to her right side, and despite the circumstances, Margaret smiled for the briefest of moments. At least Naomi had some happiness amongst all her anguish and self-recriminations.

She wished mightily her dear friend Naomi was here with her now.

His mental meanderings told Leiv he'd completely lost control of where his mind would take him. This—what could be his final "trip"—would not be controlled by rational brain functioning. Whatever part of his brain now in control, would go where it wanted to go. For good or bad, and not on a journey he willed.

Indeed, in a mental blink, he was back in Chicago, then the cold-room, then to Glover in the hospital. Returning to familiar places—reliving moments in time he would never forget

On another front, and quiet ironically, Leiv thought, here he was laying splayed to the elements, at the Mojave's mercy, and living what he figured were his last moments on earth in the company of dust, scrub grass, desert critters all standing in wait—he was still able to appreciate smelling crisp, cool, Chicago Fall night air. And taste the change of seasons in his mind. From not only across the continent, but also across the years. He even fancied he could hear oak leaves falling through tree branches under the cover of darkness. Hear the sound of their unseen gentle touch to earth. Like him, their season of life now gone. Taken by the vagrancies—or was it a plan—of Mother Nature.

He would never forget that night in Chicago with his dearest Melissa.

Leiv's painful reverie stopped as abruptly as it started, for right in front of him, he saw Melissa standing there, almost a glow, her hand again outstretched toward him, smiling, *and* Naomi was next to Melissa, *her hand* also outstretched and a welcoming smile on her face. A little to their side, looking bigger than life, his grandfather, LC also stood, his smile the biggest of all. Both his arms were outstretched—ready to embrace his grandson.

"There's a car behind us," Margaret said looking into her side view mirror.

Lloyd answered quickly, "I know. He joined us about half way here."

Margaret was glad Lloyd knew what was going on. "You know who it is?"

"Sydney Collins, I think. That's the car that was parked in front of Rhodes Castle behind Leiv's pickup."

Two motorcycles sped by from the opposite direction, heading toward Main Street.

"They're going too fast," Lloyd admonished.

Margaret wondered what fools would be driving like that on a road like this. *Running away from something?* "Hurry up, Lloyd, hurry up." She now knew for certain, Leigh-Everett was in trouble. Big time.

I need to calm myself.

Hard to do with the sun and heat rising at what she considered a phenomenal rate.

Melissa, Naomi, and LC floated away into nothingness, leaving Leiv engulfed by a wave of dizziness. He wasn't moving, so swimming in the head didn't make any sense. *Dehydration? Like Tucker?* Whatever was now going on, Leiv was sure he couldn't move, yet equally sure he felt dizzy.

Since I haven't yet joined Melissa and my grandfather— oddly, he found it a realization edged in sadness—*I haven't died yet.*

Though being alive, and not being able to move in itself, was curious; since nothing felt broken—if pain, or numbness were indicators. He "sensed" all his limbs, but his body wasn't responding to his commands—one overarching desire in particular, to get up and get out of here.

His limbs, at least his arms were intact, for Leiv felt an animal scurry across his hand; though he couldn't move to look and know for sure what animal—only hoped he hadn't been bitten.

The thought of the unknown critter, sent his mind journeying backwards once more, though this time in a different direction and more recent. Wandering around Naomi Hall's garage with Lloyd. It was there he'd seen the gigantic black-widow spider hanging in a dark corner of her garage. Probably not as large as he was re-seeing it now—but visualizing the spider again in his mind's eye, along with the hundreds of old rusty tools, trash that should have been dumped a long time ago, the exquisite little bottle he'd been drawn to, then his visit to "Le Bric-à-Brac" in Shiné where the bottle's twin now resided, and help from from Hal in Chicago—whom he'd asked to do a tox-screen as a favor for him. *Why had I done that? Naomi's garage, her little blue bottle.* Inexplicably, he'd been drawn to the bottle, and then equally unexplainable, he'd sent it off to Hal.

"Thanks for tagging along," Lloyd had opened the side door to Naomi's garage, then held it for Glover and Leiv. He and Glover stepped into the remnants of a dead woman's world.

Lying helpless in the noonday sun today, Leiv remembered that morning with a new sense of criticality. *Easy to do in hindsight.* It was a Saturday morning, and Glover was not in uniform for once, and Lloyd, dressed in jeans and chambray shirt didn't look exactly ministerial.

The pastor had seemed down, not presenting his usual positive cheerleader demeanor. He said, "Being an executor isn't fun." He felt along the wall for a light switch. "So having you two as witnesses is a good thing."

Reliving that morning, almost incomprehensible given his current circumstances—surrealistic and touched with a touch of something beyond it felt like—Leiv wanted to reach out and pat his friend on the shoulder. *Lloyd. My Saturday night companion.*

He wondered where he was now?

"Leiv, Leiv, are you alright?" *A woman's voice?* "What happened? Who shot you? Say something. Please, please, say something."

He could feel hands lifting his head, then lifting his shoulders. *More inexplicable stuff—but in the present? Events happening just in his head?* Someone was now cradling his head, and he thought he heard the sound of footsteps running his way. But no sirens.

I must have died. This must be heaven.

"Speak to us." This time a man's voice. "You have to be alive, Leiv. You just have to live."

The woman's voice again. *Margaret?* "Tell us what happened?"

"Someone shot him," the man said answering for him while running his hand over his chest, then his wounded arm. Next someone was feeling his carotid artery—the man he thought—then holding his wrist, feeling for a pulse. Leiv thought he now heard sirens in the background, but guessed it wishful thinking on his part.

"Help's on the way." *The man again. Could it be Lloyd?* "Hang in there." It *was* Lloyd, recognition confirmed by hearing him start to pray. Leiv couldn't quite make out the words.

"I went back," Leiv miraculously heard his own voice say. "To Naomi's, and to 'Le Bric-à-Brac.'" He wanted to tell them, but didn't think he had enough strength left. Tell them one puzzle had come together for him. Also, how he needed to survive, needed to live long enough to clear Tucker's name.

"Here, let me in. I can help." *Another voice. Another man?*

"You have to be careful, Sydney," Margaret said.

Sydney? Sydney Collins?

"I will, I will," Sydney said. "I used to do this, a paramedic—" his voice faded. "Can't hear an ambulance yet." Leiv couldn't tell exactly what Sydney was doing, but it felt like he was putting his hands and arms around and under his shoulders.

"I brought a blanket, we've got to carry him out of here. But we have to be very careful with his neck and spine. Can't do anything where he is now. Might need CPR..."

Quiet for a moment as three sets of hands seemed to be cradling him. Their voices were comforting. *Friends.*

"That's my blanket," Lloyd mumbled.

"Saw it in your truck and grabbed it."

"Thank goodness," Lloyd and Margaret said almost in unison.

"Yes, like that. We've got to get him up to air conditioning, water..."

Somehow, Leiv knew he must have stretched his hand out, because he felt a warm responding squeeze from one of his friends. Which friend, he didn't know, and thought it unimportant.

"I'll see you another time, Grandfather," Leiv told LC aloud, expecting his words to travel through time. *Dehydration silliness.*

Quite contrarily and out of nowhere, a most profound insight flowed through him. *Now* was the time to tell his friends. He couldn't wait. Even though his brain was fuzzy and he was sure his words wouldn't come out perfect—it needed to be done. "I have to tell you about the Mojave-Stones," he tried saying, while feeling and hearing his voice slur and fade to nothing.

"The Mojave-Stone?" He thought it was Margaret who asked, for it sounded like Lloyd had returned to praying rhythmically in the background.

Leiv knew his strength reserves were gone. But in the seconds before he lost consciousness again—he must have licked his lips—for he tasted gritty Mojave sand—and most oddly, it was sweet.

Cal Oakes told me that once.

For some reason, Leiv couldn't see very well or move his head. Maybe something over his eyes and a brace? But he thought he recognized her voice. Maybe. *Portia?*

"Can't you guys from Shiné stay out of trouble?"

Yes, it was SBC Deputy Portia Sherman. Her tone was warm, friendly—though as he squinted to bring her face into focus through what now seemed like little slits, he saw what he guessed was her characteristically uncompromising facial expression; *yet,* her words seemed to be teasing. Friendly-like. He heard a scraping, then straining his vision even more, he saw she was pulling a chair over to his bed.

"You and Tucker Oakes, both in the same hospital."

She was talking to him like he was in a coma, not expecting him to answer. *I'm not in a coma,* he wanted to shout out. *And why is she visiting Tucker?* But neither his lips or vocal chords wanted to work. Both felt dry and scratchy. But that shouldn't matter when it came to a coma, should it?

As if reading his thoughts, Deputy Sherman said, "You know, Mr. Oakes is out of his coma. I came to see if he could answer some questions."

What questions?

Once more, as if inside his head, she said, "Mainly, I wanted to ask him why he tried to kill himself? Guilt, maybe over killing Naomi Hall?"

"He didn't kill her," Leiv heard himself say. It came out squeaky and barely audible, but he'd managed to send audible sounds into the real world once again. To him a sure sign he was back on his Shiné plane of existence. *Not* in a coma.

Leiv thought he felt a pat on his hand, but wasn't sure.

"I knew you'd make it," she said. "Don't strain yourself." She patted his hand again, and this time Leiv was sure. "You and Tucker are still too out of it to make any sense." Next, he felt her squeeze his hand. "Now I'm off to Twentynine Palms." Her voice had quickly changed, more lyrical he thought. Funny how he could hear "things" while not being able to completely open his eyes. "Want to cheer up Glover—" she caught herself, and Leiv heard a touch of embarrassment in her corrected words. "I mean Chief Deers."

Deputy Portia Sherman cleared her throat. "And you, Mr. Rhodes, are a much tougher bird than I thought on first meeting you." She laughed lightly. "If you'd only seen your face when Chief Deers asked you if you wanted to taste his ostrich egg omelet."

When Leiv next realized he'd rejoined the non-coma world, a man dressed in scrubs was fiddling with his IV. There was a long tattoo of a string of skulls running down his arm.

An alarm bell started to ring, but then the man said, "Good to see you waking up again." His voice was calming, reassuring. "These drug cocktails can knock you out big time. What they're supposed to do." He looked over at Leiv, and smiled broadly. "Your electrolytes are looking pretty good. And with the blood you got, you're getting better." Then he winked. "Fast."

The man was in his forties—maybe, congenial, seemingly knowledgeable, and had a good bedside manner. Then a female nurse appeared at his side and said, "Is he all set up, Marty?"

Leiv relaxed. Prejudice, the skulls had sent him a message that wasn't accurate. He took a deep breath, then looked up at the ceiling. *I survived.* And these people were here to help him.

"Hey," he heard a female voice shouting. "Who the hell are you?" Then a loud siren-buzzer went off, next the sound of feet running and phones ringing. The last Leiv saw in those minutes before he drifted off for what seemed like the hundredth time in one day, was a fleeting vision of a another nurse and a security officer at his bedside.

Maybe it had been minutes, maybe hours, maybe days. Leiv couldn't tell, just thought there was an early-in-the-day brightness entering his room's window, and the voices he heard were familiar.

But he did *know* two things. The wyvern-type creature he was dreaming about that kept swooping down and chasing him through the desert valley between Lookout Loop and Rhodes Castle was not real. He also *knew*—he was not dead.

Yes, I'm still alive. Then most unexpectedly, not really a thought, but an emotional wave of humanity representing all the victims in *all the* criminal cases he'd presided over—*all the* deaths, *all the anguish*—overcame him, and he wanted to cry out in pain. Leiv had never experienced anything like that moment in his whole life. Sadness yes, but this, never before. For a few seconds, it felt unbearable.

Happenings over the last few days were initiating a string of "firsts" for Leiv: and they were beginning to exact a psychological and emotional toll on his psyche—pushing at him in an uncontrollable way—with this latest rush of emotion the oddest. Thankfully, just when Leiv thought he'd arrived at an unbreachable pinnacle of some sort—a breaking point possibly—the mundane broke in and brought him back from the edge.

"Just amazing," a voice Leiv recognized as Lloyd was saying, "tried to kill both of them. Leiv a second time. And they even had guns."

Leiv imagined Lloyd was pushing at the bridge of his glasses, and wanted to smile at the thought. Whatever *had been* percolating in Leiv's brain was stabilizing, allowing him to make light of his friend's formerly annoying, now endearing habit. But what was Lloyd saying about guns? Didn't yet make sense.

"We'll get 'em, Pastor." *Deputy Sherman again?* Leiv was pulled farther forward into the present, away from his earlier existential anguish. "There's an APB out for the two of them. All jurisdictions involved. The nurses and a couple of technicians got a good look at them."

She sounded strong and capable. Just like Glover. Leiv heard a door open, then close gently.

"Did you tell them what's going on?" Portia asked.

"Yes," a new male voice said. *Sydney's here, too?* "Nadya and Hester are at Leiv's huddled in the kitchen with Dobie. Waiting to hear more from us."

Now another woman's voice, "Thank you, Mr. Collins. The EMT told me your keeping him cool until they got there might have saved Leigh-Everett's life." *Margaret, of course.* "And because you knew the right way to move him."

"Leigh-Everett is more fitting than Leiv," Sydney said.

Margaret laughed lightly. More music to Leiv ears. Just the sound of her voice made him feel better. "That's because Leigh-Everett is the name his father and grandfather gave him. Leiv is the name he gave himself. Can't control what your kids do."

Silence. Leiv wondered if it had anything to do with him. "Tell me about weekend warriors," Leiv said aloud—and heard himself speak. *I can talk again.*

Another moment of silence passed, then everyone started talking at once it seemed. He heard Margaret, Lloyd, Portia, and Sydney all talking over each other.

Finally, from the general babble, Leiv most distinctively heard Portia chastise him, "About time you came back around. Got places to go, attempted murderers to track down. You need to rest. And we need to get back to work."

With bravado based on nothing, and contrary to existing circumstances, Leiv would not allow himself to be talked down. *If I can just force my eyes open.*

"Look." Margaret was the first to see. "Leigh-Everett's opened his eyes."

Lloyd started praying.

Sydney sighed.

And Portia said, "Beginning to realize how tough you really are. For a citified judge that is." Her words contradicted the relief and surprise in her tone of voice.

Leiv found his head would now turn, and he aimed his focus toward where he thought the deputy was standing. "It's important." His voice was stronger, he could hear it. But he wasn't sure for how long. "I need to know what are considered the accoutrements of weekend warriors."

"One of your endless sentences, and the word 'accoutrement,' no less.'" Margaret teased. Then everyone else laughed. Leiv didn't miss the relief he heard in their laughter.

The door opened again, and this time Leiv could see who had entered. Deputy Brad Temper from Needles. Barely in the room, he said to Portia, "I think we've lost them. Still fanning out in a perimeter search, but my gut tells me they could be anywhere by now."

Leiv's vision still wasn't topnotch, but it was clear even to his blurry eyes, the expression on Deputy Portia Sherman's otherwise attractive face was not a happy one.

He needed to get out of this bed and get to work.

"Tucker, Tucker," Leiv said, his voice barely a whisper. "I've only got a couple minutes before they track me down." His hand was sore where he'd pulled his IV out, his body ached all over, and his mind was still befuddled—but certain things had to be taken care of.

Tucker stirred, seemingly trying to turn his body toward Leiv.

"I'm going to talk fast. I'm in the hospital, just down the hall from you. I want you to know I believe you didn't kill Naomi. I also don't think you had anything to do with the dead body on your land." Leiv was talking rapidly and in hushed tones, forcing himself to stop for a few seconds to take a swallow of air. "I'm going to find out who did everything and clear your name."

He reached out to give Tucker's hand a squeeze, but couldn't readily find his hand amongst the bed sheets. Admittedly, he still wasn't seeing perfectly, lighting in the room was subdued, and Tucker's arm was hooked up to an IV.

"Mr. Rhodes!"

He turned to see the on-duty-head-nurse, two male orderlies, and a security guard, all standing in or right outside Tucker's hospital room door. They were not hiding their displeasure at his sneaking out of his room and evading them.

Leiv sighed. *The jig is up.* Then he felt Tucker grab for, and find his own hand. Tucker, his hand still feeling rough and calloused, ended up being the one to squeeze *his* hand—then hold it for a few seconds.

Tucker understands what I was saying.

Turning to face the menacing "mob" glaring at him from the doorway, Leiv said, "How'd I get here? Must be the drugs..."

He hoped his hospital gown was still tied in back.

Chapter Six

From LC's journal: *Then sometimes, things just ain't what they seem to be. And seems like mostly I get confused, lose things, or something weird happens on Thursdays. Who can forget Black Thursday on Oct 24 of '29. Bought my land right after that. Land you can count on. Bought the stones on another Thursday. Opals you can count on. Now Tuesdays though, are good days to do any darned thing on. Have a feeling I'll be leaving this here earth on a Tuesday. Don't know why, but just got that feeling.*

Thursday

Leiv wanted to leave, get out of the hospital—go back home to Rhodes Castle. Yes, LC's desert mansion was home now. A home he wanted to be in.

And "this" was not LC's library or cupola. He needed his morning sunrise-fix, his Dobie to talk to, and a cup of Hester's English Breakfast tea.

I need to get up now. But he could feel his mind drifting off again. *Drugged me again.* Still, he knew, and wasn't sure how, it was morning. He could "feel" the sun, but of course that had to be a fantasy. He tried to force his mind to work — remember what day it was. Wednesday? Thursday? *Damn.* He didn't know.

From somewhere in the world — he hoped in his hospital room, though he was no longer sure about anything — he heard a male voice say with authority, "That should keep him resting comfortably the rest of today." Then he heard a clanking of some kind. *The closing of a hospital chart, maybe?* Though Leiv didn't really know if there still were charts like that. More probably everyone used a laptop.

He wanted to smile, but his facial muscles wouldn't respond, and his brain was getting so sluggish.

Was it just yesterday? What a horrible day.

It was like the experiences of the last few days had taken him into another dimension. He realized in retrospect, a place where so many of the people who'd come through his various courtrooms over the years must have felt. Being hurt and not being able to do something about it was not fun.

Melissa yet again appeared in his mind's eye, posing for a snapshot on the rocks south of Oak Street Beach — him eager to use his brand new Nikon SLR. She was smiling, reflecting the joy of newlywed happiness back at him and his fancy camera.

Everything has changed.

The voice said, "Don't want him roaming around the hospital again like last night, now do we?" Even though drifting off to drug-land, Leiv recognized the voice. His doctor.

Well, if the doctor says I should sleep.

Leiv's last conscious thought before drifting off into drug induced la la-land again was, *I had no right being a judge. I knew nothing about life. Nothing.*

Then again he thought, *what a horrible day.*

Then again he thought, *everything is changed.*

But he still couldn't remember what day it was—though some note in LC's journal wanted him to remember what day of the week it was. Take that fact into account.

Finally, *Thursday.* That was it—*Thursday.*

Until Tucker's attempted suicide, Ida was a late morning to early afternoon swimmer. This morning, a second day in a row, she found herself floating in the early hours, though not quite as early as yesterday. Sleep had become an elusive item again, and would probably be that way until Tucker came home.

Not one for lengthy self analysis or introspection, Ida did realize she missed Tucker more than she ever expected. And especially with Georgie gone, and Calvin down in San Bernardino all the time talking with the cops, or even farther down in Loma Linda checking on Tucker. Well, she was even lonelier.

No one to be with now.

On top of all that, today was Thursday. Her day to fix a special family meal. There wasn't much family left, *now was there?*

She stood up straight in the middle of her lap pool, something she seldom did and cursed. Then Ida prayed to the world in general, "Please, please, let Leiv or Glover find out who killed that strange man so my Tucker can come home." *And Calvin, too.*

Ida very much wanted her Thursdays back. She'd fixed her life before, made everything right, but *this time,* she couldn't think of one thing she could do to get what she wanted besides wait for Leiv or Glover to figure it all out.

Margaret took Glover's hand into hers. His Cap Coleman tattoo was fully visible, and for a second, she wanted to cry out from still haunting grief. Forcibly and instantly she brought herself back to the present and her son. She knew Glover wasn't that fond of public displays of emotion like hand holding and hugging—but at the moment, she didn't care. Besides, the nurse had gone back to her circular-styled ward station. More patients to worry about than just her son.

"You look so much better." *Inane, but he did.*

Glover smiled at her indulgently, and didn't pull his hand away. "You know I'm fine now. I can leave whenever I want."

"You're lying." *Good sign,* she thought. He wants to leave, come home.

His smile broadened, but she could see in his eyes, her son was still in pain. He added, "No, for real. I can leave. It's just I like the food so much so I'm hanging around a little longer."

Margaret laughed. That was her son. *Brave, quick witted, strong.* She caught herself, indeed he was her son, but he was also a man. A concept she'd had to remind herself of for years. But here she was, yet again, thinking of him as a little boy.

Clearly intuiting her thoughts, maybe reading her expression, Glover said, "Not to worry, Mother. I'll always be your little boy."

His words were said with such lack of guile, so clearly, and so lovingly, it took every ounce of will power Margaret could muster not to break down crying. She squeezed his hand with both of hers and managed a whispered, "I love you."

Glover's unsentimental response was, "I need to get out of here, Mother. I need to get out of here today. It's Thursday, right?"

She nodded and wondered what the heck he was up to now.

"Thursdays are my lucky days," he said.

She watched as Glover turned around in bed, grimacing slightly, but managing to bring his legs over to the side of the bed. She opened her mouth once to try and stop him, but didn't.

"I'm going to need your help." He winked at her, and displayed the crooked little smile his father was also famous for. Once again, Margaret came close to emotionally caving— but managed to hold it together. She did murmur, "You know it's a Naval hospital, and the Marine base—"

"I have a uniform, too, you know." He smiled at her again. She saw pain still there in his eyes, but she also saw determination in the tightness around her son's mouth. "And like I said, Mother, Thursday is my lucky day."

Looking out from his second story Rhodes Castle bedroom window, crested on top with an elaborate stained glass motif, but fortuitously with clear glass on the bottom— Sydney thought the desert sky amazing. Chicago could have beautiful sunrises alright, but this Shiné horizon was so expansive, and such vivid colors he'd seen over his visit. *The East is the East, the sun is the sun, and the horizon was the horizon, no matter where you are.* Yet—somehow this was different.

Sydney had already called Loma Linda hospital this morning. "Mr. Rhodes is resting." The same words as last night. He'd never forget yesterday, trying to make sure a man he'd quickly come to admire didn't die before EMTs and paramedics could help him. *Risking moving him.* Sometimes a difficult decision.

He planned on calling the hospital again before lunch time.

Now, with the sun above the horizon, slight streaks of orange once again highlighting the show, he watched Hester and Nadya walk down the Pindo Palm-lined front driveway of Rhodes Castle for the second time—almost hand-in-hand, like sisters almost. Sydney was very confused. *Conflicted,* was more accurate. He knew what was going on, there was no confusion in his mind about that. *But what to do?* That was the question.

He'd been watching the two women for fifteen or so minutes as they walked, clearly in discussion, and he was sure he knew what about. The Mojave-Stone, of course. It was all he'd heard Nadya talk about for over a year at least.

He loved Nadya, and part of his love was rooted in looking at her. *Beautiful.*

And the shining black stone he'd seen, also beautiful. But another man's possession. A man that in a matter of only a couple days he'd become fond of. In addition, there was his innate sense of justice, of right-and-wrong. Somehow in his mind, Leiv Rhodes, more accurately—Judge Leigh-Everett Rhodes—was a symbol of those values.

Hell, those values were one of the main reasons he was in this predicament. He'd never forget that early Thursday morning in that back government room, signing those papers. His one little contribution to justice. *Well,* not so little. But he'd done what was right, no matter the consequences. That had been a Chicago Thursday morning.

Now Sydney stood watching his lovely wife—whom up to now, he cherished dearly—talking conspiracy and theft with a crazy lady trying to hold on to a heritage she thought was represented by, and personified in an opal.

What to do? What to do? Thursdays, days of decision.

On top of that, he knew through one of Nadya's relatives, her mother Mary Rhodes wasn't actually "a Cooper." She'd only said that to get in with the Lovel, Herne, Cooper, and Coppersmith crowds on the Northside. Be accepted. Then she'd grown up, married André to become a Rhodes, and no one cared any more.

Sydney wondered whom the last laugh would be on. He didn't want it to be Leiv.

Hester hoped Sydney wouldn't come rushing out disturbing them. In the few days Nadya's husband had been at Rhodes Castle, he'd already become a nuisance. She was always running into him, in this room, or that room, nosing around, looking at the ceilings, the furnishings—as if he were an appraiser getting ready to put the place on the market. Nadya wasn't going to be here forever. She needed to make sure their understanding was clear without Sydney around.

Before they headed outside, Hester and Nadya sat across from each other at the kitchen table. *Moments for privacy.*

"Are we alone?" Nadya asked, her voice almost a whisper.

"Yes," Hester assured her.

She does have beautiful eyes, Hester thought. *Sure,* her features were a little brutish for her taste, and her skin was less than creamy-perfect. But her eyes were captivating—no wonder sappy Sydney drools over her. Indeed, as Hester stared into her eyes, she felt mesmerized for a couple seconds.

"What does he do in there?" Nadya leaned forward. "Did you say he reads a journal LC left?"

In a contradictory movement to Nadya, she leaned back against the spindles of her red painted chair. Hester needed to go carefully. *Nadya is our future.* She tried sending her thought across the years, tried asking her mother if there was a good reason to share their secrets. Was she right trusting her instincts?

Hester spoke slowly, precisely. She wanted to make sure Nadya understood. "You know *we're* losing the battle."

Nadya nodded.

"LC tried to run away from his heritage." *He was a Cooper, not a Rhodes.*

Again, a nod from Nadya.

"And Viola ran to our heritage."

"From what you've said so far, Viola was fighting a losing battle."

It was Hester's turn to nod.

Nadya continued, "I bet it was tough for her."

Hester sighed, looked up to the ceiling for a moment. When she brought her gaze back to Nadya, she straightened her back, and like her companion, leaned forward. With fervor, she caressed Nadya's clasped hands, and felt something—her own mother's spirit maybe—flow through her into Nadya. "In the short time you've been here," she said, "I've come to think of you like a daughter." Hester looked down for a second. "You know I don't have children. And it's too late now."

"I guessed."

Hester liked that Nadya's voice had turned soft and serious, befitting the moment. They made a good team.

The Mojave-Stone needed to get in the hands of the Krisatora—the remaining Cooper representatives in Chicago—without fail. Whether LC wanted to claim his heritage or not, this stone was now a Romani treasure, an heirloom because it had been purchased and belonged for many years to a Cooper—just like with the ugly English stuff around Rhodes Castle. *Heritage stuff.* She thought LC's taste sucked in just about all respects except when it came to the Mojave-Stone. And it belonged to them. The Family. Their Chicago family since Leiv didn't care about it.

After that conversation, and now outside in fresh Mojave morning air, she and Nadya stopped at a teak English garden bench slightly tucked in among an Athol stand on the far side of the circular driveway, and facing the house. "Let's sit for a minute. I'm getting up there you know." In truth Hester seldom experienced an ache or pain of any kind associated with her bones. No arthritis, *knock on wood,* yet. Her mother was physically fit until the day she died—ironically, falling down a flight of basement stairs in Chicago while visiting the Lovels.

"We've agreed, right?" Outside of Rhodes Castle and assured privacy, Hester wanted to make sure their understanding was mutual. "At the first opportunity we have, we'll do it."

"How will we know?" Nadya asked.

"Know?"

"That it's the right time." Nadya leaned in closer, an eager expression on her face.

Hester felt gratified, and wise. *Yes,* she'd known from the very beginning, Nadya was the one. She even felt like reaching over, embracing this woman who was already like a daughter to her.

"Maybe we can do it tonight?" Nadya licked her lips.

Hester gasped slightly. "No, no, not today."

"But it's perfect. He's in the hospital."

She would have to educate Nadya. "Don't you realize? Today is Thursday."

Nadya looked at her like she was speaking a foreign language.

Hester sighed. "It's unlucky to do anything important on Thursday."

"It is?"

"Of course. Everyone knows Thursdays are unlucky."

Andreas disappeared on a Thursday. Her mother had died on a Thursday, and Everett died on a Thursday. You don't go against something like that. Of course LC died on a Tuesday. *Always was a lucky man.*

"Maybe tomorrow," she told Nadya.

Leiv heard Glover say, "You're a darned bit tougher than most think." He knew Shiné's Chief of Police sometimes considered him an effete intellectual. Clearly unsuited to desert life. So his words buoyed him a bit. *But he couldn't be in my room?* He opened his eyes. It *really* was Glover.

"What the heck are you doing here?" Leiv thought his own tone, tenor, and emotionality sounded like a kid. But he was genuinely surprised. In his mind, Shiné's Chief of Police was laid up in Twentynine Palms, just like he was here in Loma Linda. Yet, here Glover was. He tried to sit up, and surprisingly, this time, his body responded. *Too soon. Much too soon for him to be up and about.*

"I escaped," Glover said, plopping down on the side of his bed. "And I'm here to spring you. Our getaway car is waiting outside."

Glover's face said to Leiv he was still in pain—but determined. *An amazing man,* Leiv thought.

And Glover's cavalier sitting-move caused a shot of pain in Leiv's side and down his leg, but he didn't mind. Fortunately his right arm was on the other side of the bed, out of danger. All that mattered was Glover was here, and once again he felt like a kid.

Drugs still.

Glover was smiling wickedly and there was a glint in his eyes Leiv was surprised to see. *A side of Glover new to me?* "But you're a cop." Leiv pointedly eyed Glover's uniform, inferring he thought, he shouldn't be checking out of his own hospital, much less helping him sneak out of this one. It wasn't actually a criminal act, but still.

Glover however, used his uniform to emphasize an opposite perspective. "I'm not just a cop," he pulled his jacket back, to show where he'd prominently attached his badge, "I'm a Chief of Police—"

"In a dink-water town in the middle of the Mojave, almost one-hundred miles from everywhere."

Glover laughed with him, and again Leiv felt like a child on a secret mission, and out of the blue, his grandfather's diary words came to him. *"And seems like mostly I get confused, lose things, or something weird happens on Thursdays."*

"Today is Thursday, right?" Leiv asked.

"Yeah, my lucky day."

"LC thought Thursdays were weird." He didn't try to fill Glover in on all the details. "Glad you think this is a good one."

Shiné's Chief of Police stood up and walked over to the cubbyhole in the room's toilet area, "You have some clothes in here. We need to be fast. Mother's in the car, you can sleep all the way home, and Apply's gonna meet us at Mother's house."

"Sydney and Nadya?"

"They've gotten regular updates on you, I'm told." He scoffed. "Even HM's been worried about you."

Leiv made his legs slide over the edge of the bed. Forced himself to stand up, and finally willed himself to follow Glover to the restroom area. From the air he felt swirling around his body, he figured he still wasn't wearing much of anything under the cotton-thing called a robe hanging on his body. Probably untied.

Quick as he could, and with Glover's steadying hand, Leiv put on clean shorts, clean socks, his jeans, a clean Henley shirt—all thoughtfully and providently provided by someone—he guessed Margaret. "Your mother is wonderful," he mumbled, and thought he heard Glover agree. *Not his style to go mushy about Margaret.* Glover always hit him as what his own mother called "a man's man." Maybe someday he'd get the nerve to ask Glover about Margaret. Particularly, if she was the main reason he was still in Shiné.

"How am I going to get past the nurses' station?"

"The same way you got by them last night and went to see Tucker."

"It was the drugs," Leiv lied while sitting on the edge of the toilet to put his shoes on. "Don't know why there aren't covers on these things." Putting his shoes on didn't turn out to be that hard. "Who told you about me going down to Tucker's room."

"Tucker."

Leiv stopped fooling with his right shoelaces, hard to tie with your arm in a sling, but he hadn't wanted to ask Glover to help. He looked at Glover directly. "You talked to Tucker today? What did he say?"

Once again Glover smiled, accompanied by a childlike twinkle in his eyes. The effect was to transform his face. He said, "Mr. Rhodes is going to make things right."

That stopped Leiv, causing him to sit numbly for a moment, perched on the edge of a hospital toilet, evaluating aspects of his personality and current life at a most inauspicious time. He was in the middle of a "hospital escape" for goodness' sakes. *And sitting on a toilet seat without a cover with Shiné's Chief of Police staring at me.*

"I've committed myself, haven't I?"

Glover sighed, long and heavy, the expression on his face changing dramatically. "You're not alone in this." His voice seemed to have dropped half an octave, and his next words were spoken with the gravitas Leiv was familiar with and expected. "We're going to figure out who killed Naomi, and who killed that dead man on Tucker's property."

The picture of Tucker's field Sunday noonday, Tucker down on the ground, the EMTs and paramedics trying to keep him alive, and most dramatically, the still and eerily quiet pivot watering-arm standing as a monument of some sort to the basic decency of the man he and Glover knew as Tucker Oakes.

"Like I said," Glover broke into his thoughts, "we're going to Mother's. And you and me and Apply are going to lay out everything we have." He cleared his throat and pulled himself up tall. "Then you, Leigh-Everett, are going to go home and think."

Leiv opened his mouth to speak, but decided against it. Indeed, several puzzle pieces had fallen into place. *But am I right?*

"LC would have figured this out. Everett would have figured this out. Now it's your turn."

Out in the hall, a nurse's voice—talking to another nurse it sounded like—stopped their conversation, and sent Leiv back into action getting dressed.

Escape was imminent. After all it was Thursday, Glover's lucky day—and to paraphrase LC, weird things happened on Thursdays.

PART TWO
Moments

Chapter Seven

From LC's journal: *Having a town is good, having to run it ain't so much fun. And not having my Chicago relatives around is nice and peaceful. But not having a big family spread out here and there caring about you is lonely sometimes. Especially when them special times happen. The good and the bad. Contradictions. Can't get away from the darned things.*

Friday

Leiv had to strain to hear Hal's words on his cell phone, but he was fairly certain his friend said, "Got a name for you." It was a surprise hearing from Captain Hal Herman in Chicago at this time of the morning—especially since Hal initiated the call. Regardless of the time, and even with telephone scratchiness, he sure was glad to hear Hal's voice.

"Couldn't let it go, you know," Hal continued.

"You're talking about the tox-screen from awhile back?"

Hal tsked. "That was too disconnected and far out to probably have any meaning. Thailand, Burma, snakes? Couldn't mean anything for you out there in the desert. Far cry from Thailand. Though, I've certainly seen stranger connections." His voice turned excited, "No, I'm talking about your Sydney Collins guy."

Leiv heard himself intake a sharp breath. He knew instinctively Hal was about to give him a peek into Sydney's past—a real "clue," as they said in detective parlance, and he didn't want to take the time to chastise Hal for not caring about the tox-screen. He just said, "What is it? You have a real name, right?" Then Leiv held his breath.

"Anthony."

"Anthony?" Somehow this particular name was anticlimactic. He didn't know what he was expecting—but Anthony wasn't it. He listened further as Hal filled him in on the few particulars he had, which weren't many. Unfortunately, before he could press for more information on this Anthony person, Leiv heard dogs barking on Hal's end, then an exaggerated sigh by Hal, followed by a halfhearted fussing, "Get down off the couch." Finally back speaking to Leiv, he said, "I got to go." But Hal's attention was quickly pulled back to his dogs. "Stop that, how many times do I have to tell you not to do that—" The line went dead.

Slightly annoyed their connection was severed so abruptly, Leiv had to smile. Hal was always fussing at his dogs, but the lack of conviction or real anger in his voice was always there for human and canine to hear. Consequently, Hal's dogs—three at last count and if he remembered correctly—knew they could get away with anything.

I'll call Hal back later.

Leiv wondered what Dobie heard in his voice? He tsked aloud similar to Hal's, and looked over at his dog, sprawled on the west facing cupola window-seat directly across from where he was likewise and quite gingerly sprawled. They were in LC's cupola, and Leiv's legs were stretched out, his shoulders dropped back against cushions, and his arms stretched across the windowsill behind him. Margaret had made him a special concoction at their get together last night, and sent him some home. He took a shot first thing this morning—and found it a quite potent relaxant and pain reliever. He didn't plan on asking her what was in it.

He was expecting Dobie to be asleep. Surprisingly, she was looking at him intently—small pointy ears erect. *Yep*, just like with Hal's dogs, Dobie could probably get away with murder.

Murder. He needed to clear Tucker of murdering Naomi. Yet, something was still wrong whenever he tried thinking about Naomi's death. *A big fat mental clinker*, in the middle of what he thought he'd figured out. He, Margaret, and Glover talked through all the meager facts they had last night. Mostly listening on his part—some, but few new ideas swirling around in his head.

This Friday morning, the cupola as his greet-the-morning spot, Leiv was reminded once more how fond he'd become of taking in Shiné sunrises from this room. Last night—lingering pain, bandages, drugs, and all—he'd been extremely glad to escape from the hospital. With the coming of morning here atop Rhodes Castle, even more so.

Thank you, LC, he mentally whispered across time and space. Over a shorter space and time barrier he sent a, *thank you, Glover,* for helping me escape from the hospital.

Quite suddenly, Leiv's pleasant and maudlin appreciation of his cupola-view of the world felt different. *The first part of this week happened, and everything in my world changed.* Even this special experience. He'd felt that yesterday in the hospital, and now again here at home.

Unsure what to make of this moment of shifting perspective and emotion, or how to put all this week's happenings together: Tucker's attempted suicide, a dead body half buried and straddling Tucker and Naomi's land, somebody trying to kill Glover, then somebody else, or maybe the same person trying to kill him. And underlying all this "figuring out," was the recognition—who he was, why he was here, and what he should be doing—was very important to his mental well being.

This morning's sunrise was strikingly red, with striated streaks of orange, interposed with streaks of blue. Should have been awe inspiring. Indeed, *it is beautiful*—but the reality of the last few days was contrastingly stark, ugly, and evil.

"Jeez," he told Dobie. "What a rollercoaster way to start the morning." Emotionally up, down—all around. *Combined with waddling in self-centered existential soul searching.* "Good grief," he added, and looked over at Dobie again, who oddly enough still seemed to be listening.

Leiv's smile returned. Dobie did that to him—*okay*— evidently this morning was also a moment to reconcile himself to his dog-indulgent side. The humor in that was comforting, even uplifting a bit.

With help from Margaret's concoction, his drug after affects were moving on, allowing him to think about all this mishmash of information with a modicum of clarity. Everything seemed to be hitting him in a blast of bits and pieces of information, some quite inexplicable. Like the fact there was absolutely no one—at least out here in the desert— who had reason to kill *him*. And to think someone had followed him to the desert from Illinois was farfetched.

Leiv got up and walked over to Dobie's piece of the pentagon and sat by his rescued dog. He stretched out as best he could next to her, stroked her on the head a few times, then let his own head drop back, and closed his eyes.

So far since his return to Shiné, he'd mostly only had to deal with HM and her Mojave-Stone shenanigans and machinations.

"The Mojave-Stone."

He felt Dobie move, and when he opened his eyes to look at her, she was tilting her head as if his words meant something. Leiv found himself smiling again, and felt another wave of gratefulness he wasn't still in the hospital.

Indeed, after finally arriving home, *several* administrators called from intensive care in Loma Linda *several* times—very irate, and informing him in no uncertain terms they took no further responsibility for his return to health. "After all, we can't be expected to guarantee your wellbeing when you sneak out of the hospital. And your local doctor is certainly going to hear about your actions."

He wondered if HM had been listening, then found a little further amusement with the thought of Doc Walker receiving a call from Loma Linda, and not knowing what the heck they were talking about. *A hospital escapee, no less.* Visualizing the doctor's face for a few seconds took his mind back to his cardiologist, Doctor Beach back in Illinois—looking at him sternly, advising him to cut back on all the good things in life—like butter, sugar, coffee. None of that seemed very important now. Somehow, Shiné made a difference on his blood pressure, sugar level, and acid reflux. A positive influence.

Always a trade off in life. Where you live, what you do. He stroked Dobie's head some more.

Leiv felt and heard himself move from smiling to a sigh, as another pendulum shift in mood swept over him. This time, he was hit with the reality of sitting atop Rhodes Castle, looking out into his Shiné world with a strong sense of performance anxiety, trying to figure out stuff, using abilities that went beyond anything he'd done in the past. *Or was it?*

He rubbed his arm and touched his side. Neither were as sore as he expected. *I'll live.* "Bloody, but no serious organs or muscles damaged," a doctor whose face he couldn't quite remember, just his words—had explained, "You're a lucky man."

What he was grappling with now was something new. A *fear* he would *never* figure it all out. *Never* figure out who killed Naomi, who killed the body in the field, who attacked Glover, who attacked him. He hoped some synaptic connections were firing away on their own in the recesses of his cognitive brain—further trying to fit the bits and pieces together. Leiv was fearful he might be doomed to fail. *Failure.* Not an experience he was used to, liked, or wanted.

Judge L. E. Rhodes was used to figuring things out. "Judges can't fail." *Lives depended on my success.* He heard Dobie groan next to him, as if she understood.

But I have no courtroom now. No colleagues to call for advice, no assistant, no law libraries, no endless stream of eager law clerks. What was it Glover said? *"Then you, Leigh-Everett, are going to go home and think."* And after that, *"LC would have figured this out. Everett would have figured this out. Now it's your turn."*

He looked down at his hands, highlighted in an odd illumination streaming through the eastern most windowpane. Leiv noticed they were shaking a tad. *Drugs still?* He wanted to blame his sedation and pain drugs even though he knew it was his emotions shaking his hands.

My own fear of failure.

He thought he knew all those times he'd so majestically dispensed justice how defendants, prosecutors, and victims felt. *I hadn't.* Even with Melissa's death. There'd been pain. *But I didn't really know.*

"Hope I'm not disturbing you?" said a voice from his rear, from near the door he must have left ajar.

Damn. He didn't say it, but yes, Sydney was certainly disturbing him. Good manners kept him from sighing yet again. He could no longer indulge in his moments of introspection and self pity.

Leiv stood next to Sydney, looking out the cupola window and talking to his cousin-in-law. Dobie remained stretched out on the window seat between them and the window—but now with her eyes closed and ears relaxed.

"You know, you don't look like a 'Leiv.'" Sydney laughed lightly. "Probably been told that by others. Sure I'm not the first to notice your looks are not exactly Nordic."

Then after only the slightest of pauses, and without any preamble or forewarning, Sydney continued, "You know, my wife was taking pictures of the Mojave-Stone. Think she's planning on stealing it. Claims it's a gypsy thing, which is BS. I happen to know her lineage through her friends at church. She's not even Romani. No, there's no gypsy stealing-hype, prejudice, traditions there. It's all a ruse—my Nadya just wants the money."

Silence for a long moment, this time while Leiv stared at his cousin-in-law in disbelief.

"Don't know why I'm telling you this. But I may end up getting a divorce." Sydney shook his head and looked near tears. "But I loved her so much." He caught his breath. "Still do."

Leiv waited patiently. The pain in Sydney's face was palpable.

"I don't like what she's doing. Not one bit. Don't like how she's duping poor HM who really does care about all that stuff. Who just wants to make sure the Mojave-Stone is not lost to what she sees as her heritage."

Leiv was beginning to internalize what Sydney was telling him, and even with Sydney's obvious pain, Leiv almost laughed out loud. Fortunately he caught himself in time. He was certain HM was the initial ringmaster. Trying to dupe them all. And now Nadya was aiming to dupe HM—with poor Sydney caught in the middle of two connivers.

"I see you're smiling." Sydney didn't sound offended, just curious. "There really is a Mojave-Stone they're trying to steal. They sneaked in your library and looked at it. Handled it."

"Of course there's not a Mojave-Stone," Leiv said. "Fake." He paused for a few seconds waiting for what he just revealed to sink in. "And getting involved in a criminal act is not something you want to be part of. Is it, Anthony?"

Leiv watched as Sydney first sucked in air, then opened his mouth to say something, but clamped it shut.

This time, more than a few silent moments passed.

Finally, pulling himself up straight, Sydney said, "I thought all those records were sealed within the U.S. Marshall's office."

"They are. But one-time Appellate Court judges still have connections." Leiv's tone wasn't boastful, leaning more toward whimsical. Then he smiled, patted Sydney on the back, and reassured, "Not to worry. Your secret is safe with me. I've known others who've gone into the program." *Seen a lot, I guess.*

"Went through a lot of hoops just to get married." Sydney sounded sad and slightly amused at himself. "Getting a divorce is probably going to be hell." He looked directly at Leiv. "Can any of those 'connections' of yours smooth the process out for me?"

"If the time actually comes. Of course." He wondered if Sydney really would divorce his cousin Nadya for any reason. He'd seen those enraptured looks, heard how he talked to her. *The ways of love.* Of course, she just might leave him.

But he could now remove Sydney from the mix of bits and pieces needing sorting out. Similar to removing a clog in a drain, it was all he needed for some big puzzle pieces to flow freely into place.

Without much preamble, Leiv turned and abruptly—given he was walking slowly and with a lopsided lilt—left the cupola, leaving Sydney still staring out the window, and Dobie now snoring. He tried rushing downstairs to LC's library. In passing, he stopped in the kitchen long enough to tell Hester—huddled together at the table with Nadya—no lunch was required, and ask her to take phone messages—he was not to be disturbed. Once said, he didn't hang around long enough to discuss.

Inside his library, Leiv locked the door, grabbed an eye mask from his library stash, snatched an afghan from HM's stack, and ensconced himself in his father Everett's burgundy lounge chair in the corner. It took him a couple moments to get settled-in just the way he wanted, but after a bit, his eyes were closed under his mask, he was stretched out as comfortably as he could, given his injuries—with a thick yellow and orange afghan covering his body from neck to toe.

There Leiv stayed until late afternoon.

HM didn't seem to be anywhere around. *Good. Off scheming with Nadya,* he figured. Nonetheless, he used his cell phone instead of the house landline.

"Glover," Leiv said as soon as Shiné's Chief of Police answered his call, "I need to talk to you, then I need you to get Deputy Temper from Needles over here." Brad was sturdy. Comfortable. Predictable. A perfect sounding board for his thoughts.

"No 'hi', 'how are you,' or 'what 'ya been doing?'"

Leiv didn't joke in turn. "It's important."

Glover cleared his throat. "Is this your Judge Rhodes persona?" There was an edge to his tone. "Speaking royally from the bench?"

"I'm sorry, Dusty," Leiv took a communications step backwards. "I didn't mean to come across like a commander." He covered his cell phone with his hand for a couple seconds, took a deep breath, trying to pull his rushing brain back, and simultaneously calm his desire to take immediate action. "It's just I've finally figured it out."

"Which of the things we were talking about last night did you figure out?"

"Naomi's death."

Glover didn't immediately respond. When he did, his tone was curious yet cautious, "You mean if Tucker killed her?"

"Yes." Leiv wanted to blurt it all out, while simultaneously wanting to explain everything to Glover in person. See Glover's expression as he possibly made a fool of himself. "But I want to tell you face to face."

"Tonight?" Glover now sounded eager rather than skeptical. "Brad is on swing shift for a week. So he's on duty now and will be until late."

"Where are you?"

"At the Police Office."

Despite the fact he was alone, Leiv symbolically straightened his back and inhaled another deep breath. He would not only have to drive himself into town, but he'd have to do it with the prospect of returning in the dark. But he'd started it, now he needed to finish—get the truth about at least one item out. Besides, he'd survived Lookout Loop road, gunshot wounds, and hospital confinement. Driving alone at night no longer seemed quite as intimidating.

"I'm on my way," Leiv said with determination.

Next he called Pastor Lloyd Apply. "He's in a board meeting," a lady's voice Leiv didn't recognize explained.

"Please," Leiv said in a slow, measured, and as calm a voice as he could muster, "please interrupt or slip him a note saying Leigh-Everett Rhodes needs to talk to him right away. It's very important. He has my cell number." He figured using his full name would get Lloyd's attention.

He didn't call Margaret. Guessed she'd known about the whole Naomi-thing for a long time.

Leiv paid no attention to his drive into town, his mind racing through ways of explaining. He didn't notice the time he left Rhodes Castle, but dusk was already falling, not an easy time to drive.

*   *   *   *   *

235

"It was the way Tucker seemed in his field," he started explaining after they were all situated. "Thought it had to be more than just dehydration at work." Leiv was relieved how respectfully interested the three men seemed.

He was sitting across the table from Glover and Brad in the coffee area. Both Glover and the deputy insisted on a fresh pot, and the table became a logical place to talk. However, they had to wait for Lloyd, last to arrive, dressed in what Leiv called "preacher-clothes," and with the explanation a board-member grabbed him after their meeting and hence his lateness. Time was required to pull over Glover's swivel desk chair and squeeze him in at one end of the table.

Leiv continued, "I was going to try to verbally lay my mental process out logically, get to the bottom line the way I'd gotten there." He shook his head and smiled slightly. "But now that the three of you are here. One of you coming a darned long way at night." He nodded an acknowledgement the deputy's way. "I'm not going to drag out the suspense." He folded his hands neatly in front of him on the table, straightened his back, and leaned in slightly. "Naomi Hall committed suicide."

He expected to hear surprise, disagreement, disbelief. But the first to speak was Lloyd, and his tone, as always, was measured and calm. "You know, Leiv, suicide is frowned upon by many religions. You're making a serious accusation."

Leiv smiled at his friend, and said, "Not making a moral judgment. Just a statement of what I think happened." He cleared his throat and thought for a few seconds. "I'll leave the moral sorting out to you—and Margaret." Then Leiv turned his gaze to Deputy Sherman in particular. In his mind, it was the county that needed to know the truth—be convinced Tucker was innocent of this particular crime. *Then the people of Shiné would also believe.*

Glover asked, "Are you going to tell us why you think Naomi intentionally drove her car off a cliff?" his tone was measured.

To his left, Leiv heard Lloyd mumble—talking to himself mostly it sounded like—"Naomi was my cousin, a loyal parishioner. She baked cakes. I'm the executor of her will..." His voice faded.

"Malay Pit Viper venom," Leiv said.

Glover, Brad, and Lloyd proclaimed their surprise almost in unison, Glover adding a short staccato laugh of disbelief. "What?" Then Glover squinted his eyes and peered at Leiv intently. "I don't remember anything like that in the coroner's report?"

"Did they do toxic substance screens?"

"Well," Glover hesitated, "I'll have to look."

Brad joined the fray, "But look, Mr. Rhodes, snake venom is pretty far out." The deputy was in uniform, tan shirt and olive green pants—both perfectly creased.

"You're right, Deputy. I read a little on it, and it's pretty bad stuff. Toxic and destroys blood and tissues. If they exhumed Naomi—"

Lloyd objected, "I won't let them do that."

Leiv didn't let Lloyd's vehemence to what Lloyd probably believed would be defiling Naomi's gravesite stop him. "Bone samples," Leiv continued, "skin scrapings, and whatever else forensics people do." *There's an easier way to know. But no, I'll leave that alone. Leave Margaret out of it, at least for now.* "But we can ask for a panel on Tucker, right?" He looked to Glover, who begrudgingly nodded. "And I bet you a thousand dollars they'll find venom in his system."

"Why Tucker? And you must be pretty sure, Mr. Rhodes," Brad said.

"It's Leiv, Deputy. And I'm sure." *Almost sure.*

"Based on?" Glover demanded in an undemanding tone.

"Based on the facts Naomi has been to Thailand and Burma. With Margaret if you remember? And the bullets and hobnail Penny Perfume Bottle we saw in Naomi's garage."

"What?" Again from the chorus of Glover, Lloyd, and Brad.

Glover's police-cell on his hip rang, and he answered it immediately, while Leiv watched intently as Glover's facial expressions migrated from interest to incredulity. Glover nodded several times, and offered one or two words of agreement, and at the end said, "I'll see what I can find out."

Leiv hadn't ever seen Glover quite as surprised—no, the word he was looking for was amazed. *Who could he possibly be talking to?* With a deep breath, Leiv took the moment to turn his head, look out the glass front window and door, appraise the developing evening. It was now pitch black; he couldn't see a thing except the reflection of them all huddled around the station's modest break-area table. *Conspirators in the night.* Not really, but their reflection brought up that imagery. *La nuit,* as Margaret was fond of saying.

Margaret. He guessed the sly woman, his friend, had intuited, if not known, about Naomi from the start. And it must be paining her tremendously, keeping her knowledge to herself to protect her best friend's reputation, while hoping—probably praying—Tucker wouldn't be blamed much longer.

Having ended his call, Glover absently laid his phone on the table and didn't immediately say anything.

The silence in the room made the next moment even more dramatic as lightening shot across the sky from high in the night sky—and looked like it touched ground inches from the front window. Then horrendous window-shattering thunder slammed them within a couple seconds.

"Holy Hannah," Lloyd exclaimed.

Leiv had never heard the pastor say anything worse, and he thought he saw Brad clamp his mouth shut quickly to hold back words he didn't want the pastor to hear. For a second, Leiv wanted to smile, but his own heart was beating rather fast, and he needed to catch a breath himself.

Glover made a puffing sound out both corners of his mouth, shook his head, and said, "I'll be damned." Then he focused his eyes directly on Leiv. "You really are something." His tone was now kindly and deferential.

Leiv didn't have a clue what he was talking about and waited. Lloyd and Brad seemed to be in the same situation. Waiting. *More lightning and thunder? More revelations?*

Finally, after what felt like minutes—long minutes, Glover said, "That was Doctor Pauly. The one we talked to?" He looked to Leiv who nodded. "The one heading Tucker's team." Leiv nodded again. "He's heading home for the day, but before he left, he wanted to tell me something. Wanted to explain that on his team there is a Dr. Gan—with a last name beginning with S who he said no one at the hospital can pronounce—so he's just called Dr. Gan. He's from Thailand originally, and Pauly claims Gan is the best hematologist he's ever met. Evidently, Dr. Gan had a funny feeling about the swelling and tissue damage in Tucker's throat. He'd seen similar symptoms before."

Glover stopped for a moment, looking like he needed to catch his breath before finishing the retelling of his call. And while he waited, the thought Dr. Pauly had looked nothing like Chef Pauley at TGS flitted through Leiv's mind. *Silliness.*

"Well, upshot is," Glover continued, "they ended up doing blood work on poisons, I guess there's a lot to check for, but anyway—turns out Tucker swallowed a whopping amount of Malay Pit Viper snake venom before he walked out into the sun Sunday afternoon." Glover shook his head in his typical manner. "Seems the whole hospital is talking about it. Pit viper venom of all the weird things. In a patient from Shiné of all places. Gan, it seems is enjoying some fame among his colleagues over this."

Silence filled the office again for another moment before Glover finished, "He also wanted to know if I knew where he'd gotten such an unusual and bizarre poison out in the middle of the Mojave desert?" His eyes were once again boring down on Leiv. "Do *you* know?"

Leiv smiled in the corner of his mouth, sort of like Glover did, he hoped, and said, "I thought you'd never ask."

Another streak of lightning shot across the sky, but not as brightly. The following thunder was not as quick to come. Still, Leiv thought the effect dramatic enough.

"Good grief." Glover moaned. "I need another cup of coffee to get through this." He got up and headed to the coffee maker. "Anyone else?"

Leiv said, "You know, so much came from the little blue bottle."

So startling and dramatic was the lightning strike, Hester and Nadya both physically jumped and exclaimed—almost in unison—then grabbed each other's hand. Dobie, who had insisted on following them didn't seem the least bit concerned.

After deep breaths, both women cursed, then Hester asked, "Do you think that woke up your husband?"

"No, Sydney sleeps like a bear and snores like a pig."

"I know it's late, but it's still a bit early for bed, isn't it."

Nadya made a dismissive sound. "When he goes to bed early—which he does a lot—means he's really tired and will sleep even harder. Probably snore more too."

Hester thought her cousin's comments rather harsh. But that was a good thing. Easier for them to be allies—with Sydney and Leiv as the enemy.

They were now in Leiv's library, standing in the very dark room, in front of his desk. Their only light was the small penlight flashlight Hester was holding, and for the moment—pointing nowhere in particular. The night outside through the clear-paned window in front of them and to the right of Leiv's desk showed nothing, and reflected nothing—except for a tiny bit of light illuminating that stupid chess table. Hester hated that whole setup, particularly because the chess pieces were horrible to dust. Supposedly antique, she dared not just dip them in soapy water. But she didn't know where that little touch of light was coming from.

It's a full moon? Consequently, the lack of a lot of light was strange, and Hester, for a couple seconds, wondered if an unseen hand was trying to stop her progress. The word *betrayal* flashed across her mind for an added second—then was banished. Her card readings needed to be ignored—even though she'd read them *again* this morning, and betrayal had come up *again*.

This was a mission she needed to—had to—accomplish.

Indeed, and regardless of a moon missing in action, and wayward starlight effects, if you looked straight ahead, outside seemed particularly pitch-black; while the inside shadowy darkness produced by Hester's wavering penlight intensified their clandestine atmosphere. Except when the lightning struck—for a millisecond, LC's library became a modern flash-photo of brightness.

Hester would have preferred stained glass windows everywhere. At night, they blocked out most light—*more secretive feeling,* she thought, especially when skulking around Rhodes castle unawares. But tonight, in here, having just the cloak of nighttime would have to do. *Damn lightning.* Too bright, and she hoped there wouldn't be more of it.

Though their need for hand holding had passed, Hester was still taken aback. Not so much because of the lightning, but the thunder rattled her nerves. *Hate loud sounds like that.* Reminded her of the "L" in Chicago when she'd been there. Nonetheless, except for the thunder, the odd light on the chess table, her card reading, and thunder reminders of Chicago and her cousins—things were going well tonight.

Around dusk, Leiv had come to her apartment door, knocked, then told her he was leaving and asked if she would keep an eye on Dobie, but offered no explanation. Especially coming after him secluding himself away in the library all day—tonight's escapade was doubly strange. It was an unusual thing for him to go out at night—and drive himself on top of it. But she was glad, whatever the reason. Meant it was something important and he wouldn't be back for awhile: and she doubted someone was going to try to kill him again.

She would have the house to herself. Not that she wasn't curious about where and why he was going out, knowing nothing trivial would have drawn him out into the darkness; but Hester figured there was plenty of time to find out tomorrow.

Now—*tonight*—was an opportunity she didn't want to miss. *Yep,* the house to herself was too good to pass up.

Tonight they would steal the Mojave-Stone. Sydney didn't matter as a deterrent. In her mind, he was just an annoying fly to be flicked away.

To accomplish her end goal, Hester boldly let herself into the Rhodes sacred library sanctum with her passkey. Then with Nadya and Dobie inches behind her, and penlight in hand, she'd strode directly to his desk and shone her light on the ridiculous rock relief André, LC's youngest son and Nadya's father, had created as a young boy.

"That's supposed to be the tree of life, or some such nonsense your father heard in school." Ugly and stupid, in her opinion. But André had died an untimely death, so she'd never verbally made her dislike known. He was Nadya's father after all.

"Rest his soul," Nadya said, "but that *is* really ugly."

Hester's heart sang. *This woman is truly my soul mate. My spiritual daughter.*

Nadya must have realized her words about her father's creation might have been a little harsh, even for her. "Of course he was only a kid," she amended. Still, Nadya seemingly couldn't help adding, "But those rocks are *really* ugly."

"But wait until you see the 'rock' inside the safe." Hester felt her chest swell with anticipation. "The thingy André did is on hinges. Soon it will be ours." She felt for the safe's key; it was hanging around her neck where it should be. "Do you have the fake replacement?"

"Yes, here in my hand."

What a glorious moment.

*   *   *   *   *

Indeed, Leiv was very pleased with Dr. Pauly's blood test results. His conjectures were becoming more plausible. Consequently, Leiv waited for a moment, reordering his thoughts, making sure he laid it out right—and remembering that day in "Le Bric-à-Brac," more as a flash of color and emotion, rather than a saunter down memory lane. It was then and there with Mary Jones some puzzle pieces began to flicker into the realm of plausibility. Farfetched-sounding even now, though true, he was sure.

In this briefest flash of memory, with Glover and Brad staring at him expectantly, Leiv could see Mary Jones as clear as on that day in her shop. He'd been to her shop several times before, and liked bantering with her—though he suspected she took their exchanges far more seriously than he. In answer to his pseudo-philosophical and idle comment about the past and how objects can carry "it" on into the future, Mary Jones had said, "We're only here on earth for a millisecond of a millisecond in time."

He'd watched almost mesmerized as she lifted the little crater-pocked blue bottle into the air—letting what seemed like a stream of wayward sunlight find its way from her storefront glass window, then seemingly bounce around her shop helter-skelter—yet able to laser in on the little bottle she was holding high, pass through its thick glass, then bend as light does, into what looked like multi-colored sparkles. "Hobnail Penny perfume bottle I think," Mary had said.

An amazing moment.

Being pulled back to that time now, thinking about what occurred, Leiv realized he'd been captivated by her words and motions from the moment he'd entered "Le Bric-à-Brac."

"I've seen one just like it," Leiv had said. "Is the one you're holding part of a set?"

244

She smiled, and her eyes twinkled in a knowing way. "Naomi." Almost immediately, her intelligent looking face had clouded over. "She was a special woman." Mary had put the bottle back down on the highly polished surface of an Edwardian looking hutch-sideboard, with a mirrored back.

Pulling himself back from those moments in "Le Bric-à-Brac," Leiv brought all his attention to explaining what he thought to Glover, Lloyd, and Brad. "It was sitting right there on Naomi's workshop table," he said. "Well, more like a shelf in her garage." He paused, again, this time feeling his face warm—knowing all eyes were on him—expectant. "And haven't you wondered how we just happened to 'find' a dead body laying around in the desert?"

"Haven't had time to," Glover said, and waved his hand. "And go on, go on. I was there in the garage with you, remember?"

Brad, evidently processing everything he'd heard earlier, and now rushing ahead, mumbled more to himself than the others. "He was the husband of her shrink. I'm betting Martin Potter has a sizable life insurance policy."

Leiv let a few seconds pass. Allowing Brad's conjectures, sink in. *Maybe Lloyd and Glover needed a nudge on that one.* He'd come back around again to the Tonia, Martin, and Naomi connection after finishing about the antique bottle.

"Well," Leiv said, leaning in closer to Glover, willing him to visualize what he was remembering, "do you remember that ornate looking antique bottle I held up?" And with eyes still on Glover, he asked in an aside to Lloyd, "And you knew Naomi was seeing a shrink right before she died."

"Yeah," Glover said.

And Lloyd followed suit with, "Yes."

"Well, the bottle reminded me of some of the doodads Mary Jones carries down at 'Le Bric-à-Brac.'"

"And?" Impatience was edging its way into Glover's voice.

Once again Lloyd echoed Glover, "Exactly my sentiment. *And?*"

Leiv sighed, "If you want to know how I got there, you're just going to have to be patient and let me tell the story."

"Okay, okay," Glover said, gestured with his hand, and dropped back against the slats of his office-issue wooden chair. "Just hurry it up, will ya?" he glanced quickly from Brad to Lloyd, then crossed his arms over his chest. "We're waiting."

Deputy Sherman and Pastor Apply nodded their agreement.

Leiv allowed himself a little chuckle. And despite the serious issue at hand, he realized, quite suddenly and dramatically, how much better "this" was than all the seemingly endless hours arguing, bargaining, critiquing, reasoning, and politicking he'd done in his various judicial chambers over the years.

"I'm glad I came back to Shiné," Leiv heard himself say—and was shocked he had. "Sorry, about that," he quickly added. "Don't know where that came from."

Embarrassed, he looked out the front window for a second. Ink blank. No lightning.

Mentally back on track, Leiv said, "What I asked myself—well, what my subconscious asked itself—was why such a special little bottle?"

"Not much," Brad murmured.

"Yeah, not much," Leiv agreed. "But, Deputy Sherman—I mean, Brad—you weren't there to see its place in the scheme of things."

Glover sat up straighter, his demeanor seeming like he was a little more interested. "That's true Brad. Naomi's garage was not a pristine place. Mostly tools and screws were thrown in old coffee cans, cheap plastic tubs." He tilted his head a tad, and again eyed Leiv quizzically. "So now I see how that mind of yours works. I should have seen it too. That little bottle stood out, should have caught my attention. But—"

Leiv held his hand up, "You want to know, how did I find out what was in it?"

"Yep."

"I went back, stole that bottle in Naomi's garage and replaced it with another one—the one I looked at and purchased from Mary."

"You stole evidence?" Brad's voice wasn't clear on whether this was a "good thing" or a "bad thing."

Glover added, "And from under my nose." Glover's opinion wasn't clear to Leiv either.

"Well, not really evidence, and not from under your nose," Leiv said, mostly looking at Glover. "By the time of my 'appropriation,' Naomi's garage wasn't of interest to anyone anymore. Wasn't still a possible crime scene. Don't think it ever really was. What I did was just a common, misdemeanor theft. Don't you think? And it did have an 'x' on the bottom of it. Needed to know for poison control reasons, right?"

Brad tsked, but Glover asked, "But why such heightened interest all of a sudden?"

"Your mother reminded me she and Naomi had gone to Thailand."

"And from that you went to Malayan Pit Viper venom?" Glover appeared at a loss for a new way to express his incredulity—first he tsked, then he sighed, then he shook his head—finally, he rolled his eyes to the ceiling. "Unbelievable."

"Well, that wasn't exactly it." Leiv sighed himself. "To tell you the truth, I thought it was some kind of Asian drug that Naomi was hiding in plain sight. That she was using it recreationally—"

"And this recreational drug would cause her to poison herself and drive off Lookout Loop Road?" Lloyd finished for him. "How could you think that of Naomi?" He seemed genuinely surprised at Leiv's suspicion and actions. "This is a side of you that's new to me."

"Maybe one Saturday night we can go down my devious-side over a glass of Sherry—"

"You know Naomi so believed in right and wrong. Morality. Justice." Lloyd insisted, but more to himself, and now *sotto voce*.

"But that's the key, Lloyd, don't you see?" Leiv so wanted his friend to look into his eyes, see into his mind, understand what he understood. "As you say, Naomi believed in justice. Accountability. Right?"

Lloyd nodded sadly.

"And she just couldn't live with the guilt of having killed Andreas Herne. You do remember the bullets in Naomi's garage I mentioned earlier?"

Margaret was enjoying the night. From inside. Of course, thunder and lightning scared Samara and Silky witless. Even inside, behind her thick log walls, her cats wanted to be under her protection during the infrequent Shiné storms—either in her lap, or somewhere extremely close. Tonight she was indulging them, cuddling them, a knitted shawl covering their bodies, only their heads peeking out.

248

"Spoiled," she told them. Actually, she knew her current protective interaction with her cats was a matter of indulging herself. She liked seeing lightning slash across the sky, even from inside, and especially dramatic bolts like these—going from one corner of the sky across the horizon to the ground in a instant. And the colors. Blue was it? Or yellow? Both?

She closed her eyes, trying to bring the first bolt back into her mind's eye. "I'll protect you, sweetums. I'll never tell anyone you're such scaredy-cats," she soothed her pampered felines.

Exactly her words to her dearest of friends, Naomi. *I'll never tell.*

Other than her talking to her cats, her log house was silent. It was a silence, like her solitude, Margaret had not only become used to—but cherished. And living in virtually one-big-room seemed to enhance the experience of being surrounded by "silent-sound." So easy to let her thoughts flow, her mind meander.

And unfortunately, so easy to revisit the past. The loss of her very best friend in the world. Naomi Hall.

"One day soon," she informed her kittens, her log home, and the silence, "I'll have to tell Leiv the truth about Naomi committing suicide." He could tell the authorities. *Yes,* he'd been a judge, Leiv would know how to handle something like this.

She hadn't told Glover what she knew about Naomi, and she'd lied to Naomi about Glover's father. The pain of betrayal from both ends stabbed at her heart.

Another streak of lightning and pounding of thunder—both cats yowled. Margaret didn't physically jump, but her thoughts did jump back in years. To a night in Chicago many years earlier, to a faculty party, to a handsome and oh so dashing guest, to an indiscretion she'd never forget. A guest especially intriguing because his father started a town in California's Mojave Desert. Unimaginable to a young city girl like herself.

Oh, to be young and foolish again.

In the distance, she thought she heard the Burlington Northern, or was it the Union Pacific, lumbering through what was turning out to be a thick, black, and ominous night? Fancifully, Margaret wondered what it must be like to be a train engineer, speeding along the tracks and seeing a vast desert world in front of you—illuminated by slashes of lightning.

Leiv thought of Edward Hopper again. How they must look from the outside to a photographer or painter's eye. Looking through the office windows at a brightly lit room, four men, various ages and styles, huddled around an old wooden table in the corner. Planning, scheming, solving world problems? He wondered, and had to fight back the urge to get up, go outside, and look back in at his friends.

"Okay," Glover was saying, "you've dragged us all together, dropped some bombshells, which I'm not sure yet all fit together. So what is it again that you think happened with Naomi, Andreas Herne, Tucker, and my mother?"

Clearly surprised, Brad said, "The Margaret you're talking about is your mother? Maybe you said, but it didn't register."

"It's a complicated web I've woven," Leiv enigmatically answered Brad. After a deep breath, he leaned back in his chair like Glover, but not as cavalierly. *Don't have his sense of savoir faire.* Before Leiv next spoke, he took the time to look into each man's eyes directly. Brad's were the most skeptical he thought.

Finally he said, "Here's what I think in a nutshell." *Well not exactly, but close enough.* No, he was a long way from the bench tonight. He could lie a bit. "Naomi, accidently, I think, shot and killed Andreas. If I had to build a scenario, I'd say it was late at night, he was trespassing, and she planned to send a warning shot, but that warning shot turned out to be lethal. Can't be sure of that of course, but that's how I'm guessing it happened."

Therein was the lie part. Leiv was pretty sure Naomi shot Andreas meaning to do it. Probably thought it was Tucker—*no love lost there.* Much more fitting to her character than fearing a walking intruder on her property. And she had a .22 rifle just like Tucker. *Naomi was not a woman to be either trifled with or harassed.* He'd heard Margaret voice that thought more than once.

He saw Glover open his mouth as if to offer a comment, but he held up his hand and said, "Just hear me out first, okay?"

Glover nodded.

"Then she buried him. On the edge of her property. Doubt if she meant to point a finger at Tucker." *Another lie.*

Brad said, "I've often said, there's a whole lot of bodies buried in the Mojave we'll never find."

"Probably what Naomi thought, too." Now that Leiv was getting into his supposition story, he felt more comfortable with where the facts had led him. "But then," he nodded toward Lloyd, "being the moral woman she was, Naomi's conscience began to nag at her."

"Just let me make sure I have this right." Leiv heard a loud note of incredulity still in Glover's tone of voice, but mostly he heard amazement.

Glover proceeded to tick off items starting with the thumb of his left hand. "I'll go in chronological order. Maybe that will help the 'dumb cop' keep things in order."

"You don't have to be rude." Leiv interrupted. He'd thought he'd made an effort not to be condescending the whole night. Then he thought he caught a held back smile from the slight twitches in the corners of Glover's mouth. Leiv shut up.

"As I was saying, first, Naomi accidently kills a stranger."

Leiv nodded, and looking at Brad and Lloyd, saw they were all starting in the same place.

Glover continued, "*Then* she buries the body, *then* foolishly tells her shrink about it. A shrink who's in league with her husband to plot his disappearance." Glover laughed. "It's like a TV plot in little ole Shiné." His face reflected his incredulity in flashing lights. "Then Naomi felt so bad about it she kills herself?" In an instant, his expression became sour, then angry. He looked like he was about to slam his fist on their little break-room table, but caught himself. "You know what you're saying, right?"

Leiv nodded.

Glover's voice turned hard. "Those two, Martin and Tonia Potter tried killing both of us. Several times. And for what? Money?" He cursed.

Lloyd, evidently ignoring Glover's profanity, said, "That's a lot of speculation."

Glover continued, "The Potters decided to use the body Naomi told them about for an insurance scam, then tried to stop us from figuring it out."

"I believe," Leiv added softly, "Martin passed us on a motorcycle and was in the house the morning we went to Apple Valley. And after hearing what we were telling his wife—especially the part about DNA testing—they got together and decided to stop us then and there. Probably that very morning." He paused for a moment before adding, "Officer Martin was the name he gave me, remember?"

And I did hear a woman's voice up at Lookout Loop. Tonia Potter's voice most likely.

It was Lloyd's turn to shake his head. "Why didn't Naomi just go confess to a priest or something, or tell me. Why tell her therapist?" He pushed his glasses up against the bridge of his nose. "And aren't they supposed to tell the police if a patient kills someone? They were double bad." Amazement at the moral depravity of people was clear in his tone of voice and expression.

It is amazing, Leiv thought hearing it recited by Glover. Not that things like this didn't happen all the time. He'd presided over far more convoluted and nefarious crimes. And this one, they'd figured out without a bunch of legal-beagles sticking their noses into it—often muddying the waters.

Glover was on the same wave length. "What's really amazing is we figured it out."

"We?" Brad said straightening his body. And looking pointedly at Leiv.

Glover and Lloyd followed suit, and stared at Leiv for a moment.

Leiv felt an emotion he'd never experienced before. He couldn't put a name to it, or exactly explain the wherefore and why—all he knew was it felt darned good. *Quite a moment,* he thought. *Thank you, LC*—he sent a silent thank you across the dimensions of time—*for calling me home to Shiné.*

Chapter Eight

From LC's journal: *If you're talking about the 10 commandments, there's only four big ones in my mind—go to church, pay respect to your mother and father, don't kill nobody that don't deserve it, and don't steal or be envious of what other travelers have. That being said, there's always exceptions...*

Saturday

Library won over cupola, and after everything he'd experienced this last week, Leiv came to understand intensely, and with added appreciation this particular Saturday morning—sunrises over Shiné were a big part of his salvation.

The infinitely variable splashes of saturated reds, lightly brushed pale yellows, and watercolor washed misty blues—sometimes building slowly, while other times appearing fully formed it seemed, and spreading as they did across what seemed like an endless horizon—were darned near inspirational. Not a term Leiv used often, or easily. A feeling intensified by the perception the sunrise surrounded him, indeed, surrounded the whole Shiné valley.

Then there was that beautiful orange-touching-on-tangerine sunset Tuesday morning. *A lifetime ago.*

Consequently, today was quite special, and acutely meaningful. He'd survived. And having survived a brush with death gave a new and powerful import to Shiné sunrises.

Yes, I survived. Being a judge and being a victim.

Immediately, Leiv wanted to share his enhanced appreciation, trek his secret little hike up to LC's lair, pull out his grandfather's real journal, touch it, be reassured, be connected. But though his injuries were called "flesh wounds," and his arm and side were getting better fast—Leiv still thought he better not "push it." Going back into the hospital was not something he relished.

In lieu of LC's lair, he walked over gingerly and stretched out in the leather armchair tucked away in the farthest corner of the library. The same dark burgundy one he'd cocooned himself in to think. Oddly, even though its leather upholstery was soft, and its padding comfortable, Leiv seldom used this chair, usually preferring to sit in LC's desk chair and connect across the years with LC's fake diary. *Maybe I should change.*

Once ensconced in his father's chair, his legs stretched out on the ottoman, it felt "right." Leiv consciously relaxed his legs, and let his head drop back into the chair's accepting headrest. It was not a traditional yoga "Corpse Pose," but Leiv still mentally started moving through his muscles, relaxing as he could—within minutes he felt himself drift off to sleep for a mid-morning nap—and vaguely hearing Dobie snoring rhythmically from her favored spot in front of the library door.

My body needs to heal was his last thought before sleep overtook him.

*   *   *   *   *

It was a wonderful morning for Hester. The Mojave-Stone was safely in Nadya's hands, and would be in Chicago in days. Leiv had made some rumblings about taking Sydney and Nadya to Kelso Station and Amboy, now that he was out of the hospital. Thankfully Nadya said something had come up at home and they needed to get back to Chicago via Vegas tomorrow.

Sydney had remained oddly silent, and Hester thought the look on his face rather curious. But she didn't care about him. It was Nadya who would be her legacy. Indeed, she and Nadya spent most of the morning further strategizing in the kitchen—who to hand the opal over to, when, where, and how. Sydney would have to fend for himself.

Eventually Nadya went looking for her husband, leaving Hester to bask in what she considered a stellar success. The Mojave-Stone would soon be in proper and caring hands. So complete and pleasant were her reveries, Hester was caught off guard when around noon a small package was delivered for Leiv by UPS. Usually, she would have heard the truck making the turn into the driveway, and usually Dobie barked.

"Dumb dog's probably in the library with clueless Leiv," she grumbled, hurrying from the kitchen to the front double-doors, wanting to be there before Leiv. He seemed to be nowhere in sight, so Hester talked to the driver for several minutes. Not only did she like Herman, but he was supposedly a cousin of a cousin—a tenuous connection—but deserving a modicum of respect.

Once back in Rhodes Castle's kitchen with a package clearly addressed to her employer, Hester carefully opened it,

257

read the letter, and examined the enclosed item — which she thought stupid-looking and inconsequential. The letter however, was of interest. She resealed the package and put it on Leiv's desk in the library; though she'd almost walked out to the garbage-tip and thrown it away, deciding at the last minute not to. *Can't stop fate.*

In truth, the Mojave-Stone was safe, she didn't much care about anything else this beautiful Saturday morning. *Well, almost nothing else.*

Leiv woke up around noon from a stressful dream of trying to hike over a sand dune and constantly sinking into the sand. Once he shook off the distasteful dream — including physically shaking his head and making a repulsive shiver — he remembered Lloyd had organized a community prayer service for Tucker. *Oh no, was it this morning? No,* it was Sunday, and he blew out a breath of relief.

Even though Leiv was sure Tucker would be cleared of Naomi's murder, he was still on his mind in a nagging sort of way. Nonetheless, he didn't want to wait until whatever was still worrying him about Tucker popped onto the frontline in his brain; but he didn't see any option but to just wait. Maybe it was worry over Tucker's health? He was stable, but not well yet.

Leiv decided he would go see him tomorrow, and wondered if Glover was going, too? The Chief could pick him up — *No,* he stopped himself. *I'll drive myself.* Sunday morning, traffic would be light.

Tonight would be his traditional get-together time. He, Lloyd, and Margaret. Leiv caught himself again for a moment, wondering if it would be appropriate to get together since

Tucker was still in the hospital? And should he also ask Glover over this time? They'd been through a lot together this week.

Further, what about Nadya and Sydney? He hadn't been much of a host this week. He made a mental note to thank HM for entertaining and shepherding his cousin. *While Glover and I got shot.* He laughed at the bizarre nature of the week's happenings for a long moment.

After a bit, Leiv looked over at the door, and Dobie was staring back at him. So he asked his Doberman friend her opinion on his Saturday night entertaining options, and several other items still rattling around in his brain.

Leiv unconsciously fingered the lapel of his smoking jacket as he experienced the moments in his withdrawing-room Saturday night. He ended up inviting Sydney who'd declined with some nonsense about needing to help Nadya finish packing. Glover accepted and had now slid down into his armchair across from his mother Margaret and closed his eyes. Asleep or not, Leiv didn't know.

As for Lloyd sitting next to him, Leiv guessed he was about to say something thoughtful, maybe provocative even, and prepared to smile in anticipation. A quick glance over at Margaret sitting on the loveseat revealed she *was* smiling. A smile he interpreted as also "waiting in pleasant anticipation." Like him, Margaret was most probably expecting from the pastor, his usual Shiné-style *bon mots,* or philosophical insights, or some parabolic tales of wisdom.

Leiv realized he was now smiling, Maybe Lloyd would grace them with a Saturday night sermon? *Especially since tomorrow was a special "thing."* Leiv chastised himself lightly for calling a prayer meeting a "thing." However, his smile didn't fade, and somewhere inside his being he felt happy. An emotion he hadn't experienced in a very long time.

"And what the hell has happened to the Ten Commandments, for goodness' sake?" Lloyd said with emphasis, and laced with his characteristic tone of wonderment.

"If you're talking about a proposed sermon," Margaret said, "you might want to omit the profanity."

"Hell isn't profanity," he protested, "if used correctly."

The Ten Commandments? Certainly not what he'd expected from Lloyd. Another quick glance at Margaret's face said she hadn't either.

Extremely odd Lloyd was bringing them up. Leiv's thoughts flashed to his own little two-sided Ten Commandment stone-tablet plaque, with its gold-plated stand. It had adorned a spot on the credenza in his last courtroom chambers for several years. Then the package arriving today, and now Lloyd mentioning the Ten Commandments out of the blue. *Yes, very odd.* Lloyd couldn't have known unless HM told him. Leiv knew she opened everything. *Part of her charm,* he joked with himself.

The tablet-plaque was a present from a Court-recorder—back in the day. *Jeffrey.* Funny, he could still see Jeffrey leaning across his oversized desk in the small chambers-room, confiding he'd found it at a flea market. Leiv had bequeathed it to his successor as a welcome to the bench present. His predecessor had died suddenly, the accompanying note said; a heart attack. Evidently prompting the AG to send it back to him—with a most surprising, and disturbing letter.

Letter and plaque, both now sitting on his library desk.

And here Lloyd was, talking about the Ten Commandments. *Why, for heaven's sake?* Leiv felt a tingle in the bottom of his stomach.

Even stranger, in that moment of banter between friends, it felt to Leiv like a stage curtain had dropped—a scene change in a play. But *no*, it was still the four of them, in their regular places, in LC's "stone monument" dominated parlor, on a Shiné Saturday night.

But something has changed. He looked over to Glover as if his friend would explain it all. But his eyes were still closed. *Asleep, no doubt.* He wouldn't hassle him, Glover's injuries had been far more serious than his.

Silence ensued for several moments. Leiv closed his eyes like Glover, then quite surprisingly, the next thing he heard Margaret say was, "It's just too sad." Even more unbelievably, he opened his eyes and saw Margaret swiping a tear from her cheek. And Lloyd was shaking his head in agreement.

"We never really knew the man." Margaret took a deep breath. "Georgie and Naomi, sweet wonderful people they were—at least they have us to grieve for them." She took another breath. "He's unknown with no one to grieve for him."

Leiv tried to mentally jump to where they were. *What was sad?*

"Of course," Lloyd said, and looking at him, "you've probably seen a lot of that in your time on the bench." Before Leiv could answer, his friend clarified, "Pain and heartbreak, that is."

"You're talking about?"

Margaret asked, "The body buried in the desert. If it wasn't Martin Potter, then who was it?"

Lloyd looked away and Leiv guessed Margaret already knew Naomi shot Andreas Herne on purpose. She was trying to find out what he knew, but Leiv looked away too.

Hester couldn't believe she was crying. So far this had been the happiest day in her life—then out of nowhere, pain, grief, sorrow—all slammed her at once. Poor Andreas, her one and only love. Probably the one in that grave. Probably killed by Kizzy Lovel, Bersch's sister. *Evil, evil, Kizzy.*

And no one to know, no one to mourn Andreas but her. So so sad.

At least we have the Mojave-Stone.

Several long moments passed before from yet another hidden spot in Leiv's psyche, a stream of pictures, memories, emotions from his previous life as a judge—flooded and captured him. Finally, his surprise ball of emotion moved on, and he thought, *I'm glad I left. The Midwest and the law.* The past passing on? He sure hoped so. "Sorry," he mumbled. "Got caught in my own thoughts."

"No problem," Lloyd said, his tone mirroring his.

Margaret finished the chorus, "Me, too. Memories." Her eyes were riveted on the fireplace.

Glover opened his eyes and said, "You know they're trying to get DNA from the body buried in the desert. Would be funny if it really was the gypsy HM said went missing." Then Glover stretched, smiled, and said in a tone Leiv wasn't used to hearing his friend use, "Thanks for inviting me." Glover smiled. "But I must tell you, that stone thing in the middle of your fireplace is really ugly. Almost as bad as the one over your desk."

Everybody laughed. Music to Leiv's ears.

Chapter Nine

From LC's journal: *Yep, I saw to the tavern. And Viola saw to the church. Even the altar was her idea. She's got the smartness in the family alright.*

Sunday once more

Once again wide awake in predawn hours, Ida Oakes went straight from her bedroom to floating in the warm watery arms of her lap pool. *It's true*, she reflected, the water held her safe, cupped almost like a hand to protect against the outside ravages of reality. Here she was good, right, and safe.

It was Sunday, a week since Tucker went loony-tunes and tried to kill himself. Occasionally she felt guilty about that—*could have talked to him more*. But how did she know he'd try to kill himself?

Thank goodness for Judge Rhodes. She'd already heard on the Shiné grapevine he figured it all out—well Tucker's part at least. So when her husband came home, Tucker would be able to leave all that guilt crap behind him. Enjoy life with her and Calvin.

And yes, he would be coming home. Soon she thought. Hell, they hadn't kept the Chief and Judge Rhodes in the hospital long—and they'd both been shot. The words from Loma Linda this morning when she'd called were, "Doctor is much more optimistic. The venom treatment is working."

Snake poison of all things. She could barely wrap her mind around it all. Chief Deers had patiently explained it to her though. Twice. *Nice man.* And easy to look at. If her face wasn't turned down in water, Ida would have smiled.

On top of that, a prayer meeting today for Tucker. She couldn't ask for more. Though she didn't actually believe in God—covering all your bases was a good idea.

Ida expected they would all be there. Rhodes, Deers—and Calvin of course.

Cupola or library? As usual, it was Leiv's ritual morning decision. Experience the sunrise from his open pentagon to the world, always appealing on a Sunday morning; or from his comfortable and richly adorned library—*this morning in particular*—a good place to continue his good feeling from last night. As always, both spots would be easy for him to connect to LC across the years. Health wise, Leiv felt much stronger, but still not quite up to walking back to his grandfather's hillside secret hidey-hole—the third and best place.

This morning he chose the library, preferring a connection not only to his grandfather, but also to his father, Everett—and several thousand law books.

All bringing him quite firmly to the conclusion, *yes,* he was Leigh-Everett Rhodes, a Rhodes descendant, on Rhodes property, and determined to carry on LC's desire to move past being a Cooper and fulfilling Viola's grand design for a "special little desert town."

Viola's vision, besides insisting on the layout of Shiné, and insisting there needed to be a church, a tavern, a restaurant, a gas station, and some kind of specialty shop to be a "proper town." It was Viola who also insisted on the handling of the Mojave-Stones.

LC had the vision, but Viola made it happen.

This morning, as Leiv had so often sent a thankful message across the universe to his grandfather, LC, he took the time to send a special note of gratitude to his grandmother.

Thank you, Viola. He would keep their secrets safe.

A knock on his library door woke Dobie up, and caused him to sigh. "Come in," he said absently.

De ja vu, Sydney was again breaking into his reverie— standing next to Dobie in the threshold of the library's open door. Leiv forced down a sigh, stood up, and asked in a congenial, "What can I do for you, Sydney?"

His cousin-in-law, a rather wistful cast to his features, came farther into the library and walked over to Leiv's plain glass window-to-the-world. "I'm going to miss Rhodes Castle," he said, his back to Leiv. "Especially this view, and the one up high in the five-sided room."

In some ways, he and Sydney were simpatico, he thought anew.

"And I wanted you to know Nadya and HM have done the deed." Sydney turned his back on another beautiful Shiné morning, straightened his stance, took a deep breath, and looked at Leiv. "They've stolen your fake Mojave-Stone," he said, and glanced at the safe behind Leiv for a second. "My wife is taking it back to Chicago."

Leiv opened his mouth to speak, but Sydney held up his hand, asking for more time to talk. "HM thinks she's taking it to some big gypsy clan honcho, but I know Nadya plans on stealing it for herself." He sighed wearily.

And probably leaving you in the process, Leiv speculated with more certainty this time. "I wouldn't worry about the stone." *Poor Sydney.* It was still written on his face how much he loved Nadya.

Silence fell while Sydney cocked his head and made a curious face before finally smiling, and saying, "I should have known you and your grandfather are much smarter than HM thinks you are."

Leiv smiled in return and made a gesture with two opened hands.

Sydney shook his head and chuckled a little more. He said, "Nadya and I are heading out in a few minutes, and I wanted to say thank you and goodbye for both of us."

Leiv stood up. "I'll walk you out." He was sorry to see Sydney go. Nadya not so much, though he really hadn't had time to get to revisit with her. Knowing she was a thief was not endearing. Still, he said, "I wish we'd had more time—"

Sydney laughed. "Your friend and you almost got killed, for Pete's sake."

"Well, there is that." Leiv came around the desk and extended his hand. After the two men shook hands, Leiv said, "Let's go see the ladies and get you on the road."

"Still have a little more packing to do."

"I'll come down in maybe half an hour?" Then he remembered his Aunt and other cousin. "What about Mary and Kate? Does Nadya plan on bailing on them?"

"I don't know about Mother Mary and Katey." Sydney

paused for a few seconds, as if he wanted to add something. Instead, he just agreed, "Perfect on the timing. Yours that is." Then without preamble, he asked, "There really isn't a Mojave-Stone, is there?"

"Of course not," Leiv answered as always, without hesitation, and with nary a second thought.

After Sydney left to finish packing, Leiv sat back down, and Dobie, returning her allegiance to Leiv, nonchalantly came over and laid down at his chair's side.

"Not by the door?"

She woofed once, put her head down, and closed her eyes.

Leiv again found a smile spreading across his face. Not just over Dobie's actions, but thinking about the Mojave-Stones.

He hadn't really lied to Sydney, he rationalized. There was not *"A"* Mojave-Stone. There were *five:* One rather large one in the center of Shiné Community Church's huge altar, one over the tavern bar wall at TGS, one in the center of André's ugly collage behind and above Leiv where he was now sitting, one over Rhodes Castle withdrawing room's massive fireplace, and one over the inside threshold above Rhodes castle's stained glass entry doors.

Indeed, LC himself often slipped up and said *stones*— in both his journals.

Funny about HM and Nadya, he thought, then after a few seconds added, *and rather tragic.* He shook his head at HM stealing and replacing the fake Mojave-Stone in the safe behind him with another fake. While disparaging the real one staring back at her. He knew she hated André's creation. *Dear,*

dear, HM.

Thinking about HM—who emphatically stated she wasn't going inside any church no matter who they were praying for—reminded Leiv, the prayer service was beginning within the hour.

Nonetheless, Leiv took a few more moments to marvel at his grandfather's "smartness" in recognizing a hand full of rocks were precious Mexican fire opals, and his willingness to take a chance. Most of all, Leiv marveled and heralded Viola's "smartness" and unabashed audacity to hide such precious gems in-plain-sight.

He looked over at his ten commandment plaque seemingly staring back at him, and his hand unconsciously went down to pat Dobie on the head. He couldn't quite reach the top of her head, but the action brought out clearly how much he liked the darned mutt. *Like her a lot.*

Then Leiv pulled out from his top drawer the letter that came with his plaque. A letter from the Illinois Governor asking him to return. Asking him if he was interested in the bench again. This time, on the Illinois Supreme Court. What he'd thought when first reading the offer yesterday was—what a hard decision. Now the answer was so easy.

What he had loved, and still loved with all his heart were Melissa and the judicial process. He could not abandon those loves—ever. But he certainly should be able to figure a way to work around them. Right here in Shiné.

No, he hadn't run back home. LC's legacies had called him.

Called me back to Shiné.

From the front row, as he took in and settled into the

church service, Leiv remembered both Lloyd's words from last night, and his little plaque. *"And what the hell has happened to the Ten Commandments, for goodness' sake?"* Leiv couldn't take his eyes off the altar, or pull his thoughts from Lloyd and his plaque. Maybe he should have a larger version of it produced for Lloyd's altar? Then there was one of the Mojave-Stones, right in plain sight. A monument to wit, intelligence, sneakiness, and hubris. He made himself not stare at it.

Everyone was seated, but they were waiting for Pastor Lloyd Apply to begin. He was still walking around shaking parishioners' hands. It was a big crowd, considering Shiné's actual population wasn't very large. Evidently a wide swatch of desert dwellers had taken the time to come and pray for Tucker.

Leiv's own visits to Shiné Community Church were few, so he didn't often have time to just take-in this altar. Indeed, remembering back to the actual altar-event as described by LC, it wouldn't have happened without some timely intervention from Viola; soothing some hot and tired haulers trying to get the behemoth-of-an-altar placed just right. *They did well*—Leiv acknowledged without staring at it now. LC, Viola, and all the workers involved had accomplished quite a feat. Especially the front fresco scene stone craftsmen. As for the center piece stones, knowing what he did about the Mojave-Stone, Leiv would have smiled broadly if it were a different occasion.

His lack of church attendance in Shiné wasn't due to a particular aversion to churches. In fact, at one period in his younger days, he'd planned and completed a round-robin of sorts, going to a weekend service for every religious denomination in the town he was living in at the time. Bloomington Normal.

He ended up missing one small Baptist congregation,

but didn't realize until after he'd moved. Indeed, he wasn't a stranger to churches and religion. Unfortunately, he finally recognized and accepted, he didn't have a religious soul—if he could use the word soul. Back here in Shiné, Leiv finally felt comfortable with his lack of church-going fervor. Even risking offending Lloyd by not attending his services.

Today, however, I need to be here. He couldn't let Tucker down.

Leiv took a breath and looked around again. The church was full, from the first row to the last. Margaret and Glover were sitting with him, but he also saw quite a few faces he recognized: Chefs Jack and Pauley from TGS in chef-attire, no less, Mary Jones from "Le Bric-à-Brac," Doctor Walker, paramedic Walker Johns, even Deputy Brad Temper. Of course Tucker's wife Ida, and his brother Calvin.

Finally, with his usual dignity and composure, Lloyd went to the front and turned to face everyone. Somewhere, someone was playing an organ, but Leiv didn't see any pipes or organ or speakers. Lloyd began by saying, "This prayer meeting is to give thanks that two of our community are alive and with us." Lloyd nodded toward him and Glover. "And to pray for Tucker Oakes to return to the same good health."

Leiv had never been to, or heard of this type of "meeting," but he sure did appreciate the sentiment—and he was more touched than he expected. Especially because of the round of applause following Lloyd's statement. Sure, Glover and Tucker were well known and well liked, but him? His only notoriety was being the grandson of LC.

"In his goodness, our Father in heaven has blessed our patron Leiv Rhodes and eminent alfalfa farmer Tucker Oakes, and our renowned Chief of Police, Glover Deers."

Patron? Eminent? Renowned? Lloyd was laying it on pretty thick, he thought.

"Tucker is still in the hospital, but the continuing healing hand of our Lord is watching over him."

"Amen," a soft voice in the rear said. He thought the voice familiar and reflexively, Leiv looked to his right and slightly to the rear. What he saw, changed everything.

Indeed, he had to force his attention back to the service—when what Leiv wanted to do was grab Glover by the shoulder, drag him out of church and tell him what he'd just seen and realized.

But he couldn't. Not this moment. He was too honored, and Tucker deserved his respect.

Lloyd continued, "Let us bow our heads in prayer."

Though he dropped his head, Leiv, couldn't stop moving jigsaw pieces around. Unfortunately he didn't like the picture the pieces were forming. Even in Shiné, evil existed.

Could he never get away from it?

"I saw it in her eyes," Leiv insisted.

As soon as the service was over, and under Margaret's curious eye, he'd dragged Glover away out into the church's parking lot.

Once again, Glover was incredulous. "You're trying to tell me she's a crazed killer?"

Indeed, it was hard to image. He'd seen her float into both TGS and Shiné Community Church this morning — reminding him of a leaf riding on the water's surface.

"Okay, okay, I know it's hard to take in and I'm not explaining it that well," Leiv insisted. For privacy sake he was standing very close to Glover, but he tugged on his uniform shirt sleeve, guiding him even farther away from the gaggle of parishioners talking in somber tones around the church's entrance. No one seemed to be paying much attention to them, even hearing the occasional laugh, but not many. Still, what he was trying to tell Glover needed privacy.

"The way she looked at Calvin, Glover," Leiv said, almost at whisper level, "was pure, unadulterated lust." A moment he knew she thought unguarded, and was consequently not lacking in intensity.

"Doesn't mean she's a murderer."

"It did to me." Leiv looked away for a moment, trying to find the right words. "It was the kind of desire that said 'I'll do anything to have you.'"

"I've never heard anything to suggest Ida wasn't happy with Tucker." Glover's voice clearly said he wasn't convinced of Ida's murderous intent.

It seemed clear and simple to Leiv. "She wants them both."

"Both? You have no proof."

Leiv made a face. "That's your department. You're a Chief-of-Police in a 'premier' high desert town with connections down below. Didn't you just assist in solving a weekend warrior insurance fraud—with a faked death, no less?"

Leiv thought Glover was going to come back with some kind of witty and sarcastic put down. Instead, he said, "I could call Portia and see what she can do—" Glover narrowed his eyes and peered into Leiv's. "And just how do you think this murder of Georgie Oakes went down?"

"Here's a couple things for you to think about—why was there only one towel poolside? Brings to mind several scenarios. How about the fact they both learned to swim together."

"Flimsy." Glover crossed his arms across his chest.

It is flimsy—but I saw that look. Leiv sighed. "Well, are

you going to do some digging or not? "

Glover nodded slowly.

Tucker would be heartbroken. But killing Georgie was not a "nice" thing to do.

A Couple Weeks Later

From LC's journal—last page: *Didn't that Shakespeare guy, yeah, I done some reading on my own, say something about tales told by idiots, and strutting and fretting on stage?*

"Tucker is resigning now that Ida's been indicted," Glover said, coming to the end of their whispered discussion about Ida's charges and Tucker's improved health condition. "Says he needs to be at her side through all this."

"Even though she confessed?" *Retracted of course, per her defense attorney.* "Even though she thought it was just fine to kill a man's wife because she wanted him? And what about Calvin? At her side, too?" Leiv puffed noisily out both sides of his cheeks. "What with killing his wife and all."

Judge or not, people were still amazing him.

Glover shushed him, "Not so loud, Tucker will hear you." He lowered his own voice. "No, not so much. I think it's hard for him to take in Ida actually killed Georgie, but I know for sure he really loved Georgie." He shook his head. "Not going to be a pretty trial, I don't think."

"I never saw that before," Leiv said, his eyes drawn to Glover's forearm. "In all the time I've known you." Another little piece of life's drama revealed.

Glover had both his uniform shirt-sleeves rolled up, having just finished wiping spilled coke off the counter, and had turned back to look at Leiv. He held his arm up allowing Leiv to have a better look at his tattoo, and clicked out the corner of his mouth before saying, "I don't much roll my sleeves up. Or wear short-sleeved shirts." He laughed lightly. "And damn sure you haven't seen me naked."

Leiv laughed too. Had to. *Father clicked out the corner of his mouth just like that. And so do I sometimes.* All the while a curtain in his brain was rising, revealing the actors and the set. "Is it an eagle?"

"Yep."

Leiv was sitting behind the spare desk in Glover's office. He was waiting for Glover to finish wiping up Tucker's overturned soda—fortunately not much was left in the can. Tucker was in the restroom washing up.

As soon as Glover finished, Leiv planned to ride with him to pick up Margaret and Lloyd and take both to lunch at TGS. Tucker was going to hold-down-the-fort. Leiv was sitting in the wooden slat roller desk-chair—now he leaned forward and felt his shoulders tightened as he said, his words slow and careful, "LC had one just like that. So did my father, Everett."

Then there's you and father's favorite meal, steak and eggs. Funny, Leiv further thought, *what gets passed on.*

"An August Coleman look-alike tattoo I'm told."

"Yep, 'Cap' Coleman," Leiv said, slowly.

Glover turned his head slightly, squinting his eyes and looking at Leiv intently.

For Leiv, the curtain had risen—he just had to wait for Glover to look out into the audience. *Or look at the actors on stage?* Like him lately, actor and viewer. "And Everett's nickname was also Dusty." He didn't explain he just read that in LC's journal. "Not used much, though. Only by people real close to him. I seldom heard it myself."

He also now remembered several moments with Margaret when she was about to say, "Your brother."

Minutes of quiet passed. Glover rubbed his arm, and Leiv waited.

Finally, Glover said, one of his trademark wry smiles starting to form in the corner of his mouth, "Do you think we should mention this to my mother, Margaret?"

It wasn't the response Leiv actually expected, but it seemed right, now that Glover's curtain had evidently risen. Leiv found himself smiling in return. A real smile, not a corner-of-the-mouth Glover variety. Having a brother opened a whole new world of possibilities for Leiv. *A confidant? A co-conspirator in whatever?* For a moment, he felt wonderful, like a kid. And he guessed—knew really—Glover planned to hang around Shiné to keep an eye on his mother, Margaret.

"You know, I think it was your blood I received at Loma Linda. The nurse said it came from Twentynine Palms."

Glover smiled slightly, but didn't say anything.

"From someone who shouldn't have been giving blood."

Now, having a *secret* brother—and a blood brother in every sense of the word—was even better. "I think the wise course of action is to keep this to ourselves." He looked outside, through the Chief's storefront window. A bright beautiful Mojave winter day was developing. "And we should respect Margaret's privacy, don't you think?" He could hear Tucker returning from the bathroom, then rustling around with paper towels at the coffee station. He'd be joining them in a few moments.

Their minds evidently still in lockstep, Glover looked over toward Tucker's back. Next he nodded, with his prior promise of a smile, turning into a full reality just like Leiv's. "On another secretive front," he said as he turned his head back, lowered his voice, and looked most pointedly into Leiv's eyes, "Does the Mojave-Stone actually exist?"

"Of course not," Leiv answered without hesitation, and with nary a second thought.

END NOTE

On page one-hundred-and-two in LC's journal, he explains the origin of his town's name—Shiné.

Viola likes to show our boys the stones in morning light. Sitting as they do in the room up top of the house, mornings usually, letting the sun make them glitter, sparkle, and shine. André calls it shiny, and it comes out his little mouth as shy-knee. Viola's got a soft spot for that one, and has started saying the name of our place shy-knee like the boy. She may have made shy-knee a reality, but it's little André who really named the place.

Thinking I'm gonna be changing the spelling too, and with one of them little marks at the end. Make it fancy, befitting a Leigh Cooper Rhodes kind of town.

Then he'd printed, in block letter across a whole page:

SHINÉ

ACKNOWLEDGEMENTS

As always, my gratitude goes to my excellent editors — Mike Foley, Virginia Moody, and Kitty Kladstrup. This story would not be published without them.

To my relatives, friends old and new, fellow authors, and readers—thanks for your continuing words of encouragement. I can never properly say how much your support means to me.

I'm also most grateful to my Route 66 and Public Safety Writers Association (PSWA) friends and business owners who always so graciously provide information on animals, politics, law-enforcement, Route 66, and local lore.

And thank you, Wilkie Collins, for giving the world The Moonstone.

Madeline (M.M.) Gornell's mystery novels include—PSWA awarding winners **Uncle Si's Secret** and **Lies of Convenience** (also a Hollywood Book Festival honorable Mention), **Death of a Perfect Man**, and **Reticence of Ravens** (a finalist for the Eric Hoffer 2011 fiction Prize, the da Vinci Eye for cover art, and the Montaigne Medal for most thought provoking book). Her latest, **Counsel of Ravens** (a London Book Festival Honorary Mention and LA Book Festival Runner-Up) is her first sequel, and was a continuation of Hubert Champion's Mojave saga. She continues to be inspired by historic Route 66, and Rhodes reflects that continuing fascination.

She lives with her husband and assorted canines in the Mojave High Desert near the internationally revered Route 66.

Made in the USA
Charleston, SC
24 June 2016